Amulet

by

Kathryn Amurra

Heart's True Desire Series

Copyright Notice
This is a work of fiction. Names, characters, places, and incidents are either the product of the author's imagination or are used fictitiously, and any resemblance to actual persons living or dead, business establishments, events, or locales, is entirely coincidental.

Amulet

COPYRIGHT © 2023 by Kathryn Amurra

All rights reserved. No part of this book may be used or reproduced in any manner whatsoever without written permission of the author or The Wild Rose Press, Inc. except in the case of brief quotations embodied in critical articles or reviews.
Contact Information: info@thewildrosepress.com

Cover Art by *Lea Schizas*

The Wild Rose Press, Inc.
PO Box 708
Adams Basin, NY 14410-0708
Visit us at www.thewildrosepress.com

Publishing History
First Edition, 2024
Trade Paperback ISBN 978-1-5092-5409-5
Digital ISBN 978-1-5092-5410-1

Heart's True Desire Series
Published in the United States of America

Dedication

For my three lovely daughters, Maye, Jemma, and Penny, who have taught me that there is no limit to the love we are capable of giving, and my husband, Ken, the hero of all my stories.

Praise for Amulet

"Kathryn Amurra's *Amulet* is an absorbing tale of re-evaluating what's important in life, of choices between what one has always wished for versus one's true heart's desires, and discovering that magic comes in many forms. Thoroughly enjoyed this enchanting story!"

—Joy Allyson, Author of *Whiskey Love* (Published by The Wild Rose Press)

"I loved it! I was speed-reading near the end—so anxious to see how the romance worked out! What a great ending! I look forward to more in this series."

—Kel O'Connor, Author of The DAG Series

"For anyone who loves clean, contemporary romance with a hint of magic! Kathryn Amurra writes a story that will appeal to readers who enjoy contemporary romance combined with just the right dash of magic to their stories! She spins an engaging tale of a family heirloom that grants whoever possesses it their greatest wish."

—Leanne Davis, Author of the River's End Series

Chapter One

Val Nikolov surveyed the grand hall he had rented out for the evening and began to relax. The sparkling lights and festive chatter of his employees and their families filled him with a mixture of pride and appreciation. It was hard not to be in a good mood with Christmas just around the corner. Harder still when he considered what a great year it had been for Span Global. If all went according to plan and the acquisition of his company went through, there would be even more for all of them to celebrate before too long.

An exasperated sigh escaped loudly from the ruby-red lips of the woman standing beside Val, taking a little of his joy with it.

Turning to the tall blonde to find her glaring in the general direction of the happy masses, Val couldn't help stating the obvious. "You look bored, Ginny."

His girlfriend turned slightly to look at him, a wry smile twisting her otherwise flawless face.

"Not really. I'm just contemplating which one of your employees picked out the wine for this party. Was it Judy?"

"As a matter of fact, it was."

Flipping her curls back, she managed to expose more of the cleavage that was already on generous display in the low-cut red dress she wore. "No wonder it tastes like it came out of a box."

It had been like pulling teeth to get Ginny to agree to come to his company's holiday party, and now he wondered why he'd even bothered. Their relationship had run its course. He was miserable with her, and clearly, the feeling was mutual. It was time to face the facts and end it. But not tonight.

Val picked up his glass of wine from the high-top table and took a long sip, savoring the flavors just to spite her and resolving not to let Ginny's sour disposition ruin his evening.

"Who's that?"

Certain he would regret it, Val glanced over his shoulder, following her gaze.

"The one in the dark blue dress that looks like it came off the clearance rack at a discount store," she clarified.

He spotted the young woman across the room. She was maybe five-foot-seven in her strappy heels and looked rather good in the lacy cocktail dress, regardless of where Ginny thought it came from. Her light brown hair was pulled back with only a couple of tresses falling naturally on either side of a picture-perfect face to caress a graceful neck and delicate collarbone.

There was something familiar about the woman, in her unassuming stance and warm expression, but Val knew she wasn't someone he'd met before. He knew everyone in the company—all sixty-two employees. Not to mention this woman was not the type to slip anyone's mind.

She stood alone, a few steps from the bar, with a subtle, welcoming smile in the hopes that someone might come to talk to her, Val guessed. Now and then she took a sip of her drink, then returned to smiling, in search of that brave soul.

But most men weren't that brave. A beautiful woman no one seemed to know standing alone in a crowded room was intimidating, to say the least. Nope, she was going to have a hard time finding company at this Christmas party, which didn't seem right at all.

"I don't know who she is," Val finally said in response to Ginny's question. "But I do like that dress."

"You're an ass," she hissed, walking away. Val laughed for the first time that night.

Looking over again at the lovely young woman, Val felt a pang of sympathy. He knew what it was like to be an outsider, someone who didn't fit in. That description pretty much summed up his childhood. With parents who hated each other, an older brother and two older sisters who despised him, and classmates who bullied him relentlessly, he'd had no one on his side except for his kind-hearted grandmother.

Spotting his secretary nearby, Val made his way over to the rather large fifty-year-old and put a hand on her shoulder. She stopped talking mid-sentence and, realizing it was him, instantly beamed in welcome. "Val! Haven't seen you all night! Where've you been hiding, hon?"

Judy was the only one at the office who spoke to him in such an informal, almost affectionate manner. And he wouldn't have had it any other way.

"I've only just now succeeded in getting away from Ginny."

Judy chuckled. "You should have called me over to help you with that."

Judy also was the only one who told Val exactly what she thought of his choice of women. And it was never anything good.

"I think I upset her. She said something about me being an ass and stormed off."

"Good," said Judy, without hesitation. "Maybe she'll be so upset she'll break up with you."

"It doesn't matter how upset she is," replied Val, raising his glass to take another drink. "I'm breaking up with her on Monday."

Judy threw her hands up in the air. "Goodness gracious, Val, that's the best Christmas present you could have given me!"

"Really? So, I guess I can just hold on to that bonus check I was going to give you next week."

Judy slapped him hard on the arm. "You'd better not, or I'll have to agree with Miss Ginny's comment about you being an ass."

Val laughed, then looked over at the young woman who had piqued his interest a few minutes before.

"Hey, Judy, who's that woman standing by herself? She doesn't work for us, does she? Is she someone's forgotten date?"

"Oh, hon, she's the new contract attorney that started last week. She technically works for Advance Legal, but she's coming into the office every day to help with the due diligence work for the acquisition. And by 'help' I pretty much mean 'do all of it herself.'"

"I see." He remembered authorizing his Human Resources Manager to find a contract attorney. They needed help cleaning up their books and making sure everything was squared away before the documents went out to FiberTech's attorneys for review. He didn't want to risk any last-minute technicalities or legal hang-ups derailing the acquisition. It had taken Val eleven years to build Span Global into the company it was today, and the sale to FiberTech would make him a very rich man. More than that, it would free him up to start a new project, and at thirty-six years old, he was ready for something new.

"I think I looked over a few résumés for that position. None of them were from women, though, as I recall."

Chuckling, Judy dabbed at the beads of sweat forming near her temples with a napkin. "You probably thought you were reading a man's résumé when you picked it out of the pile. Her name is Alex. Alex Weaver."

Val nodded. "Yes, I remember that résumé. She has an undergraduate degree in engineering, took some business courses while in law school, and still managed to get a J.D. in three years, top ten percent of her law school class. I think she's proficient in a ridiculous number of languages, too, if I'm not mixing her up with someone else."

"That ridiculous number is six, by the way," Judy clarified.

He looked over at Alex once more. The welcoming smile had faded somewhat, and her attention had turned to the band that was playing holiday songs in the corner of the large indoor courtyard.

"I feel bad I haven't had a chance to talk to her," said Val, almost to himself. "There's just been so many meetings and phone calls with this acquisition going on and end-of-year planning. I didn't even know we'd officially hired someone."

Just then, Kurt Donovan came toward him, hand outstretched and a huge grin on his face.

"Val, I've been looking all over for you. Great party."

Val shook his key product manager's hand warmly. "Glad to see you're enjoying yourself, Kurt. You, of all people, deserve to let off some steam during the holidays. The work you and your team did on the re-design of the reflective lenses really brought us to the forefront for next-gen fiber optic systems. It's been a great year for us, thanks to you."

Kurt accepted the praise with an awkward nod. "A lot of people showed up tonight, it looks like. Word is getting out about your Christmas parties."

"Word gets out about everything," replied Val.

"You don't know how true that is," said Kurt, all humor suddenly gone from his expression. "Say, I need to have a little chat with you about something. Do you have time Monday morning to talk?"

Val quickly went over Monday's schedule in his mind. He had a nine o'clock call with FiberTech's General Counsel in Israel, which would last about an hour, and back-to-back meetings in the afternoon. He was hoping to squeeze in a quick lunch with Ginny in between to break the news that they were done. Now that he had decided to end the relationship, he didn't want to wait a second longer than needed.

"Why don't you stop by at ten-fifteen?"

"Hey, sounds good. I'll leave you to your hobnobbing. Enjoy the rest of your party and the weekend, and I'll see you Monday morning, ten-fifteen sharp."

"All right, Kurt. Enjoy."

As Kurt walked away from him, Val turned his attention once more to Alex, intending to go over to introduce himself. Unfortunately, she was no longer standing near the bar, or anywhere in the vicinity.

"Judy," Val interrupted his secretary's conversation for the second time that night.

She answered, unperturbed. "Yes, Val?"

"Did you see where Alex went? She was standing right there a minute ago."

Judy looked toward the bar area. "Oh, hon, I think she just left. I saw her walk over to the coat check stand."

Val nodded, suddenly irritated. That was one more thing to add to Monday's list.

Chapter Two

Alex quietly opened the door to the townhouse and stepped into the darkened living room,
shutting and locking the door behind her. Letting her eyes adjust to the lack of light for a moment, she shuffled past the kitchen and into the bedroom, trying not to bump into anything.

"You can turn on the light, Lex. I'm not asleep yet."

Instead of turning on the overhead light in the bedroom, Alex took a few steps into the bathroom and turned on that light to keep from accidentally blinding her boyfriend.

"Why are you still awake, Billy? I thought you had to get up early tomorrow morning to work." She unzipped her dress and stepped out of it, then moved over to the closet to hang it up.

"It's only nine. And I'm not eighty years old."

Alex chuckled, but his answer irked her just the same. Billy hadn't attended the party because of a deposition that needed to be prepped the following morning, and yet here he was, claiming it was too early to be asleep.

She stomped softly to the bathroom to take a quick shower, hoping the hot water would relax her. Ten minutes later, she was climbing into bed. The shower had only been marginally helpful.

Curling onto one side, facing away from Billy, Alex closed her eyes. There was no reason to be upset. She knew Billy didn't like parties, especially ones where he didn't know anyone. But she hadn't known anyone at the party that night, either, and it would have been nice to have her boyfriend there, for support. It was a new job, and he knew it was important for Alex to make an appearance. He should have gone with her. Then at least they could have stood there being awkward together, sharing a glass of wine and enjoying the music. They wouldn't have had to stay long.

Instead, she had stood there alone, searching in vain for someone to talk to and lacking the courage to interrupt anyone's conversation to introduce herself. All her high school insecurities had come rushing back, and she had stayed planted in one spot, feeling like an idiot for over an hour before calling it quits.

Billy rolled over and inched closer, fitting his body to her backside and putting an arm around her. Apparently, he still wasn't asleep. And from the way he began rubbing her arm, it wasn't sleep that was on his mind.

He passed a hand under her oversized shirt and touched her stomach, working his way up.

This is what he wants from you. And you keep giving it to him. It's no wonder the boy doesn't want to get married. Why should he? Her mother's voice was loud in her head tonight, and being annoyed at Billy only seemed to make it louder.

When she made no move to reciprocate Billy's advances, his hand stilled. "Are you mad at me?"

That innocent question was all it took to diffuse Alex's aggravation, and she sighed. Billy loved her; she knew he did. How could she be mad at him for being truthful about not wanting to go to the stupid holiday party? After all, Alex hadn't said how much she really wanted him to be there. Instead, she had smiled and told him to stay home. How could she fault him for doing just that?

"No," she finally answered. "I'm not mad. Just tired."

"Oh."

Withdrawing his hand, Billy wrapped an arm around her waist, then kissed the back of her head. "Get some rest, Lex. It's Saturday tomorrow—you can sleep in. I'll try to finish up at the office before lunch so we can do something together in the afternoon."

Alex reached for his arm, squeezing it tenderly, then closed her eyes.

****

On Monday morning, Val woke up to one of the worst sore throats of his life. Accepting the fact that sleeping in was not an option, he took a long, hot shower, breathing in the steam to soothe the searing pain that accompanied each swallow. After getting dressed, he forced down a glass of water that felt like tiny daggers shredding his esophagus to flush whatever virus this was out of his system. He made himself a piece of toast with a generous coating of butter and tried to eat, but then simply gave up, deciding there was nothing he could do to make his throat feel better. He just had to tough it out.

What was worse was that he had a full day of meetings and phone calls, which meant a lot of talking.

It was going to be a hell of a day.

The traffic that morning seemed to be on Team

Sore Throat, and Val ended up getting to the office almost a full hour late. A stop at the drugstore to get a bag of throat lozenges meant that by the time he finally sat down at his desk, he had only ten minutes to prepare for his first call.

Fortunately, there were no surprises from the general counsel of FiberTech. Aside from the fact that Val had to reach into his bag of lozenges every five minutes to pop another one into his mouth, the call went off without a hitch.

His next call, however, did not go as smoothly.

"Ginny, we need to talk."

"You don't sound good. Are you sick or something?" Ginny was as sympathetic as ever.

"Yes, I woke up with a terrible sore throat."

"You weren't sick at the Christmas party, were you?"

Val sighed, which hurt. He popped another lozenge.

"No, I wasn't sick at the Christmas party."

"Good, because I'd hate to get sick a week before Christmas. Are you at work?"

"Yes," Val answered.

"If you're sick, you should stay home and keep your germs to yourself, don't you think?"

"So, you're worried about the people I work with getting sick because of me?"

"No," replied Ginny, "I don't really care. I'm just saying. So why are you calling me? I hope you don't want me to come over tonight because there's no way I'm getting near you if you're sick."

Val rolled his eyes. "I know. You'd hate to get sick a week before Christmas. You mentioned that already.

In any case, I'm not calling to ask you to come over tonight. I just wanted to meet you for lunch. I want to talk to you. Are you free?"

"Val, I already told you, I can't get sick for the holidays. Whatever you want to talk about, we don't need a face-to-face."

He really didn't want to break up over the phone. In all his years of dating and breaking up with women, he'd never done it other than in person. No matter how bad things had gone or how much he dreaded it, Val always paid his soon-to-be ex-girlfriend the courtesy of looking her in the eyes when he broke it off.

"Ginny," he tried again, "I really want to see you today. There's something I need to tell you, and I don't want to do it over the phone. We don't have to have lunch or anything. We can just meet for coffee or go for a walk or whatever you want."

"Listen, Val, you're being a little creepy about all this. They invented the telephone so you could tell people stuff without actually being with them. Just tell me what you want to say and let's be done with it."

If she wanted him to do it over the phone, then so be it. There was a first time for everything.

"All right, Ginny. You win. What I wanted to tell you is that this just isn't working for me anymore."

"What's not working for you anymore?"

He marveled at the genuine lack of understanding.

"*This*. *Us*. *We're* not working anymore."

"What?" Ginny's voice suddenly rose an octave. "What do you mean? You're breaking up with me? Over the phone?"

Val didn't have the energy to point out that the over-the-phone part was at her request.

"Yes, I'm breaking up with you. I don't think we should see each other anymore."

"*You're* breaking up with *me*?" she repeated, with emphasis. "You son of a bitch!"

"Ginny, it's not like we both didn't see this coming. It's not like you were actually enjoying the time we spent together. It's not like you were ever happy being with me."

"Are you saying you didn't have a good time with me? Are you saying I meant nothing to you?"

Val started unwrapping another lozenge. "I'm saying it was fun for the first couple of weeks, and that was about it. I'm sure you felt the same."

"Don't *presume* to know how I felt! How I *feel*! I can't believe you're breaking up with me. Do you know how many men tried to hook up with me while I was dating you?"

"Well, maybe you can call a few of them back now." He put the unwrapped lozenge in his mouth.

"You heartless bastard. You have no feelings. You feel nothing, and you're going to end up alone. Old and alone. And you're going to deserve it."

Val took that as the end of the conversation. "All right, well, take care of yourself, Ginny. Merry Christmas. I'm sure I'll see you around."

"Fuck you."

With that, she hung up.

Val set the phone down and leaned back in his chair. Maybe he should just take a break from dating. At thirty-six years old, he didn't have the patience for this stuff anymore.

Looking up at the clock on the wall, he noticed it was five minutes past ten o'clock. Kurt would be coming by to talk soon.

He rose from the comfortable chair and walked out of his office, closing the door behind him. Judy sat outside in the area between his office and the main hallway that led past the break room to the various engineering departments and conference rooms.

Val stopped in front of Judy's workstation and started rifling through the pile of mail waiting for him on the corner of her desk.

"Did I miss anything important while I was holed up in my office?" he asked, looking up at Judy and flashing an innocent grin, despite the knives in his throat.

"No siree," replied Judy. "So, are you going to do it? Are you going to break up with her?"

"I already did. I was talking to her just now."

"You did it over the phone? Poor Ginny."

"Hey, whose side are you on?" He paused, looking over at her. "Besides, I tried to get Ginny to meet me somewhere so we could talk in person, but she refused. She didn't want to get any of my germs. So, as requested, I just told her over the phone."

"I'm guessing she didn't take it well." Judy put a letter in front of him to sign.

"What makes you say that?" replied Val, his lips curving into a subdued smile.

"Prissy, spoiled brats never take well to being dumped."

"You're right about that." Val signed the letter and slid it back toward her. "I'm going to see if we have any ginger ale in the fridge in the break room. Do you want anything?"

"No thanks, hon. I'm fine."

Val turned left down the hall and walked past a handful of offices to the break room. One of his engineers, a bright young woman only a year out of school, smiled at him as she poured coffee into a mug.

"Good morning, Wendy."

"Good morning, Val. How are you?"

"Sick, unfortunately," he replied casually. "I woke up this morning with a terrible sore throat."

"Oh, that's too bad. And what, with everything that's going on right now."

He nodded. "Yeah, it's going to be a rough week."

Wendy stirred some creamer and a generous amount of sugar into her coffee while Val opened the door to the fridge.

There were no cans of ginger ale, so he settled for a can of cola.

Throwing the wooden stirrer into the waste can under the counter, Wendy looked back at Val as she started to leave. "Well, I hope you feel better soon."

"Thanks. I hope so too."

Val grabbed a package of crackers from a small basket on the counter before walking out of the break room and back to his office. Kurt was chatting with Judy when he arrived.

Looking up at Val, Kurt smiled tentatively. "Hey, Val, is now still a good time to talk?"

"Yeah. I wouldn't get too close to me if I were you, though. I have a terrible sore throat that I wouldn't wish on anyone."

Kurt followed Val into his office and shut the door behind them. At the sound of the door closing, Val realized this would be a serious conversation. No one came into his office and closed the door unless they were about to complain about something or someone. Or about to announce their resignation.

Sitting down, Val motioned for Kurt to take a seat and looked across the desk at the man he was about to "have a talk" with. Kurt was only a few years younger than Val, thirty-two or thirty-three at most, but the gray in his hair made him look at least forty. Hands down the best engineer Val had working for him, Kurt had a wife and two kids—a girl who was four and a boy who was about two. In addition to his technical skills, Kurt was a people person. He was a good communicator, eliciting the trust of everyone he met.

To see him now, though, avoiding all eye contact and nervously arranging and rearranging the pens in the mug on the edge of Val's desk, one would think the man had been kept chained to his computer in a dark basement for the last ten years.

Val finally broke the silence. "So, Kurt, what's going on? I hope there's nothing wrong."

Kurt stopped fidgeting and clasped his hands on his lap. "No, nothing's wrong, really."

Letting out a deep sigh, Kurt lowered his head and gazed intently at the front of his own shirt. Then, apparently finding courage somewhere within the woven threads, he looked back up at Val. "I'm giving my notice."

Val knew the disappointment was clearly written on his face. "What are you talking about, Kurt? You're quitting? You're leaving the company? Why? Are you unhappy here? Is there something going on at home?"

"Everything's fine at home, Val. Joanie and I have just been talking a lot about stuff lately, about what I'm doing, where I'm headed."

Joanie. Val should have known Kurt's wife was involved. Over the years, hearing Kurt talk and seeing Joanie at social functions from time to time, Val had gathered that Joanie had Kurt on a tight leash. A couple of years back, Kurt requested to switch secretaries because Joanie thought his was "too pretty."

"You don't like where you're headed here, Kurt? You're the product manager of the Optoelectronic Components Group. You're the best engineer I've got."

Kurt shook his head. "That's just it, Val. That's how you see me—as an engineer. But that's not all I am. That's not all I want to be. I want to start making decisions, calling the shots. I want to lead people."

"You are leading people." Val tried to keep his voice down, but he was frustrated. "I've been taking you with me on important visits to meet with important people, and you've been doing great. You don't think I recognize that? You don't think I'm trying to get you more opportunities to use those skills?"

"You've had the opportunities, Val, but you passed me over." From the tone of Kurt's voice, it was obvious Kurt was getting frustrated, too. "When Arnie left and the Engineering Director position opened up a couple of months ago, I told you I was interested. You know I would have been great in that role. But instead, what did you do? You gave it to Kelly Jacobs, who's wet behind the ears and can't tell the difference between a VCSEL and a flashlight."

"That's not fair," said Val, a little too loudly. "Kelly is more than qualified for the Director's position, and I've mentioned several times that the decision to give the job to her was a strategic one. You know if this acquisition goes through, each unit director will go with the business to FiberTech. You know I wanted you with me, to help me with my next project. *Our* next project. I didn't want to lose my best engineer to FiberTech, Kurt."

"Yeah," replied Kurt, sardonically, "well now you've lost him to Pierce."

Val froze and just stared at Kurt for a second. Then he said with admirable composure, "You're leaving Span Global to go to Pierce Industries?"

Kurt nodded. "That's right. They've been after me for years, and I've always said no, that I was happy here, that I couldn't just leave. But then I realized I could. They're making me their Vice President of Research and Development, Val. How could I have refused that offer?"

"Kurt, I know you're no fool. You weren't swayed by that title, were you? Everyone and their brother is a vice president at that company. Even the janitor is the 'Vice President of Sanitation.'"

"You don't understand, Val. They're giving me real opportunities, a platform to build something great."

Val stood up abruptly, pushing his chair away from the desk. "You had something great *here*, Kurt! How can you throw all of this away? This acquisition alone would have made you twice as rich as you are right now. You've just forfeited all of it—don't you realize that?"

Kurt leaned back in his chair and looked up at Val, arms folded across his chest. "The keyword there is 'if,' Val. *If* the deal goes through."

"What are you saying, Kurt?" Val placed his hands on the desk and leaned in a little closer to study Kurt's face, trying to read him. "What exactly are you saying?"

"I'm saying," replied Kurt, emphasizing each word, "that I know Gideon Krantz, too. I've met him, and he knows me. He *trusts* me. And the main reason Gideon was interested in acquiring *your* company is because he knew *my* work and liked it. But now, if I no longer work with you and instead I work with Pierce, well, it's going to be a whole other story, isn't it?"

Somehow, Val managed not to utter a string of curses in response to Kurt's rhetorical question.

"The whole reason *you* know Gideon Krantz is because *I* introduced you to him!" Val hissed through gritted teeth. "I brought you to Israel with me. I brought you to the meetings with Gideon and his team. And now you're saying the whole deal is going to fall apart just because you're leaving? Do you really think that highly of yourself, Kurt?"

Val paused, suddenly remembering a conversation he'd had with his lawyer when Arnie left. "You have no right to go to a competitor, Kurt. You signed an employment agreement with me, and that employment agreement precludes you from working for a competitor for two years following your departure from Span Global."

Kurt chuckled. He didn't seem so nervous anymore. "You don't think I reviewed my employment agreement before I pulled the trigger on this, Val? Arnie may have signed a non-compete clause in his employment agreement, but I didn't. I was your third employee, Val. My employment agreement consisted of a one-page document, and there are no non-compete provisions in there. I guarantee you that."

Val had a sinking feeling that Kurt was right, but

he couldn't back down. "I think we're done here, Kurt. You should pack your things up and leave as soon as possible. If you're not gone in thirty minutes, I'm having security escort you out."

Kurt smiled and nodded his head. "Understood. We all have to do what's best for us. I've got a family to take care of."

"And I've got a company to run. So, if you'll excuse me, I have some phone calls to make."

Kurt rose from the chair and walked to the door. With a hand on the doorknob to open it, he looked over his shoulder at Val, who was already back at his desk typing.

"Take care of yourself, Val."

Val nodded curtly. Then Kurt opened the door and left.

A moment later, Val flew out of his office and went to Judy's desk. She looked up with tremulous eyes as he approached.

"Do you know what just happened?" he asked, point blank.

"Something bad," she responded.

Judy had likely only heard muffled voices through the door when Kurt and Val were exchanging words, but it didn't take a genius to figure out something unpleasant had just gone down.

"Yes, something very bad. Kurt just gave his notice. He's going over to Pierce Industries. Those bastards. Poaching from us!" He shook his head, angry at Pierce for making the offer, angry at Kurt for accepting it, and angry at himself for not being able to stop it.

He shook his head again and continued.

"Whatever—what's done is done. Now we have to deal with it. I gave Kurt half an hour to clear out. I want someone from security up here immediately to watch him as he packs up his office. I'm sure he's already taken whatever files he wanted over the past few weeks leading up to this, but damned if I'm going to let him take anything else."

"I'll call security right now," she said, reaching for the phone.

"And I need you to pull his file from HR."

"I'll walk down there myself and get it," Judy replied. She was just the calm, efficient presence Val needed to get him through this mess.

"Thank you, Judy," he said softly, verbalizing in some small way the enormous gratitude he felt for his assistant. "I'm going to be on the phone for a while."

"I'll let you know if there's an emergency, or rather, a bigger emergency. I won't let anyone interrupt you otherwise."

He nodded, then re-entered his office and closed the door.

Chapter Three

Val emerged from his office over two hours later. It was almost one o'clock. He hadn't eaten lunch, and, considering his increasingly sore throat, he didn't particularly want to.

"I know you're not in the mood," said Judy, gingerly testing the waters, "but there's a stack of files and papers here for you to look at and sign when you get a chance. The ones on top have to go out today, unfortunately."

"That's fine," he replied, taking the files. "I need a break from this other stuff, anyway."

He was about to retreat to his office when Judy stopped him.

"Hang on a minute, hon. Alex Weaver left this for you."

Judy reached for a napkin that had what looked like a wrapped tea bag on it and handed the packet to Val.

"She said she overheard you talking about having a sore throat in the break room this morning and thought this might help. It's green tea with mint. The girl lost me when she started talking about antioxidants, but the long and short of it is that the tea makes her throat feel better when she's sick, and she thought you ought to give it a whirl. I told her I would give you the message. And the tea bag."

"Thanks, Judy." Val stared at the tea bag in his

hand before returning his attention to Judy. "Where does Miss Weaver sit? I had intended to go introduce myself, but the morning sort of got away from me."

"Obviously," said Judy, cracking a smile. "Alex has the little office right next door to the break room, which is probably how she overheard you. She spends a lot of time in Records, though, going through boxes of old documents."

Val was about to head into the hallway when Judy added, "If you're planning on talking to Alex now, you won't find her. She said something about needing to drive her boyfriend to the shop. He's getting his brakes fixed or something, I can't remember. She wanted to ask your permission to take a long lunch break to do that, but I told her not to worry about it—I hope that was okay."

This woman, Alex Weaver, never seemed to be around when he wanted to talk to her.

"Of course, it's fine. Thanks, Judy."

"No problem, hon."

Val turned away from the hallway and went back into his office.

It was well past six o'clock when he reemerged. Judy had gone home about an hour earlier, but not before knocking on his door and asking if he needed her to stay. Val had told her everything was fine and had encouraged her to go home.

Now, stepping into the empty hall and heading toward the break room, Val wondered what he would do if Judy decided one day to up and quit on him, too. Kurt's departure was one thing, but if Judy left? Well, he would seriously consider retiring at that point.

He walked past one dark, empty office after

another on his way to the break room. Rounding the corner, he heard the sound of fingers typing on a keyboard. It was coming from the small room just past the break room, which, unlike the other offices, was well-lit.

Val slowed down as he walked past the break room and peeked into the tiny office, which he was pretty sure used to be a janitorial supply closet.

Inside the room, a woman sat with her back to the door behind a desk that took up nearly the whole office. Folders and papers covered every inch of the desk, arranged in piles according to some method of organization that probably only she understood. Her light brown hair was pulled back in a ponytail, and she stared at a half-finished sentence on the computer screen in front of her, one hand balled into a fist under her chin, one foot tapping the ground.

"Excuse me?" said Val softly, feeling bad for interrupting her.

The woman gasped and involuntarily jumped out of the chair as she turned to face him.

Val chuckled. "I'm sorry, I didn't mean to frighten you."

Alex Weaver smiled and stepped forward. "Oh no, you're fine. I just get a little jumpy when I'm sitting by myself, concentrating on something in complete and utter silence, and then someone sneaks up behind me."

"Completely understandable," he replied, amused. "I'm Val. Val Nikolov." He reached out to shake her hand. "You must be Alex Weaver."

"Very nice to meet you, Mr. Nikolov."

"No, please, it's just Val. Everyone calls me Val."

"Okay, Val. It really is very nice to meet you. I

came by earlier, but your secretary said you were busy today and that later in the week might be better."

Val took a step back and silently evaluated the young woman standing in front of him. The lateness of the hour was evidenced by her disheveled hair and half-untucked blouse, but there was still an air of casual grace and effortless beauty about her. Beige eye shadow, long since faded, and remnants of the mascara that still clung to sweeping eyelashes made her light brown eyes look like warm pools of honey. A heart-shaped mouth formed an inviting frame for the perfect white teeth that showed each time her lips curled into a smile, which was often.

"Yes," Val replied, pausing his silent commentary on the lovely lady's appearance. "We had a bit of drama that caused a lot of firefighting to be required today."

"Oh, really? I hope it wasn't too bad."

"It wasn't great, but we'll be fine. I've been on the phone with my lawyer most of the afternoon trying to figure out how to minimize the damage."

It hadn't occurred to him until that moment that Miss Weaver was his lawyer, too. She should know what was going on. After all, it might affect her work, and she could even have some legal advice for him.

"Hey, if you have some time, I'd like to fill you in on what's been going on. Maybe get your take on it."

Alex looked at him for a moment, as though she wasn't sure she had heard him correctly, then answered with an eager head bob. "Sure. That would be great. I'm free whenever it's convenient for you."

Despite being locked up in his office all day, scrutinizing the effect of Kurt's departure on the deal with FiberTech with the taste of countless throat lozenges in his mouth, Val felt suddenly light and energetic. And hungry.

"How late were you planning on staying tonight?" he asked, immediately adding, "And why are you here after hours to begin with?"

"Oh, I'm sorry," she said, having mistaken the question for a reproach. "I can shut down and get—"

"No, no," Val said, smiling. "It's not a problem. I'm just curious. I mean, you only started…last week?"

She nodded.

"And you're not actually even employed by Span Global."

She nodded again. "That's true, but I'm here to do a job, and it's time-sensitive, and I had to leave for a couple of hours today to take my boyfriend to get his car from the shop. You all were nice enough to let me take time out of the workday for that. I have to make up that time, you know?"

"Well, I appreciate it," he replied warmly. "That's very conscientious of you. I wish more of our employees had the same work ethic. And loyalty." Val paused. "What I was going to say is that if you don't mind staying here for another forty-five minutes or so, we could have some dinner delivered and I could brief you on what happened today. Do you have time?"

"Of course," she replied immediately.

"Great. The Chinese place downstairs is good and fast, and they'll bring it right up to us. Does that sound okay?"

Alex smiled brightly. "That sounds great."

"All right. Do you want to look at a menu?"

"I've eaten there before," she said. "It's all pretty

good. I'm just not a huge fan of shrimp and other sea critters."

He laughed. "Okay. I'll order a couple of different things, all landwalkers, I promise. Let's meet in the conference room across the hall?"

"Sure, I'll just grab a notepad and I'll be right there."

Val turned to leave, then remembered the tea Alex had left for him earlier that day.

"By the way," he said, looking back at her, "thank you for the tea bag you left with Judy. I used it this afternoon, and the mint actually did make my throat feel better. For a few minutes."

She laughed. "I hate sore throats. Sometimes the tea works. Sometimes nothing works."

"Hey, I'll take a few minutes of relief. It's better than nothing."

"Is it still pretty bad, your throat?" Her eyebrows came together in genuine concern, and he found the sympathy selfishly therapeutic.

"It's not as bad as this morning. Hopefully, it'll be a little better tomorrow."

Alex smiled. She had a sweet smile.

As Val walked back to his office to call down for the food, he found himself grinning. He liked Alex Weaver. She seemed to be a hard worker, thoughtful, and, yes, strikingly beautiful. It was a tempting combination of characteristics, and he was, as of ten o'clock that morning, a single man. Still, even though he was single, Alex wasn't. Plus, she worked for him, directly or indirectly. He had never dated any of his employees, for good reason—it wasn't a particularly smart move from a human resources perspective.

Val shook his head—what was he doing? He didn't need another girlfriend. Even if Alex hadn't been off limits, he just didn't have the time. Not for her or anyone else.

There were more important things to think about.

****

As Val's steps echoed down the hall, Alex quietly clapped her hands together in excitement. For the first time since law school, she felt important, like her skills mattered. *She felt like a lawyer.*

She was reaching for a yellow legal pad when her cell phone rang from under a pile of papers.

Moving the papers to the side, she saw Billy's name on the display and put the phone to her ear.

"Hi, Billy. Everything okay?"

"Hey, Lex." His voice was more animated than usual. "Everything is great. You'll never guess what happened today."

She chuckled, putting the notepad under her arm and leaning against the edge of the desk. "Well, you sound pretty happy, so I'm guessing whatever happened was good."

"Jon Winters called me into his office today." Jon Winters was the head of the litigation group. Alex remembered meeting him at one of Billy's firm's social events the previous summer.

"You remember the case I got pulled into as a sub for the attorney who just had a baby?"

"The one with all the property damage at the nightclub and implicating some senator?" Billy had spent three days working into the wee hours of the morning writing a brief for that case a couple of weeks earlier. Alex had slept on the couch in the living room while he worked at the dining room table, feeling bad about abandoning him for the comfort of their bed.

"Yeah, that's the one. Jon is directly involved with that case because it's his client. Well, apparently he read the brief I'd spent all that time writing, and he liked it. I mean, really liked it. Jon said it was better than some of the stuff he's seen senior associates write. He wants me on the case full-time. I might even end up going with them to trial."

"Wow, Billy, that's huge!" Billy had often complained that junior associates hardly ever got actual trial experience. This was a big deal and would be great for his career.

"I want to celebrate. When are you coming home?"

Alex saw the light come on in the conference room across the hall. Val was already in there. He was waiting for her.

"I need a little more time, Billy. The owner of the company just came by and wants to meet with me to go over some stuff. It'll probably only be another half hour. An hour, max."

"Aw, come on, Lex. What could the owner possibly need to talk to you about right now that can't wait until morning? You're a temp. Wait—is the owner a man? Is he trying to hit on you or something?"

Alex felt a sting of disappointment at Billy's words. Did he really think the only reason Val would want to meet was to hit on her? That she had nothing else of value to offer?

"Something big happened with the company today," she tried to keep the tremor from sounding in her voice. "He said it could affect the deal I'm working on and wants to fill me in."

"Is he a young guy, this owner? Or maybe a creepy old guy. Does he smile a lot at you?"

She pushed away from the desk and clutched the phone tighter. "He is not hitting on me, Billy. I'm a lawyer, and he wants to talk to me. That's what businessmen do—they talk to their lawyers."

Billy was quiet on the other end. Alex hoped that meant he understood how important this was to her.

"I want you to come home, Lex. I just got home a few minutes ago. It's lonely here without you. Are you sure you can't get out of this meeting?"

Alex thought of all the times she got home before Billy and was waiting for him. There were often weeks, when she was in between job assignments, when she'd stay home all day. Never once had she told Billy to ignore his responsibilities and come home.

"I have to go. Val's waiting for me." She paused, suddenly feeling a twinge of sympathy for Billy. He wasn't used to being the one to wait on her. Billy just wanted to spend time with her, to share his happy moment. "I'll be home as soon as I can. I promise."

He didn't argue, and they said their goodbyes. Taking a deep breath to clear her thoughts, Alex headed for the conference room.

Chapter Four

"So, after working with you for eleven years, this guy decides to screw you over right when you're on the verge of closing this big deal. I can't believe he would do that to you."

Val and Alex were sitting in the conference room half an hour later, talking over nearly empty containers of Chinese food. Val had just finished explaining his history with Kurt Donovan, and Alex appeared genuinely disturbed by the situation. He found that somewhat amusing and extremely gratifying.

"I mean, you trusted him," she continued, finding a stray water chestnut in one of the containers and plucking it up with chopsticks. "You brought him with you on these meetings, gave him every opportunity, and now he seems to think that you're nothing without him. It sounds to me like this guy just got too big for his britches, if you don't mind me saying so. It's just a very conceited, ungrateful way to behave. Maybe you're better off without him."

"I would be," Val said with a slight smile, "except for the fact that now he's going to my biggest competitor, and they've specifically hired him to give them a shot at the deal I'm trying to get with FiberTech."

"He didn't have a non-compete clause in his employment contract?"

"No, unfortunately. I had his records pulled from HR this morning, and he was right about that. Kurt was one of the first people formally employed by Span Global, and I knew a lot less than I know now. Plus, I didn't have the money to get legal advice when I was first starting out. I wrote up his employment contract myself. Is there any way the non-compete clause can be read into the contract because of his continued employment and the fact that everyone a year later—up until today—has a non-compete in their agreement?"

Alex shook her head slowly. "I'm not an employment lawyer, and you probably can't even call the document review I've been doing 'the practice of law,' but, if I remember correctly from my contracts class in law school, non-compete clauses are not something the law favors. It's like specific performance—making someone carry through with what they said they would do. The courts just don't like to force people to do or not do anything. I hate to say it, but I don't think you can keep this guy from working for whoever he wants, including your competitor. But you should check with your attorney on that."

"I have," Val said, "and she said almost exactly the same thing."

"So, you're testing me?" Alex arched her eyebrows. The smile that broke out across her face just then reassured him that she took no offense.

"No. Just hoping my attorney was wrong."

They sat there for a moment, not speaking. Val was oddly at peace with the events of the day, and pleasantly surprised with his dinner companion and newest employee.

Alex started picking up the empty containers, and

Val rose to help her. The night cleaning crew had already been through to empty the trash receptacles in the conference room, so they took their garbage to the break room and threw it out there. Alex stopped at the sink to wash up, and he waited a couple of steps away until she had finished before doing the same.

"Thank you, Val, for telling me about Kurt Donovan leaving the company."

Val stopped drying his hands and looked over at Alex. Her mouth was a straight line, and she was almost, but not quite, frowning. It was the most serious expression he had seen on her. "I thought it was important for you to know. After all, you're handling the due diligence for this deal. Who knows how what happened today is going to affect all that stuff?"

"I understand that," she replied, "but I just want you to know that I appreciate being part of your company and helping in any way I can. It's why I went to law school, but I haven't had the opportunity to really be engaged at this level with any of the staff attorney assignments I've had until now. So, thank you."

Val wondered how a woman with such an impressive résumé, and an impressive presence, for that matter, could have ended up reviewing documents for a living, but he had enough sense to simply accept her thanks and leave the questions for another time.

After gathering their respective belongings, Val turned off the lights, and they rode the elevator down together to the lobby floor.

"Where are you parked?" he asked as they stepped off the elevator.

"I'm at the el-cheapo lot next to the courthouse,"

Alex answered, smiling.

"Well, I'll drive you then."

"Oh, no," she replied, shaking her head. "You've done enough already. You wouldn't even let me pay for my dinner."

"The company paid for that. I know you are woman, hear you roar and all that, but please do me a favor and let me drive you to the parking lot. It will allow me to sleep much easier if I don't have to worry about you getting mugged on the way to your car."

She chuckled, then relented. "I suppose I don't want to have your insomnia on my conscience. All right, I'll let you drive me. I appreciate it."

"It's no problem, really. I'm parked in the building. We just have to take another elevator down two levels."

She followed him quietly as they stepped onto the shuttle elevator that went down to the parking spaces beneath the building. They rode in comfortable silence. Despite polite elevator etiquette dictating he should keep his gaze to the ground, Val couldn't resist looking at Alex. He took in her shapely legs and the curves of her figure, silhouetted by her coat, and finally her face. Thankfully, Alex had turned toward the elevator doors and didn't notice his perusal.

"Here we are," he needlessly announced as the doors slid open.

He walked ahead of her to his 1968 Camaro SS convertible. Val loved that car. He had driven to Arizona in a rental to get it, then spent two summers restoring and modernizing it between college and business school. Whatever money wasn't needed for food or rent he had put into that car. It was white with blue rally stripes, and the seats were black leather. It was beautiful.

Val opened the passenger side door for her, silently grateful for having just cleaned the interior.

Thanking him, Alex got into the front seat. He couldn't help noticing as Alex's coat parted at the bottom and her skirt slid a couple of inches up her thighs in the process.

He shut the door before she could realize where his eyes and thoughts had been and went around to the driver's side.

"I'll try not to breathe too much on the short ride over to your parking lot," he said, starting the car. "I'd hate it if I got you sick."

"Oh, don't worry about that. I've got a pretty robust immune system. Plus, if I'm choosing between catching a cold and dying in a fiery car crash because you held your breath and passed out, I think I'd choose the former."

Val laughed. "It's always good to put things into perspective."

He reached over to the stick shift and put the car in reverse. It was only after grasping the shifter that he sensed how close his hand was to Alex's left knee. Indulging himself, Val glanced at her face in profile as he turned his body to look behind them and backed out of the parking spot. She was looking down at her lap and trying to adjust her coat.

Val shifted again, driving toward the exit. Alex was quiet, and he hoped she wasn't uncomfortable sitting next to him. After their dinner and a pleasant conversation, she couldn't possibly be worried that he was trying to put the moves on her, could she?

"We'll have to see about getting you a parking spot

in the building. I'll talk to Judy about it tomorrow."

Alex looked over at him. "That's really nice of you, but I can't afford to park here. It's more than twice as expensive as the lot I'm in right now, and I can hardly afford that."

Val knew that contract attorneys made less than in-house counsel or attorneys in big law firms, but he was curious how much less. "What are they paying you at Advance Legal?"

"Thirty dollars an hour."

He was quiet for a moment. "They're making a killing on you, you know. I should have hired you directly—you could have made more money, and I could have spent less money. Anyway, don't worry about the cost. The company will pay for your parking."

The unexpected offer had her eyes widening in surprise. "I can't ask you to do that!"

"You're not. It's a business decision that I'm making. Look, it's going to be crazy the next few weeks with this deal. I might need you to come in extra early on some days and stay late on others. And the days are short this time of year. I can't be worrying about the seven-block walk you have to make to your car in the dark every night."

Alex pressed her lips into a straight line, and even relying only on peripheral vision, Val could tell she was skeptical. "So, you're saying I'd be doing you a favor by allowing the company to pay exorbitant amounts of money for me to park in the building."

He could hear the smile in her voice as she said the words, and he wished he could take his eyes off the road for more than just a moment to see it.

"Yes, that's exactly right."

Sighing, Alex relented. "All right, then. I'll do it. For the company."

He laughed. "You might just get employee of the month at this rate."

She chuckled softly in response, and the sound made Val feel lighter somehow.

He drove onto the shoulder at the front entrance of the open-air parking lot she'd indicated and turned on the car's hazards. "Thanks again for dinner and the ride," Alex said, pushing open the car door.

"Thank you for staying late and listening to my work woes."

She smiled widely at him, then stepped out of the car with her large purse slung over her shoulder. He couldn't help watching as she maneuvered herself up and out of the low sports car, then chastised himself for doing so.

He lowered the window on the passenger side as she pushed the door closed and called out to her. "See you tomorrow, Alex."

"See you tomorrow, Val," she replied, leaning down to look through the window. "I hope you feel better soon, and thanks again for everything, really."

He didn't feel the cold chill of the air coming through the open window as he watched Alex walk briskly toward her car. She hurriedly put the key into the driver's side door, unlocked it, then opened it and jumped in. He continued watching as her car came humming to life and slowly backed out of her spot. Alex waved to him as she drove toward the gate to exit the lot, and he took that as his cue to leave. As he drove away, Val realized he had forgotten all about his sore throat.

It was almost nine o'clock in the evening by the time he got home to his spacious, clean condo. After a long day that, admittedly, ended much better than it began, Val was glad to have a little peace and quiet.

Grabbing an empty glass from the cupboard and filling it with water, he popped another lozenge in his mouth before taking a sip. His throat really did feel much better than it had just a few hours ago.

Despite the unfortunate turn of events with Kurt's announcement that morning, Val felt at peace with the situation. Part of that feeling came from just having spent some time with a very attractive and equally personable young woman, but he knew that wasn't the whole reason for it.

Deep down, he knew everything was going to be all right. As that realization sunk in, Val found himself moving from the kitchen to the study, his sock-clad feet making no sound against the shiny hardwood floors. He had faced some serious challenges in his life, but he had always come out on top.

The study was dark, but Val left the switch on the wall untouched as he entered. He stepped carefully around the leather couch in the center of the room, his eyes slowly adjusting to the darkness, and took a few more steps to the desk and credenza that were arranged across from each other, at the far end of the room.

Laying a hand on top of the desk to guide himself, he moved around to the other side and lowered himself into the swivel chair. Only then did he reach for the metal cord hanging from the desk lamp to turn it on. The little lamp filled the room with light, causing him to squint until his eyes adjusted again.

Amulet

Moving to the second desk drawer down on the right, Val grasped the handle and slowly pulled. Then he reached into the open drawer and felt around inside until his fingers landed on what he had been looking for—a rolled-up pair of socks.

They were navy blue dress socks, to be exact, and he had held on to them since high school—not because he cared particularly about the socks, but rather because of what he kept hidden inside them. It was the secret of Val's success, the reason he led such a perfect life. It was his guarantee that Kurt Donovan's departure would turn out to be nothing more than a temporary annoyance.

As Val pulled a black velvet bag from within the folds of the rolled-up socks, he thought about his grandmother. Just as the old woman had done eighteen years ago, Val tugged on the silver ribbon that held the bag closed and loosened the cinch. Then, turning the bag upside down, he poured the contents of the sack out into the palm of his hand.

Curling his fingers around the smooth stone of the necklace his grandmother had given him, Val closed his eyes and let out a slow breath. Yes, everything would be fine. His grandmother had made sure of that.

Chapter Five

Eighteen Years Earlier

"Val! Stop dickin' around and take the third register. Don't you see there's a line out there?"

Val cringed at the sound of Mr. Albright's voice, then set down the mop he was using. Stepping over to the sink, he turned on the faucet and squirted some soap onto his hands.

Keith Albright, the second shift manager at the shitty fast-food restaurant where Val worked most days after school, was short, skinny, and balding, and he was neither married nor dating, as far as Val could tell. According to his grandmother, that was the reason the man despised Val and rarely spoke to him without barking out some command or insult. Maybe she was right and Mr. Albright was jealous of Val's physical appearance and quiet confidence. Or maybe the old woman just saw Val with her heart rather than her eyes.

Regardless of why Mr. Albright treated him so poorly, Val never talked back or got angry. If he had learned anything from being bullied all his life, it was that the greatest reward you can give a bully is a reaction. Val simply followed orders and kept coming back for more. Besides, he didn't want to give Mr. Albright an excuse to fire him. He needed that paycheck every two weeks if he was going to have any chance of going to college. And without a car, the fact that Val could walk to work from his house made it the best job he could hope for.

Val dried his hands and walked over to the cash register. He swiped his ID badge and entered a passcode to unlock it, then looked up to summon the next customer in line.

"What can I get for you tonight?" he asked, trying to sound pleasant.

He took the middle-aged woman's order, helped her use a credit card to pay, then handed over a receipt with a number printed at the top. "We'll call your number when your order's ready."

The woman stepped aside, and the next customer stepped up to order.

It was a busy night. The after-work crowd was out in full force, and Val marveled at the number of familiar faces he saw, sometimes two and three times in the same week.

At around seven, the crowds died down, and Val considered closing his register and going back to cleaning the floors that Mr. Albright had ordered him to clean earlier in the shift. Just then, however, a group of girls entered the place, giggling and bouncing their heads from side to side in animated conversation.

Val recognized the girls from school. They were seniors, like him, and they were in the brainy, but somewhat popular crowd. Three of the four of them were in his English class and his history class.

One of the girls, Terri, was in almost all his classes. In fact, she had been his lab partner for a time in physics, and she had always talked to him in class and said hi when they passed each other in the halls. Val had wondered on more than one occasion if perhaps

Terri had a crush on him, which would have been wonderful.

"Hi, Amanda, what can I get for you tonight?"

In addition to knowing how to deal with bullies, Val also knew how to talk to girls. He had watched enough boys in his classes and in the hallways to know what worked and what didn't. Granted, he hadn't had much practice applying what he had learned from his hours of observation, but there was no time like the present. Besides, girls were much more likely to talk to him, and even flirt with him, when there weren't other guys around and there was no one to keep up appearances for.

One by one, Val took their orders and their money, then assembled their trays of food as each order came up. The last girl to order had been Terri, and so she was the last one lingering at the counter, waiting for her food.

"So, how's it goin', Val?" she said as he came back to the counter with her drink.

"Oh, not bad. Can't complain," he replied, flashing her a quick smile.

"Can you believe prom is next week? It seems like the whole year has just flown by. Only a few weeks and we'll be done with all of this, graduated and off to make our way in the world. Kind of scary."

"Yeah," he replied, setting a box of fries and a sandwich on the tray. "It goes by fast. But I can't say I'm not happy to be moving on."

Terri's order was all there, on the tray, but rather than move the tray toward her, Val stood there, trying to think of something else to say.

Luckily, she spoke first. "Speaking of prom, are

you going?"

Val would have bet his minimum wage job that she knew full well he didn't have a date to the prom, but he went along with it. "Nah, I don't think so. You?"

Terri smiled shyly. "I was hoping to, but I haven't asked the guy I had in mind yet."

Was she asking him to go to prom? Could that actually be happening?

He swallowed. "So, who did you have in mind?"

She looked Val in the eyes, and his heart almost stopped. "You."

He laughed to cover up his utter amazement and excitement. "You don't say. So, you're asking me to go to prom with you?"

"I am. Do you want to go?"

"Sure," he replied, letting a little of his excitement spill out. "I don't think I'm working next Saturday night, but let me go check the calendar in the back, just to be sure."

"Okay," she said, beaming.

Val walked as fast as he could without running to the wall where Mr. Albright posted the schedule every two weeks and searched for the nights he was working. Sure enough, he was off next Saturday.

Val had a huge grin on his face when he turned to walk back to the front counter and almost ran right into Mr. Albright.

"What are you doing back here? Didn't I ask you to man the registers?"

"Yes, Mr. Albright. I was, but there's no one in line right now and I just wanted to check my schedule for next Saturday."

"Why? You have a hot date or something?" The

man looked at Val with utter contempt.

"Maybe," was all Val said in response. The contempt was easily reciprocated.

"Well, I'm afraid I need you here next Saturday."

"No, you don't. I'm not on the schedule."

The color in Mr. Albright's cratered face rose, and, nostrils flaring, he took the pen that was behind his ear and marked up the schedule. Then he turned to Val with a self-satisfied smirk. "Now you're on the schedule. You'll be here, right?"

Val seethed with anger. How could this little man ruin everything for him, just like that? Just when things were starting to work out. It wasn't fair—it wasn't right.

Val could have just quit, right then and there. He could have told Mr. Albright to take the job and shove it up his ass. But he didn't. Val needed that job. He needed that $4.25 an hour to pay for classes at the community college next semester. He gritted his teeth and turned around. He couldn't bear to look at Mr. Albright's pock-marked, big-nosed, sickly pale face anymore. The man was disgusting, inside and out, and at that moment Val hated him.

Val walked sullenly back to the front counter. Terri was still standing there, and half her fries were gone.

"Sorry it took so long," said Val. "I talked to my boss, but unfortunately I do have to work on Saturday night, and I can't get out of it. I'm really sorry."

Terri swallowed the food. "Oh, don't worry about it. It's probably going to be lame, anyway. I should go find the girls before they send a search party for me. Anyway, see you on Monday. Bye, Val."

She turned away before Val could even say "bye"

Amulet

back. Terri had gone out on a limb and asked him out, and he had rejected her. She would never ask him out again. And if he asked her out sometime over the next few weeks leading up to graduation? Would she say yes, or would she give him a taste of his own medicine and reject him in front of everyone?

Half an hour later, at the end of his shift, Val left quietly and walked home.

It was mid-May, and the days were getting longer. The sun had just set, but there would be at least another twenty-five minutes of light in the sky, and it only took ten to get home.

With each step Val took, anger over the events that had transpired that night bubbled within him anew. All he could see was the pock-marked face of his terrible boss; all he could hear was cruel sniggering as that odious man wrote Val's name onto the schedule for next Saturday night.

The worst part about it all was that there was nothing Val could do to defend himself, nothing he could do to make things turn out the way he wanted them to turn out. Val was helpless, at the beck and call of a sniveling, hateful man. He never wanted to be in that position again. He never wanted to turn away from something he wanted just because he couldn't pay the price.

The house was dark and quiet when Val slipped inside, and he found his grandmother had fallen asleep in the ratty armchair in her makeshift bedroom. Poor woman. What did she do all day?

It had to be past eight, and Val was hungry. He went to the kitchen, opened the refrigerator, and sighed. His parents hadn't been to the store in at least a week, probably more like two. There was a container of cream cheese and a tub of margarine on the top shelf; a jar of apricot jam, a jar of mayonnaise, and an almost empty bag of bread shoved all the way to the back of the second shelf; three cans of beer and a half-empty bag of corn tortillas on the bottom shelf; some wilted lettuce in the crisper; and a pitcher of water, a bottle of ketchup, and a bottle of mustard in the door.

So many condiments, and nothing to put them on.

Val contemplated pouring the cans of beer down the drain so his parents' trip to the grocery store would be expedited, then decided against it. The beer would likely be gone by morning, anyway. He shook his head and sighed again, pulling out the bag of bread and the jam.

There were two slices of white bread left in the bag, and one of them was an end piece, which didn't really count as a full slice. Val got a paper plate out of the pantry and put the slices of bread on it, side-by-side, then started spreading the jam on the bread before putting the two pieces of bread back together to make a sandwich.

The selection of canned foods in the pantry was just as depressing, but Val found a can of green beans hiding behind the crushed tomatoes. After heating the green beans in a bowl, he put the food on the kitchen table and sat down. Just as he was picking up the sandwich, however, it occurred to him that his grandmother had likely had very little to eat all day.

So, he reached for a butter knife on the counter and cut his sandwich in half, then got another bowl from the cupboard and spooned half of the green beans into it. He carefully made his way to his grandmother's room, balancing the plate of sandwiches in one hand and the two bowls of green beans in the other.

His grandmother was awake now and had moved to the folding chair by the door, next to her nightstand, where she sat knitting something that vaguely resembled a blanket.

"Baba?"

The old lady looked up from her knitting and beamed in welcome. "Valentin, come in!"

"Hi, Baba," he said, walking over to her. He set one of the bowls down on the nightstand, then picked up one of the sandwiches and held it out for her to take. "Sorry, Baba, I couldn't find anything else for us to eat."

She looked at him thoughtfully, then took the sandwich.

"What your sister eating?" she said in her comforting version of the English language.

"I don't know. She's not home yet."

His grandmother shook her head. "She at boyfriend house. She gonna end up like other one, with baby. Stupid girls."

Val didn't respond. The old woman was probably right. His eldest sister, Gabriela, had followed in their brother Dimitar's footsteps a few years ago, leaving the house only a week after graduating from high school to live with her boyfriend. Shortly thereafter, Gabriela found out she was pregnant and got a job at a daycare center a couple of hours away. She then dumped her boyfriend, who may or may not have been the father of the child, anyway.

Eva, who was only a year older than Val at nineteen, still lived at home, but only because she had no money and her boyfriend didn't have his own place. It wasn't a secret that Eva dreamed of the day she could follow in her older siblings' footsteps and be out on her own. She rarely spoke to Val or their parents. Sometimes, Val was amazed at how, even in a house as small as theirs, they could all live under the same roof and avoid each other so thoroughly.

He sat on the edge of his grandmother's bed, and they ate in silence. When Val was finished, he waited patiently while his grandmother took the last few bites of her sandwich, then finished off the green beans.

"Thank you, Valentin. You good boy," she said, putting down her fork.

Val smiled and stood up. He was about to reach for the empty bowl, but she waved him back down to a seated position.

"Stay for minute. Talk to Baba. Here, I provide dessert while we talk."

Chuckling, he watched her open the drawer of the nightstand and pull out an open box of vanilla wafer cookies. She slowly reached into the box and withdrew four of the cookies.

Val took the cookies from his grandmother, then leaned over to kiss her cheek. "Thank you, Baba."

She reached for his hand and squeezed it. "You are good boy, Valentin. Do not let anyone tell you different."

He smiled at her. His grandmother always knew how to make him feel special and loved. No matter what kind of day he'd had, no matter what insults he had endured, Val always felt he was enough when he was with her. "What would you like to talk about, Baba?"

Amulet

"You. What you gonna do with life?"

Val leaned forward to put his elbows on his knees and rubbed his chin, thinking. "What am I going to do with my life? I don't know, Baba. Something. I want to do something. I just don't know exactly what yet."

His grandmother sat there watching him, as though contemplating how to say what was on her mind, then finally spoke again.

"Come. I show you something special."

Val watched as she opened the drawer of the nightstand again and pulled out a small sack made of black velvet material. The sack was tightly cinched with a silver ribbon. Carefully, she loosened the ribbon, opened the sack, and poured out its contents.

Into her hand fell what looked like a necklace. Placing the black bag on her lap, she held the necklace up for him to see. The necklace had a thick, cumbersome-looking silver chain with a large, oddly shaped blue stone mounted on the flat piece of silver that was hanging from it. There were several hairline cracks in the stone, and those cracks had turned black over time. The stone itself, however, looked very smooth, as though someone had been rubbing it with their finger for the past hundred years.

Val looked at her, puzzled. "What is it, Baba?"

She looked at him again, her expression pensive, although he had no idea what the old woman was considering. "You ready, I think."

"Can you understand if I speak to you like this?" she continued, speaking in her native Bulgarian, which he knew was her way of making sure her words weren't lost in translation.

Val nodded. "Yes, Baba."

"Good. Because I have a story to tell you, and it is important that you listen, understand, and remember what I say."

"Okay." Val couldn't help being intrigued.

At that, his grandmother looked at him, eyes wide with excitement. "This is an amulet," she said simply, as though stating the obvious. "It has magic—it can give you what your heart most desires. You believe in magic, don't you, Valentin?"

Val shrugged. "I don't know. I'm a little too old to believe in that kind of stuff."

His grandmother huffed. "Luckily, whether you believe it makes no difference at all. The amulet does have magic—magic that has been passed on in our family from one generation to the next. Well, more or less—I am about to skip a generation because your father and your aunts and uncles are all idiots and do not deserve to have this amulet."

Suppressing his laughter at the old woman's frank assessment of her children, Val looked at the amulet again, trying to determine if it could really be magical. The idea was nothing short of ridiculous, and the amulet itself was rather plain and ugly-looking. But his grandmother wouldn't be making up stories, would she? There had to be a reason she at least thought the necklace possessed some sort of power.

So, Val simply replied in Bulgarian, "Tell me, Baba."

His grandmother smiled and nodded approvingly. Then she began to tell him the story of the amulet.

"In the last decades of the Ottoman Empire's rule in Bulgaria, there lived a jeweler in one of the biggest cities in the country. This man had a daughter and a son—twins—and he loved them more than anything else in the world. You see, his wife had died giving birth to the children, and he had no one else. On the eve of his daughter's wedding, the man decided he wanted to give the girl something special to remember him by. He found a rare stone in his collection that he had obtained in a trade with another jeweler from the Orient years before, and he proceeded to make the girl a necklace. As the man began to fashion the chain and the mount for the stone, a thought occurred to him. He could not give his daughter such a gift without giving something to his beloved son, as well. So, he carefully cleaved the stone to obtain two similarly-sized stones. With one, he finished the necklace for his daughter. With the other, he made a ring for his son."

Val said nothing as his grandmother paused, reached for the cup of water sitting on the nightstand, and raised it to her lips. Setting down the cup, she continued.

"Once the necklace and the ring were ready, the jeweler took the pieces to the parish priest, who was also a good friend of the family, and asked the priest to bless them. When the priest gave the jewelry back to the man, the man could sense great power in the items—a power that he did not feel in them before. He asked the priest about what this might mean, and the priest explained that sometimes a thing that is physical absorbs a thing that is spiritual. It embodies it and becomes a vessel for it. The priest said that when he held the necklace and the ring and recited the blessing, he could sense the man's great love for his children.

"That was all the priest would say on the subject, but based on those few words, and what the man felt holding the two pieces, he grew to believe these trinkets had become the embodiment of his love for his daughter and for his son. And just as the father would do anything for his children, he believed the necklace and the ring now had the power to do anything his children asked."

Val could feel himself frowning. "Is this true, Baba?"

"Of course it is." Her tone left no room for further questions, so Val shut his mouth and listened to what else the old woman had to say.

"My great-grandfather, my mother's grandfather, told my mother this story on the morning she was to be married. The necklace had been given to him by his own mother on her deathbed, because, you see, *she* was the twin daughter. The necklace had been created for her. My great-grandfather, who had raised my mother after both her parents died, in turn, gave my mother this necklace, this amulet, and told her to keep it safe always. He told my mother that whatever she asked of the amulet, the amulet would grant to her—but she could only ask for one thing, the thing she most desired. So long as she kept the amulet, that thing she most desired would be hers."

The old lady looked down at the necklace she held tenderly in her hands for a moment, then looked back up at Val and smiled.

"You understand story so far, Val?" she asked, confirming in broken English that he was understanding the tale she wove in her native tongue.

"*Da*, Baba," he answered.

She nodded, satisfied, before continuing in her comfortable Bulgarian prose.

Amulet

"My mother married my father, and a few months later my father moved her to a tiny village in the Balkan mountains, where my father had been born and raised. My mother had lived in Burgas all her life, a beautiful city on the Black Sea that was one of the largest cities in Bulgaria and still is today. But she adjusted to life with her husband's kin around her, and over the next ten years, she had four children—three boys and me. I was the youngest."

It was hard for Val to picture his grandmother as a young child, running around her parents' house, chased by three older brothers. All he could see was a wrinkled old woman who could do nothing but sit in a chair all day. It was only when his grandmother looked at him, her eyes sparkling with excitement, that he caught a glimpse of the person she used to be—the person she still was, somewhere under all those wrinkles.

"I was two years old when my eldest brother, Konstantin, died. He was nine years old, and to this day, I don't know exactly what he died of. My mother used to say he caught croup. There was no doctor in the small village where they lived, and my brother got sick during a very bad winter storm. As a result, they could not reach the closest doctor until the storm had passed and the weather warmed enough to allow passage into and out of the mountains. By the time the storm ended, poor Konstantin had died.

"After my brother died, my mother begged my father to move them back to Burgas, or any city for that matter. But my father refused. You see, my father liked to drink. He liked to drink and gamble, and he liked to do those things with his cousins and his friends, all of whom lived in that little village. He had no desire to go elsewhere, even for his wife. Even for his children."

The old woman shook her head slowly, eyebrows raised, silently reprimanding her father for his weakness, no doubt.

"My mother was a strong woman and did something few women did back then. When spring came, she gave my father an ultimatum. She told him that she was going to take her children and move back to Burgas, and my father could either come with us or stay behind in that little village drinking and gambling. He chose to stay behind and let his wife and three surviving children go on without him. But he warned my mother that he would come for her someday, that she was his and always would be.

"Well, that night, as my mother was packing up all our belongings for the journey, she found this necklace. She hadn't set eyes on it in years, having hidden it for fear that her husband would gamble it away, just as he had done with many of the other pieces of jewelry she had brought with her when she married. And when she saw the necklace, my mother remembered what her grandfather had said about it. Whatever she asked of the amulet, the amulet would grant. She need only ask for the one thing she most desired. It was clear to my mother that this was the moment she was meant to use the amulet. What's more, she knew without a doubt what she wanted most in her life, and that thing was freedom. She wanted freedom from her husband's selfish ways; freedom from being told where she could live and what she could do; freedom from the feeling that everything was beyond her control.

"My mother spoke those words out loud, then placed the necklace around her neck. And she knew at once that it had worked, and that she would be free for as long as she kept that necklace."

Here, the old lady paused, reaching for the water to take another sip. As she placed the cup back down, she looked at Val and smiled.

"And that is how we came to live in Burgas again. Not once did my father come to visit. And never again did he threaten to take us or my mother back to the mountains.

"Years later, I married your grandfather. I was twenty-eight—an old maid by the standards of the day. Soon after we were married, I got pregnant with your uncle Georgi. The pregnancy was easy, and your uncle Georgi gave me no problems. Two years later, I got pregnant again, with your father, and it was a different story. In my seventh month of pregnancy, I fell ill—very ill. I had a high fever that lasted several days, and I could not eat. Ironically, none of the doctors that came to see me could help. My mother, of course, saw my illness as punishment for leaving my father, as though God were saying to her, 'Do you think I can't take another of your children just because you've moved to the big city? You see, even the doctors cannot help her.'

"But then my mother remembered this necklace. She came to my bedside and told me the story of the amulet, of what it had done for her, and what it could do for me. She told me that as long as the necklace was mine, I would keep that which my heart desired most, but that once I gave the necklace to someone else, I would no longer have the amulet's power in my life.

"We had heard years earlier that my father had died in that same little village where I was born. So, when I took the necklace from my mother and wished for my health and the health of the child that grew inside me, I had no fear of my father coming back to claim my mother."

At this, the old lady shook her head from side to side, eyebrows raised and lips pressed together, as though she still had trouble believing what had happened next.

"Val, I tell you, the very next day I woke up as a new woman. My fever was gone, and by the afternoon I was up and about the house, as though nothing had happened. It had worked. The amulet's power had saved me and your father. But my mother, she had made a great sacrifice for my sake.

"Your grandfather and I had been living with my mother when we first married, but a few weeks after your father was born, your grandfather's aunt died and your grandfather took possession of her house. We moved into that house a month later, and my eldest brother Nikola said my mother could not live alone in the house where we all had lived together. He said my mother was too old to be on her own, and he moved her to his house to live with him, his wife, and their three children.

"My sister-in-law ruled her house with an iron hand, and my mother was treated like one of the children. She was told when to rise in the morning, what to wear, what to eat, and where to go. You see, Val, my mother lost her freedom because she gave me the amulet."

His grandmother paused for a moment, then sighed.

"Do you understand what I am telling you, Valentin?"

Amulet

Val didn't speak right away but instead looked at his grandmother's eyes. They peered at him expectantly and expressed a strange combination of sadness and excitement, of satisfaction and eagerness to see what would come next.

Finally, Val answered. "I think I understand, Baba. I think you're saying that what your mother believed about the amulet was true, that it's special somehow."

The old lady grinned from ear to ear and nodded several times. "Yes, my dear Valentin. It is very special, just as you are special. And that is why it must now belong to you."

Val looked at her, puzzled. "What do you mean? You're giving it up? Why?"

"It's time, Valentin. It is not mine, I only borrowed it. Like my mother before me and her grandfather before her, I must pass it down. It's time."

"But what about my father, or my uncles or aunts or cousins? Why me?"

His grandmother gazed tenderly at him and brushed his cheek with her fingers. "Because, my dear boy, you are the only one who deserves it. Of all your aunts and uncles, cousins, siblings, your father even, you are the only one who has love in your heart. And if this amulet derives its power from love—my great-grandfather's love for my mother, my mother's love for me, and now my love for you—how can it belong to anyone who cannot feel love, cannot know it or recognize it in himself or in others? It must be you, Valentin. It always has been, and it always will be."

"You think too highly of me, Baba," replied Val, shaking his head.

"I most certainly do not!" said his grandmother,

almost angrily.

He was quiet for a moment. "Baba, what if I ask for the wrong thing?"

His grandmother's stern expression relaxed into a knowing smile. "This is why you are the right choice. Not only love resides in you, but wisdom, patience, and compassion. Tell me, what will you not accomplish if you maintain these virtues?"

Val leaned in and hugged his grandmother tightly. "Thank you, Baba. Not just for the amulet, which I'm very grateful for, but also for how much you've loved me over the years. If I have love in my heart, it is only because you put it there."

At those words, his grandmother hugged him again, with more strength than he expected.

"Are you sure, Baba? Are you sure you want to give it to me now? I can wait."

"Is time," she said, slipping back into her broken English. "No worry about me. I am eighty-five, no longer young woman. And I wish for health, not life. I not die tomorrow, I promise."

Val took the old woman's hand and, in a surge of emotion, kissed it and held it to his cheek for a moment.

"Go on. Take it." His grandmother pressed the necklace into Val's hand, and at the feeling of cold metal against his skin, an inexplicable sense of peace came over him. She reached out her other hand and gave him the bag. Taking the bag, Val slipped the necklace back inside it and cinched the silver drawstring closed.

"Baba," he said, looking up at her, "you said there was a ring, also. Does it also grant a person's greatest desire?"

Amulet

The old woman raised her eyebrows in a look of surprise, as though she hadn't expected the question. "I suppose yes, but I not sure. Twin brother who got ring, he marry a few years later and go to America. I hear no more about him."

As Val considered all that his grandmother had just told him, she smiled lovingly at him. "You know what you want, Valentin? What you will ask amulet?"

"Yes, Baba. I think I do. After tonight, I think I do."

His grandmother's face smoothed in a most peaceful expression, and Val felt she approved of what he would be asking for, even though he never told her.

He leaned in and hugged her one more time before saying goodnight and leaving the room. As he walked down the hall to his bedroom, Val wondered how his grandmother's life might now change without the amulet, if what she had told him were true. Of course, it probably wasn't—there was no such thing as magic. But what if it were? How might his own life soon change, now that the amulet was his, if his grandmother was right? Was it possible that he could be rich and successful in his life? Could all his hard work at school and work actually pay off?

Back in his room, Val opened his sock drawer and tucked the little black bag into the folded-over end of the navy blue dress socks he hardly ever wore. He hated to let go of the amulet, but he smelled like french fries and greasy burgers—he had to take a shower.

The bag was still there when he emerged minutes later. Throwing on a white t-shirt and a pair of boxers, Val got into bed with the lights turned off and the bag in his hand. He pulled the covers over himself and waited until his eyes adjusted to the darkness. Then he slowly opened the bag and reached in with his thumb and forefinger to draw the necklace out.

The silver chain sparkled as it caught the light coming in from the almost full moon outside his window. He turned the necklace around until he could see the front of the stone hanging from the chain.

It was not as ugly as it had first seemed. He traced the imperfections in the curvature of the silver mount and followed the black scars on the face of the stone as he imagined his ancestor making the necklace so many years ago. Somehow, holding that necklace, Val felt part of his family for the first time, part of that history. The life of the amulet would continue with him, and then after him, just as it had with his grandmother, and in some way a little piece of his own life would go on with it, as well.

Val nervously slipped the loop of the chain around his neck and held the stone in his hand. In that moment, with the words of his wish unspoken on his lips, he thought about how he had felt when Terri asked him to go to the prom and when, for thirty seconds, he thought it would work out. He had felt like a whole person, like he was worthy. Because for those thirty seconds, Val had felt how wonderful it was to have someone who wanted him.

He shook his head, clearing away the distracting thoughts. He knew what he wanted. "*Iskam uspekh*," he said in the language of his ancestors. Then, lest the amulet not understand his mediocre Bulgarian pronunciation, Val repeated in English: "I want success."

Feeling satisfied and exhausted at the same time,

Val tucked the necklace inside his t-shirt and rolled over onto his side, closing his eyes and quickly falling asleep.

****

Now, sitting at his desk in his comfortable study in a condo that was over four times the size of his childhood home, Val once again traced the cracks in the blue stone of the necklace cradled in his hand.

"I have had success in my life from the moment I uttered those words," he said, speaking to the amulet, remembering that day as though it were yesterday. "I know you won't fail me now."

Chapter Six

Val groped blindly toward the source of the blaring sound that woke him. He found his cell phone on the dresser and, eyes shut, silenced the alarm.

Rolling over onto his back, he laid there for a few minutes, not quite awake but no longer asleep. Finally, he summoned the will to sit up and open his eyes.

The room was still dark; the sun wouldn't rise for another two hours. He switched on the bedside lamp and instinctively raised a hand to shield himself from its brightness.

After a few moments, he reached again for his phone, this time to check emails. As expected, messages had come in overnight from the Israelis. Their workday had started over four hours ago.

There were three emails this morning—one was from Yaakov Goldman, the GC of FiberTech and one of Val's closest contacts at the company, and the other two were from Gideon Krantz, the president and CEO of FiberTech.

He read Yaakov's email first, which was short and blunt:

What the hell is going on, Val? Krantz called me into his office and said that a key member of your team just quit to go work for Pierce. Give me a call when you can.

The emails from Gideon Krantz were a little more

formal:

Dear Val,

Hope all is well. I received a voice message from Michael Elburrow of Pierce Industries last night. He said that Kurt Donovan is leaving your company and going to work for Pierce. Is this true, or is it just a ploy by Pierce to disrupt the progress of our deal? Perhaps a telephone conference is in order? Let me know your availability.

Regards, Gideon

Gideon's second email, sent only an hour later, was even more to the point:

Val,

Let's talk when you get into the office on Tuesday. 9 a.m. your time works for me.

Gideon

Val had known he would need to tell FiberTech what happened with Kurt today, but he hadn't expected Pierce would be so bold as to call FiberTech and tell them Kurt was making the switch the same day Kurt gave his notice. Bastards.

He responded to Gideon's second email and then Yaakov's email, then got dressed and ready to go to work.

Val's throat was noticeably less sore than the previous morning, but he stopped at the grocery store on the way to work to pick up a box of mint green tea anyway. Who knew how his throat would feel as the day wore on? Plus, the stuff Alex had given him the day before actually hadn't tasted half bad.

He was in the office by seven, well before anyone else. Val preferred at least an hour of peace and quiet in the morning to finish the tasks left undone the night before.

The first thing he did was to call Yaakov Goldman to get the inside scoop on what was going on. According to Yaakov, who, to his credit, was very candid with Val, Gideon Krantz was more than a little disturbed that Kurt Donovan was no longer working for Val. In fact, Gideon was questioning the whole deal. Apparently, Gideon was under the impression that Kurt Donovan was the heart and soul of the engineering operations at Span Global and that without him, the product would fall apart.

"You know that's not true, right, Yaakov?"

"Yeah, Val, I know that, but this is Krantz we're talking about."

"Kurt wasn't even part of the deal. He wasn't going to go over to FiberTech after the sale."

He could hear Yaakov sigh on the other end of the line. "I think he was planning to talk to you about that."

So, the whole value of his company was tied to one guy, and that one guy had decided to quit yesterday. Val could feel his blood pressure rising.

"You know Pierce's products are crap, Yaakov. Their technology is at least a generation behind ours, and they hold half as many patents as we do. We have more experience with fiber optics, we use better materials, and we have better contacts with vendors and customers. I don't understand how Kurt is even a consideration. This is not a one-man show. It never has been. Was he good, yes, but we've got twenty other engineers who are just as good. Gideon just hasn't met them."

Yaakov was sympathetic and at least outwardly agreed that Kurt's leaving shouldn't affect the deal. But then there was the reality of human psychology and perception. There was the reality of Gideon Krantz, and in the end, it was Gideon's recommendation that would be relied upon when FiberTech's board of directors voted on whether to sign off on the deal.

"What if I came and met with Gideon in person? Would that help?"

Yaakov was silent for a moment as he considered Val's proposal.

"Yes, Val. Yes, I think that might help. But bring someone with you. Someone who can make a good impression on Krantz. Someone he can trust."

Someone he could fall in love with more than he was obviously in love with Kurt Donovan, Val added silently as he finished the conversation with Yaakov.

At nine o'clock, Val got the call from Gideon Krantz. Gideon was pleasant enough on the phone, but it was obvious the man was concerned. Val explained the capabilities of his engineering team and the superiority of their optoelectronic components, trying to impress upon FiberTech's CEO that Kurt's departure had not diminished the value of the company. Gideon listened patiently and asked questions, and Val answered as well as he possibly could.

At the end of the conversation, Val offered to come to Israel to meet with Gideon and answer any other questions, and Gideon seemed receptive to the suggestion.

"When can you come?" asked Gideon. "Your holidays start tomorrow, don't they?"

"Yes," replied Val. "Our office is closed at noon tomorrow for Christmas Eve, then all day Thursday and Friday. But we can fly out Friday night and be in Israel

Saturday afternoon your time, if we can get the same flight through Munich that we took the last time we came. Are you available to meet on Sunday at your Tel Aviv office? Perhaps we can take you and Ayala, and Yaakov and his wife, Mara, to dinner Sunday night, as well. Would that work for you?"

Gideon thought for a moment before answering. "Yes, I believe so. I will check with Ayala and confirm, but I think that would work out. Who will you be bringing with you?"

Now it was Val's turn to think. He had to bring someone who would appeal to Gideon, someone Gideon could trust. Val quickly ran through the list of senior engineers in his head to see who might fit the criteria, but none of them seemed to stand out. Could it be that Kurt really was the only one on his staff who could bridge the gap between technical aptitude and social grace?

Alex Weaver. Her résumé, and if Val was being totally honest, her face, came immediately to mind. He had read through Ms. Weaver's résumé again the night before and had been pleasantly surprised the see that she held an undergraduate degree in electrical engineering. True, she only worked as an engineer for a couple of years before going to law school and knew very little about his company, having been there for only just over a week, but her combined engineering and legal training was a major benefit. Her acumen for languages would likely prove useful, as well. If Val wasn't mistaken, Gideon grew up in France, and there was no faster way to trusting someone than hearing them speak in your native tongue. All those qualities, coupled with charm, personality, and work ethic, made

Alex seem like the obvious choice.

"I have someone in mind, but I need to make sure she would be available, it being the holidays and all."

"A woman?" said Gideon. "My wife will like that."

Ten points for Span Global, thought Val, smiling.

After finishing up with Gideon, Val immediately went out to talk to Judy.

"Judy, can you check on flights to Tel Aviv leaving on Friday and arriving there on Saturday? Try to see if we can get the one through Munich. Two tickets, coming back Monday or Tuesday, at the latest. See what's available. Please."

"Sure thing, hon. Emergency meeting with FiberTech?"

"Yes. Let's see if we can't salvage this thing."

Judy finished taking notes on the flights and looked up at him. "Who are you taking?"

Val hesitated for a moment, wondering how it would look to others that his newest, least experienced, and most attractive female employee would be accompanying him. "Alex Weaver. I have to see if she's available, though. It's not exactly the best time of year for a spur-of-the-moment business trip."

"Good choice." Her response surprised him. "She'll make a great impression, and that's what you need right now, in my humble opinion."

"We'll see," replied Val, secretly relieved to have Judy's approval.

Val went down the hall, past the break room, to Alex's closet-like office, which was unoccupied at the moment. Val sighed. His employee's habit of not being around when he needed her was starting to get old.

He walked down the hall to Records, hoping she

would be there.

"Records" consisted of an interior maze of narrow hallways created by rows of tall metal shelves, upon which were stored boxes upon boxes of documents, some of them dating back to the creation of the company eleven years ago. Val couldn't help feeling sorry for the enormity of the task Alex had been hired to handle.

He spotted her a few rows in, standing on a step stool, reaching over her head to the top row and trying to ease a box off its dusty shelf. The pencil-length dark purple skirt and matching silk blouse Alex wore flattered her fine figure, or perhaps it was the other way around.

Val cleared his throat. "Can I help you with that?"

She spun around to look at him, eyes wide as the step stool wobbled beneath her. "Oh my gosh, you scared the crap out of me. Again. You're like a ninja or something."

He laughed. "Not really. It's just these sound-dampening carpets we have."

Abandoning the stubborn box, she stepped down to ground level, smiling at Val. "Were you looking for me?"

"Yes." At that moment, Val couldn't help noticing how unconcerned he felt about the very serious issues his company faced.

"How can I help?"

"First, let me help you. Do you need to get that box down?"

Alex nodded. "Tax records from 2015."

She moved aside as he got up onto the step stool and brought down the heavy box of papers. "We should have gone paperless years ago, but everyone is so against it. It's just difficult to get people on board with such a new and different process, you know?"

Smiling in agreement, Alex took the box from him and set it down on the ground. Then she looked back over at Val, waiting patiently to hear the purpose of his visit.

"So," he began, "this thing with FiberTech is coming to a head. They're being courted by Pierce, Kurt's new company, and FiberTech's CEO is concerned that Kurt's leaving here is an indication that we've got some fundamental problems, that he shouldn't buy us."

Head already shaking and eyebrows drawn together in annoyance, Alex put her hands on her hips and huffed. "Figures. That's exactly what Pierce wants."

The fact that this whole thing pissed her off was unbelievably gratifying.

"What are you going to do?" she asked.

"I'm going to go meet with him, the CEO. In Israel."

"That's a good idea. People like it when you go out of your way to make them feel important. And Israel is pretty out of your way."

Taking a quiet breath, Val got to the point of his visit. "I'd like you to come with me."

Alex just stared at him, her lips parted slightly. He imagined that if she were a cartoon, her jaw would be stretched down to the ground and her eyes would be popping out of her head.

"Why me?" she asked bluntly.

Val sighed. "Because you have an engineering

degree—"

"I never worked more than a couple of summers as an intern doing that, and my job before law school can hardly count as a real engineering position," she countered.

"I know, but you have other skills I think would be useful, and I think you'll make a good impression. You've got both legal and business training, in addition to your engineering degree. You also speak French, and the CEO is a French native. Plus, you're well-spoken, you can think on your feet, and you know how to make people feel at ease."

"You know all these things after meeting me just yesterday?"

"Half of it is on your résumé, and the other half isn't too hard to figure out."

She smiled, blushing slightly.

"The problem is," Val continued, "we would have to fly to Israel on Friday afternoon, the day after Christmas. I don't know what your plans were for the holidays, but I'm sure they didn't include international travel."

She thought for a moment. "The timing won't be a problem. My boyfriend's folks live half an hour away, so that's as much traveling as we had planned on doing. I have a valid passport. Do we need a visa or anything like that?"

"No. A passport is all we need. I'm glad you have one. That would have thrown a wrench in the works."

"I can take a stack of your vendor and customer contracts with me and summarize those on the plane and in our downtime," she thought out loud. "I think I can still finish everything by the deadline. When are we coming back?"

"Monday or Tuesday. Judy's checking on the flights now. So, does that mean you can come?"

She smiled again. "Yes. I'm glad I can help. I've always wanted to make use of my French. And I can pretend to be an engineer for a couple of days. Plus, I've never been to Israel before, or anywhere in that region." Pausing briefly, she added, "Is it safe?"

At this, Val hesitated. "It's not the U.S., but it's not a war zone, either. There are some parts we'll want to stay away from, but we won't be near those areas, anyway. We'll probably stay at the Ritz-Carlton in Herzliya, which is less than twenty minutes away from FiberTech's offices in Tel-Aviv. Herzliya is a small beach town. It's quiet and tucked away from the hustle and bustle of the city. I think it's better than staying in Tel-Aviv. And the Ritz is relatively new and very nice. You'll like it."

"Sounds like a vacation, not work," she said, tucking an errant lock of hair behind her ear.

"It'll be work," Val assured her, "but there's no reason why we can't try to enjoy ourselves while we're out there. I'll have Judy send you your itinerary once everything's all settled. Where do you live?"

"On the south side of the city, about five miles out, in a townhouse."

"I can come by and pick you up so we can ride to the airport together, if that's all right with you."

Alex nodded. "You did a pretty decent job driving me to the parking lot last night, so I'm okay with that."

He laughed. "Good. It'll be easier that way, I think. Thanks for agreeing to this on such short notice. I really do appreciate it."

"I know," she replied, softly. "You don't have to keep thanking me. I just hope it all works out."

"We'll give it our best shot. That's all we can do."

Val tried not to grin as he turned to make his way out of the labyrinth of shelves and into the hallway to head back to his office. To take his thoughts away from his traveling companion's captivating looks and sweet disposition, Val began listing in his mind all the tasks yet to be accomplished. Sufficiently sobered, he sighed.

There was a lot to do before Christmas.

****

Alex had a lot to do before Christmas if she was going to be flying halfway around the globe to Israel on Friday.

She knew she was grinning like an idiot carrying the box Val had retrieved back to her office, but she couldn't help it. He'd asked her to go with him. The fate of the company was in the balance, and of all the employees at his disposal, he had asked her. It was unbelievable.

Entering her cramped office, Alex set the box down on a pile of papers at the corner of her desk and sat down. After absently staring at the darkened computer screen for a few moments, she reached for the phone. She was about to dial Billy's office line when she reconsidered.

How would Billy react to her agreeing to travel to Israel the day after Christmas with a man she barely knew? Billy had been none too pleased with her staying late at the office the night before. She doubted he would take this news any better.

Putting the phone down slowly, Alex logged back onto her computer. She would send Billy an email and see if he could spare a half hour for lunch. It would be easier to explain the situation in person. That way, Billy would see how excited she was to be doing something useful, to be contributing at work, and it would offset any negative feelings he might otherwise have about being left alone in their townhouse for a few days or Val's intentions.

Everything would be fine.

Chapter Seven

The next day was Wednesday, Christmas Eve, and between handing out bonus checks, preparing for international travel, and actually getting work done before everyone disappeared for the holidays, the morning whirred by on fast-forward for Val.

Judy had somehow managed to procure two business class tickets for the flight through Munich leaving Friday night, but coming back they would be on a flight through Newark, and they would have to wait until Tuesday morning to leave Tel-Aviv. Although Judy proclaimed that finding the tickets was a Christmas Miracle, the miraculous nature of the booking was tempered by the fact that Val would have to pay through the nose for the last-minute flights. He reminded himself that it would be well-worth the expense if they succeeded in keeping the deal together.

Val dismissed everyone at noon to start the holiday break and was packing up his laptop to head out himself when Alex stopped by.

"I forgot to ask you what I should pack," she said, standing in his doorway.

It was a little after one o'clock, and Alex was probably the last person leaving the office, aside from Val. The sun slanting in through the large windows behind Val's desk caused her to squint a little, at the same time making her light brown eyes glow like embers.

"That's a good question," Val replied, trying not to let himself get distracted. "You'll want something comfortable and in layers for the flights. It'll be Saturday afternoon when we get to Tel Aviv, and we'll probably want to change clothes. The weather there this time of year feels like the beginning of fall here, hovering around sixty degrees Fahrenheit during the day, cooling down significantly at night. It is the desert, after all. So maybe bring a fleece or light jacket with you for the evenings. We'll take FiberTech somewhere fancy for dinner on Sunday, so maybe a nice dress for that night. And for our meeting with them, I'm going to wear a suit, so you can either wear a suit or a dress, whatever you feel more comfortable in. We'll have Monday there without any meetings, so maybe we'll go sightseeing or something. We'll see."

"Okay, great, thanks. That's really helpful." She hesitated for a moment, then added, "Should we exchange phone numbers, maybe? That way if you need to get in touch with me or something happens with the trip…"

"Sure, good idea," replied Val.

He recited his phone number and watched as Alex typed it into her cell phone. Then she sent Val a text, and he added her name to his contacts.

"I'll pick you up around two-thirty in the afternoon to drive to the airport on Friday," he said after an awkward pause in their conversation.

"Yes, I'll be ready. You got my email this morning with my address?"

Val nodded. "I did."

There was another uncomfortable moment of

silence.

"Well," said Alex, her face lighting up in a smile, "Merry Christmas."

"Merry Christmas," replied Val. As Alex began to leave, he abruptly added, "Any plans for the holiday?" He cringed inwardly, hoping his attempt to keep her in his doorway just a little longer was not obvious. "I think you mentioned going to visit your boyfriend's family, perhaps?"

"Yes," Alex replied, turning her body toward him again. "Billy's family only lives twenty miles north of here. He has three older brothers, all of them married with a couple of kids each. They always go to his mom and dad's on Christmas morning. They open presents, eat all day, and play with the kids. It's a lot of fun, having kids there, you know." She paused, smiled again, then added, "How about you? Any big family gatherings to attend?"

Val felt foolish for not anticipating the question before bringing up the subject of their holiday plans. As a result, he hadn't prepared an answer. He had no choice but to tell some version of the truth.

"Nothing like what you have planned. My niece, who's turning twenty-one next month, is planning to stop by for dinner tonight on her way to my sister's house."

"That sounds nice. You're going to cook for her?"

"If you call heating food that's been prepared ahead of time by a professional chef cooking, then yes."

Val could tell Alex understood there were things he was leaving out—family drama and messiness that were the reasons he was usually alone on Christmas, but she was well-mannered enough not to pry. Val had enough to do and think about that he wouldn't even feel the loneliness this holiday. It was, perhaps, the only silver lining in this whole business with Kurt Donovan leaving. Well, he thought, looking over at Alex again, perhaps not the *only* silver lining.

"So," said Alex, breaking the silence, "I hope everything goes well with your heating up of dinner and that you enjoy the visit with your niece tonight. And I hope you get out of here soon."

"Thanks, Alex," he replied warmly. "Hope you have a good time, as well. I'll see you on Friday afternoon."

"Yes, see you then."

She smiled again, then turned and walked away. There was something about that smile. It was both contagious and addictive. She was generous with it, and yet Val was always left wanting more.

Val chided himself for having such romantic notions and reminded himself, again, that he was going on a business trip with Alex in two days. Regardless of who technically employed her, he was her boss, and she had a boyfriend and was off limits. He knew that.

Val left the office with some papers and his laptop a few minutes later and went home.

His housekeeper Edith, who just happened to be an amazing cook, had left two Cornish hens and a colorful assortment of vegetables in a basting pan in the refrigerator, along with instructions for the temperature to set the oven and the length of time to cook the meal. The food looked so good, it was almost edible just the way it was. Edith had made a salad, also in the fridge, and had left a small jar of homemade dressing on the counter. For dessert, a dozen perfect-looking Christmas cookies were arranged on a large dish, covered with red cellophane.

By the time his niece Liza rang the doorbell at five o'clock, there were only ten cookies under the cellophane.

"Uncle Val!" The dark-haired twenty-year-old flung her arms around him and tenderly kissed each of his cheeks.

"Hi, Liza." He chuckled, disentangling himself from her embrace. "How's my favorite college student?"

"Doin' great. I can't believe I had to stay on campus until yesterday for my chemistry final. That professor has been a jerk all semester. It's like he has a god complex or something. Everyone's been gone since last Wednesday, except for us. I hope I aced it, just to spite him."

Val laughed at his niece's youthful exuberance. "I'm sure you'll get an A, just like you have been getting in all your other classes."

He was so proud of Liza for doing well in high school, deciding to go to college, and going to one of the top 25 schools in the country. She made it all seem so easy, but Val knew better. He knew her mom. He knew what Liza had to deal with growing up. Val's sister Gabriela wasn't even twenty when she brought Liza into this world. She didn't know anything about taking care of herself, let alone another little life. It was a wonder Liza had survived, let alone thrived.

"Something smells amazing, Uncle Val. I might be coming here every Christmas Eve, to hell with what my mom says."

"Don't talk about your mom that way. She's just

worried about you driving late at night after you have dinner here."

Val knew his sister had been against Liza visiting him, insisting instead that she come directly home to spend Christmas Eve with her, Liza's two younger brothers, cousins, aunt, another uncle, and grandmother—Val's mother. Val was no more a part of the family now than he had been twenty years ago. Perhaps even less so.

"Well, come on in," said Val, squeezing Liza's shoulder in a paternal way. "I'll get you a drink and you can fill me in on what you've been up to while I get everything ready."

"Wow, that's really progressive of you," said Liza, following him into the huge kitchen and looking with obvious wonder at all the gray marble, hardwood floors and cabinetry, and stainless steel appliances, illuminated in the most artful way by a generous number of recessed lights set in the ceilings at least five feet above her head.

"What do you mean?" asked Val, looking over at her as he reached for some hot pads in a drawer.

"I mean I'm not twenty-one yet. I thought you'd be a stickler about serving alcohol to someone who was under-aged."

"Oh," replied Val, his lips curling into a smile. "Well, you're right, I am. I was talking about soda or juice, not alcohol. So, what's your poison?"

"Figures," she said, rolling her eyes for effect and sitting down at the marble island in the center of the large kitchen. "I'll have some Sprite, if you have it."

"I can put it in a wine glass for you, if you'd like. After all, it is Christmas."

"Geez, Uncle Val, I'm not ten!"

They both laughed. Val took the Cornish hens out of the oven and set them on the hot pads he had placed on the counter, in front of Liza.

"Wow, those look great. You did all this?"

"Not really," he replied. "But I don't mind taking the credit."

After pouring Liza a glass of Sprite and himself a Coke, Val brought out the salad and drizzled the salad dressing on top. He mixed it all, then set out the plates and the silverware. Liza helped herself to some salad while he cut up the Cornish hens and placed a portion of one on her plate, along with some vegetables.

As they ate, Liza told him about her classes and professors. She told him about the boyfriend she broke up with a month ago and her new admirer, who she was considering dating next semester.

"Is he a good guy, Liza?"

"Yeah, he's a good guy," she replied. "He's just not exactly my type."

Val looked at his niece, taking in the wavy, dark brown hair that hung loose past her shoulders, the dark, expressive eyes framed by long lashes, and the thick, but well-groomed eyebrows, and wondered what her type might be.

"Is the boy smart? What's his major?"

"*The boy*," she replied, poking fun at Val's words, "is studying chemistry. He's like a cool nerd, super smart, but kind of cute, too."

"Well," said Val, "just be careful. You're still very young. You don't want to make any mistakes, you know?"

"Yes," sighed Liza. Val knew she'd heard this

speech before because he had given it. "Don't worry, I'm not going to end up like my mother. I'm in college, aren't I?"

"Yes, but that doesn't mean you're out of the woods yet. Anything can happen if you're not careful."

"Geez, Uncle Val, even my mom doesn't lecture me about sex."

"I know. That's why I feel the need to do it."

Val had always seen himself as Liza's guardian. Even though his sister Gabriela, and the rest of his family purposely excluded him from all family functions and gatherings, Val had managed to become close to Liza over the years. He had advised her on what classes to take in high school and what colleges to apply to. When Liza was accepted to her top choice, Val had even managed to convince Liza to tell her mother that she had been awarded a full scholarship. The only part Liza had to leave out was that the scholarship was sponsored in full by Uncle Val.

Perhaps he was more like a fairy godfather.

Val knew Gabriela would never have allowed him to pay for Liza's college education. His sister had made her views on Val's success very clear from the beginning—he had "won the lottery" by going to the right school, meeting the right people, and starting the right company. He was just lucky, and he didn't know a thing about how hard she had it or the sacrifices she had to make every day for her kids. Val didn't even have any kids. He couldn't just expect to throw money at them in exchange for their love and respect. They weren't his employees. He had to earn their affection, and in Gabriela's book, Val had never done a thing in his life to earn anything.

So, Val stayed away.

His sister Gabriela was currently unmarried, mother to three children, and living on a depressing combination of alimony and state-sponsored aid. The only good thing Gabriela had done in her life was to be so preoccupied with herself that she never noticed Val's positive influence on her oldest daughter, which Val hoped would someday trickle down to Liza's brothers and, possibly, her cousins.

As for his older brother, Val had watched Dimitar go from one minimum wage job to the next, married to a woman he couldn't stand to be with, father to two kids he barely knew, and following in his late father's footsteps in every aspect of his life.

His other sister, Eva, had fared only slightly better than her older brother and sister. Eva worked as a receptionist at an insurance agency and was married to a kind man she berated at every opportunity. She had two children as well, the oldest of whom had dropped out of school last year to shack up with her boyfriend, who was three years older. Val had abandoned his practice of staying out of their lives only briefly by advising his sister Eva to go to the twenty-one-year-old boy's apartment and take back her daughter, but his sister had just laughed at the suggestion.

Val hadn't spoken to any of them in years, including his mother. He kept up with their general news by exchanging emails and visits with Liza, which gave him some level of comfort, but they knew nothing of that. To them, Val did not exist, but he cared about them just the same and would have given them whatever they wanted—money, cars, jobs, advice—had they only asked.

"So, you're going to be here alone for Christmas?" Liza's question pulled him out of his thoughts.

They had finished their meal and were relaxing in Val's spacious living room in front of the fireplace.

"I have a lot to do," replied Val, not really answering the question. "I'm leaving for a very important trip the day after Christmas, and there's a lot that needs to be done between now and then."

"Yeah," she said. Liza understood how it was for him. She was quiet for a moment before turning to look him squarely in the eyes. "You shouldn't be afraid of getting married, Uncle Val. Your family is not going to be dysfunctional like ours."

He stared at her, shocked. Val had never talked to Liza about his girlfriends or his desire to get married or not get married, and Liza had never asked him any questions about what he planned to do with his life, long term.

"What makes you think I'm afraid of getting married?"

"Well," she answered, "you're like forty years old—"

"Thirty-six, actually," Val corrected, with raised eyebrows.

"Whatever. Most people your age have been married and divorced at least once. I know you're not gay because you've dated like a hundred gorgeous women."

"You realize I'm your uncle, right? Your elder?"

"I'm not trying to be disrespectful, Uncle Val. I'm just telling you that you shouldn't let your messed-up family—our messed-up family—keep you from being happy with someone, you know? I can guarantee I'm not going to end up alone or stuck with someone who makes me miserable. I deserve better than that, and so do you."

And there it was. There was the spark, the magic element that made Liza different from everyone else in the family: self-esteem. Val wondered where she had managed to pick that up. Whatever its source, he was grateful to see it, and he wholeheartedly agreed—Liza did deserve better.

"It's not easy to find a person you're willing to spend the rest of your life with, Liza," he replied, owing her some sort of response. "And unfortunately, the older you get, the harder it is to see the good in people and overlook the imperfections. That's what you need to do when you decide you can't live without someone—you need to see all the good they bring to the relationship and get over all their shortcomings. Like you said, I've gone out with a lot of women, and I still haven't found the one whose imperfections I could overlook."

"Yeah," she said, her lips curling into a sly smile, "but you've gotta admit your dating criteria hasn't exactly been set up to find you a wife, judging from the only girlfriend of yours I happened to meet. I just don't think 'busty' and 'superficial' are generally recognized as 'future mother of my children' characteristics."

"Come on, now," laughed Val, "just because a woman is well-endowed and cares about her appearance doesn't mean she won't be a good mother. Now let's stop talking about this nonsense before I have to remind you again to respect your elders."

"All right, Uncle Val. I just hate the thought of you being alone on Christmas."

"I won't be alone," he replied, picking up a cookie from the plate he had set between them. "I'll have all these delicious sugar cookies to keep me company."

She laughed, plucking a cookie off the plate, too. "Not if I can help it!"

Chapter Eight

Alex woke up on Christmas morning with a huge smile on her face. She knew even before opening her eyes that it was too early to get out of bed. Then again, it was Christmas. If little kids could get up early and run to the tree to see what Santa had gotten for them, then why couldn't she?

Except, Alex didn't have to sneak a peek at what was under the tree. *She knew*. She knew what Billy was getting for her, and it was exactly what she wanted. What she had wanted for a long time.

"Why are you sitting up in bed?" asked Billy, groaning and pulling the covers up to his chin. "It's not morning yet, Lex. Go back to sleep."

"It is morning," Alex replied with a quick glance at the clock at her bedside, just to confirm. "It's almost seven. And it's Christmas morning. Time for us to open presents."

"I thought we were going to open presents at my parents' house."

Alex paused. It would make sense that he would want his parents to be there. They had wanted this to happen almost as much as she did.

Unfortunately, Alex just couldn't wait.

"Let's open presents now, then we can open them again with your parents," she suggested, slipping out from under the covers and getting down on all fours to find the box she had wrapped and hidden under the nightstand.

"Here," she said, almost shoving the shiny red package with a lopsided silver bow in his face. "You go first."

Knowing what Billy had gotten her, Alex wished she could have thought of something better to give her boyfriend than a set of cufflinks from his alma mater. But she couldn't do anything about that now. She'd only found out about Billy's present for her the night before while putting away Billy's underwear. The box, which was from the best jeweler in town, was peeking out from in between layers of Billy's boxer shorts.

Alex hadn't opened it, of course—she did have some modicum of self-restraint—but she didn't have to open it to know what was inside.

He was going to do it. He was going to propose.

She should have guessed Billy would do it even before she'd found the box. Alex had heard him on the phone the week before talking to someone about 'availability' and 'taking him through the process.' It hadn't even occurred to her then that he might have been calling potential venues for the wedding. It was only after she'd accidentally uncovered the velvet box hiding under Billy's striped blue boxer shorts that she had put two and two together.

Billy heaved a sigh as he took the present from her, pulling himself into a sitting position. With a flick of his fingers, Alex's poor attempt to wrap the gift was completely undone, and Billy lifted the lid of the box to reveal two glossy blue and white cuff links depicting the profile of a lion.

"Where'd you find these, Lex? They're great!"

He leaned over and gave her a quick kiss. "Thanks, babe."

Alex fixed her eyes on her boyfriend expectantly, hoping he wouldn't make her ask outright for her present.

Billy sighed. "I suppose you want to open your present now, huh?"

She nodded, hardly able to keep from squealing with excitement. She would call her mom and dad first to tell them. They would probably insist on having some sort of engagement lunch or something at a fancy restaurant near their house. With the trip to Israel the following evening, her parents would have to wait until the following weekend for a visit, but that was okay. They'd waited years to celebrate their daughter's engagement. What was a couple more weeks?

Alex started smiling again, not that she had ever truly stopped. Billy was going to be *her husband*. She was going to be his wife. Her mother would finally acknowledge Billy's existence and welcome him as part of the family. Everything would change. Everything would be right. It would be the way it was supposed to be.

Caught up in her musings, Alex didn't notice that Billy had slipped out of bed to retrieve her present until the black velvet box suddenly appeared in her hands.

"Go on," said Billy, excitement shining in his own eyes. "Open it."

She almost asked him if he wanted to say something first but then stopped herself just in time. Billy was proposing to her. He should be allowed to do it in whatever way he wanted to.

Holding her breath, Alex cracked open the box,

smile growing wider and pulse racing faster. Then her heart stopped. It stopped and it squeezed and it fell from her chest as she sucked in a sharp breath. Almost immediately, tears welled up behind her eyes, building pressure even as she willed herself not to fall apart.

"Do you like them?" asked Billy, timidly.

She nodded as the tears blurred her vision, making the two diamond earrings look like one stone.

"They're beautiful," she managed to reply. And they were. The diamonds were huge—at least half a karat each—and prominently displayed on rose gold mounts. But they were not an engagement ring.

"Excuse me," she whispered, sliding out of the bed and running into the bathroom across the hall. As Alex locked the door, she heard Billy's footsteps approaching.

"Lex, what's wrong?" He sounded confused, and she didn't know which was worse—the fact that he hadn't proposed or that he really had no idea why she was upset.

"Nothing," Alex squeaked, her tears flowing freely as she suppressed a sob. "I'm fine. I just—I just need a minute."

"Don't you like the earrings?" he asked, causing her to choke down another sob.

"Yes, I like them." Her voice came out high-pitched. She sounded hysterical.

Alex shook her head to clear it and drew in several slow breaths in succession. She had to calm down.

"That's not the only thing I have for you."

Alex paused her breathing exercise. Could the earrings possibly be a prelude to the real proposal?

Hope stirred within her again, and she swiped at

her eyes with trembling hands.

What if he was building up to the big question? What if her outburst had just ruined what Billy had been planning?

Ashamed, Alex set the box of earrings down on the counter and turned on the faucet to splash cold water on her face. Toweling off and taking another deep breath, she unlocked the door and opened it.

"I'm sorry," she said. She felt she should elaborate, but Alex knew there was nothing she could say that wouldn't make the situation worse.

Thankfully, Billy didn't press her. Instead, he handed her an envelope.

"I know you've mentioned doing this in the past," he began, "but it didn't seem to be the right time. I didn't want to commit, and you have to commit so you can do it right, you know?"

Alex nodded wordlessly as she took the envelope. Her breath came in short spurts as she tore open the flap.

She had barely taken the paper out of the envelope when she realized what it was.

"A gym membership?" Alex looked at Billy incredulously. "You bought me a gym membership?"

"Us," he clarified, clearly missing her point. "I bought us a membership. So we can work out together, like we talk about doing every year." Billy shook his head, frowning. "I don't get it. Are you mad at me?"

"Am I mad at you?" she repeated, tears welling up again. Alex let the envelope and its contents fall out of her hands and ran for shelter in the bathroom once more. This time, however, Billy grabbed her arm to stop her.

"Don't go back in there," he said sternly. "Talk to me. Tell me what's wrong."

"What's wrong?" Apparently, she was only capable of repeating his last statement in the form of a question.

"Yes," he replied patiently. "Tell. Me. What's. Wrong."

She shook off his grasp. "I thought you were going to propose to me," she cried, unable to control herself. "That's what's wrong!"

Then she dashed into the bathroom and slammed the door in his face, immediately sinking to the floor, back against the door. Alex wrapped her arms around her legs and brought her head down to rest on her raised knees. Sobs racked her body—guttural sounds that she hardly recognized as her own—but she didn't care. Not anymore.

"Lex, baby. Please."

She could hear Billy slide his body down the other side of the door, assuming a seated position similar to hers, if she had to guess.

"I don't understand why this is happening," he continued.

Alex squeezed her eyes shut and held her legs tighter.

"You know I love you, Lex. I just don't want to get married. You've known that from the beginning."

"Why not?" she replied in a small voice that was not hers. "We've been out of school for five years, Billy. We've been together for almost eight. When I heard you on the phone talking to someone about 'taking you through the process,' well, I just thought…"

"What? You thought I'd suddenly changed my

mind?"

"Yes!" she admitted, suddenly feeling very foolish. Billy was right, after all. He'd never been unclear about his position on marriage. How could she have let herself think that now, out of nowhere, he was going to propose to her? "I thought you'd changed your mind," Alex whispered, wishing she had never found the box with the earrings or overheard his conversation on the phone. If she hadn't let herself believe that he was going to ask her to marry him, she would have been thrilled to get the diamond earrings and excited to be starting a workout routine with him. She wouldn't have felt this—heartbroken.

"Lex," he said, his voice soft and soothing, "I love what we have together. I love being with you. I love coming home to you. I love that you're the last person I see before I go to sleep, and I love waking up beside you. Being married or not being married won't change how I feel about you. It won't make any difference. It just doesn't matter."

But it does matter. It matters to me.

Those thoughts, however, Alex kept to herself.

****

Val had to admit that the timing of his break-up with Ginny was not ideal. Despite having a lot to do to plan for his trip the following day to Israel, it would have been nice to have somewhere to go, someone to meet, on a day when almost every store was closed and every movie on TV was about family, peace, and joy.

Merry Christmas to me.

Shrugging off his self-pity, Val tried his best to spend Christmas Day getting up to speed on everything Kurt Donovan had done since Val had introduced him to FiberTech. IT had downloaded all of Kurt's work emails onto a flash memory stick, and Val spent most of the morning and early afternoon reading one email after the next and getting more and more frustrated and angry with what he hadn't expected to find: Gideon Krantz had developed what seemed to be a very strong relationship with Kurt Donovan. Gideon trusted Kurt's opinion, went to him with questions big and small, and connected with him even on a personal level.

Yes, the situation was much worse than Val had expected.

By the time he pulled up to Alex's townhouse the following afternoon, he was convinced that they were fighting a very uphill battle. If not for the amulet, Val would have canceled the trip altogether and resigned himself to defeat. The amulet, however, had carried him through many a tough situation, and although part of his adult self naturally doubted that a rough-cut stone could possibly possess any type of "magic," the other part of him believed, just as his grandmother had before him.

Alex must have seen him drive up through one of the cozy townhouse's windows because before he could get out of the car to knock, the front door opened. Val smiled as he watched her balance a laptop bag and a purse on her shoulder, hold the storm door open with her foot, and drag out a carry-on roller bag that looked like it was packed to the gills.

Quickly exiting the car, Val took a few long strides and was at her side in moments. "Let me help you with that," he said, reaching for the carry-on.

She opened her mouth to protest, but Val had the bag in his hand before she could utter a sound. "Thank you," she said instead.

He carried the bag easily to the car, popped the trunk, and placed it carefully beside his own bag. She approached and placed the laptop in the trunk, as well.

Once the bags were loaded, Val closed the trunk and went over to the passenger side to open the door for her. "Is this because I'm a girl, or do you always treat your passengers with such care?" Alex rolled her eyes playfully as she stepped into the car. Laughing, Val shut the door behind her.

A few seconds later, he was sitting beside her and putting the car into drive.

"So, are you ready for this little adventure?" he asked, allowing himself a quick glance in Alex's direction as they came up to a stoplight.

Alex must have mistaken his question for an inquiry as to whether she was prepared for the meetings with FiberTech because she began to give him a report.

"I did a lot of research yesterday afternoon about FiberTech online—the history of the company, the key players and their backgrounds, the products and services they provide, that kind of thing. I went through their last five years of Annual Reports for investors..."

"Wow, five years' worth," Val remarked, amused.

"...just to get an idea of the company's goals and strategy for growth and how this acquisition is going to help them meet those goals. I also tried to learn more about the history of your company, but there wasn't that much information on the Internet, and I figured I could just ask you about it in person, so I didn't spend too much time on that. I developed a list of questions for you, instead."

"So, you're not going to let me just watch movies and sleep on the plane?" Val looked over at Alex and gave her a mischievous grin. She hesitated for a moment, unsure of whether he was being serious or joking, then smiled tentatively.

She was nervous, Val observed to himself. She wasn't her relaxed, confident self. Was it him? Was he making Alex nervous? Val had only been in the car with her for a few minutes. He was wearing a polo shirt and jeans, and he had a small red scratch on his face where he had cut himself shaving a few hours ago, for crying out loud. His mere physical presence couldn't possibly be making her nervous. Any thoughts to the contrary could only be attributed to vanity, and possibly also some wishful thinking.

Val watched her out of the corner of his eye as he accelerated onto the interstate. Her hair hung loose down both sides of her face, and she was looking down at her hands, which were folded in her lap. Hands clasped firmly together, she was rubbing her thumbs on the backs of her hands, almost absentmindedly. The air felt heavy all around her.

Val modified his theory—Alex wasn't nervous. She was preoccupied. She was thinking about something, something unpleasant or disappointing. And she looked—tired.

"Did you sleep well last night?" he asked, searching for some clue as to her current disposition.

Alex glanced at him, then attempted a half-hearted smile. "Not really. I kept waking up. That always happens to me before I travel. Even if my flight is at night."

"That's understandable," Val replied. "Well, you'll have plenty of time to sleep on the plane, if you can tear yourself away from the annual reports you're committing to memory."

She looked down, as though she hadn't even heard his teasing remark. What was going on with her?

During the twenty-minute ride to the airport, Val prattled on about the weather and other inconsequential matters, pausing only once he'd parked and began unloading their bags. They checked in and got in line for security within ten minutes, but Val was still unsure of what was bothering her. He had also run out of things to say, and they had been creeping forward in line in relative silence.

"Do you travel a lot?" Alex asked as they picked up their bags to move one more step forward in line, then put them back down again. It was the first time she had initiated conversation since he had picked her up, and Val was relieved.

"A fair amount, but not too bad," he replied. They moved forward and stopped again.

"How much?"

"Oh, maybe once every three or four weeks," he answered.

"For how long?"

"Sometimes a week, sometimes only a couple days. It depends."

Alex glanced over at the TSA Pre-Check Lane, where passengers seemed to walk right up to the TSA agent and go through security in a matter of a couple of minutes. "How come you don't have the Pre-Check thing if you travel so often?"

"I do," replied Val, "but you don't. We have a lot of time until our flight boards, anyway. Wait here or wait in the lounge. It's all still waiting."

"The lounge?"

Val smiled. "You'll see."

They finally made it through security, and Val grabbed his bags, shoes, and other personal belongings and moved to the bench where Alex was already standing. Her back was to him, and he watched as she slipped on her shoes and put a thick black leather belt back around her waist. Val liked her outfit—a turquoise blue short-sleeved button-down shirt with black dress pants that fit nicely, and that black belt that went around the smallest part of her waist, over her shirt, pulling the whole look together. It felt strange to watch Alex get dressed like that, but he couldn't tear his eyes away. Alex left her sweater and jacket off, and Val was secretly grateful that she hadn't decided to cover herself back up with all those extra articles of clothing.

Finally, Val forced his attention to his own shoes and belt and tried to push the image of Alex dressing out of his mind.

They followed the signs down the hall, past shops and restaurants, until they came to the airline lounge.

"Am I allowed to go in there?" Alex asked, looking up at him innocently.

"Of course," he said. "It comes with our business class tickets. It's part of the reason the tickets are so ridiculously expensive."

He led the way through the doors of the lounge and up to the hostess at the counter. The well-coiffed woman looked at their tickets briefly, then welcomed them in.

Val motioned for Alex to enter before him and couldn't help smiling as she looked around in wonder. There was a buffet of fresh fruit, nuts, and other snacks, as well as a few hot foods and a variety of drinks. Alex turned her eyes to him after surveying all of it, and Val knew what she was thinking: Is this all free?

He grinned and motioned toward a large room past the food, near some windows. They put their bags down near a couple of empty seats. "You can go get something to eat," said Val. "I'll stay here with the bags until you get back."

She nodded, and he watched as she walked toward the food. A few minutes later Alex came back with a plate full of fruit and nuts and a glass of water. She sat down next to him, then leaned closer and whispered, "I'm not even hungry!"

Val laughed. "Well, you'd better pace yourself. All they do in business class is feed you, and it's all actually pretty decent food, especially on this flight."

Alex smiled as she picked up a pistachio. "I have a feeling I'm going to enjoy the next few days."

Chapter Nine

Less than an hour later, Val and Alex were making their way to their gate to wait for the call to board. The easy conversation with Val had done wonders for Alex's nerves, and she no longer felt like a tightly wound ball of stress, ready to come undone at any moment. Still, she wished the big blowout with Billy hadn't happened the day before this huge international business trip. Alex couldn't stop thinking about all the things she'd said. And all the things Billy hadn't.

She'd only managed to take refuge in the bathroom for a few minutes before Billy had coaxed her out and dried her tears. He loved her—she knew he did. He just didn't see things the same way Alex did, and she was beginning to think he never would. Alex just had to accept it and move on. That was all there was to it. Billy wasn't going to marry her, and that was that. She couldn't keep finding hope in places it didn't exist. She couldn't keep thinking that every jewelry box held a secret engagement ring or that every whispered phone call was with a catering hall. She couldn't keep setting herself up for disappointment, time and time again.

"Come on," said Val, looking over his shoulder at her and smiling. "They're boarding business class."

Lost in her thoughts, Alex had completely missed the announcement.

The flight attendant at the door to the plane greeted

them warmly and directed them to a wide aisle on the left, behind a curtain.

"I've never been on this side of the curtain before," she whispered, making Val chuckle. "I feel almost guilty coming up here."

"Don't feel guilty," he replied, stopping at the third row of seats. "Just enjoy it."

Alex tried not to look like a country mouse as she casually took in her surroundings. The seats alone were a sight to behold—wide, comfortable sleeping pods that held little resemblance to the seats Alex was used to seeing on planes. Their two pods were next to each other but oriented such that, when reclined, there could be some privacy between them. It was a clever design.

Val put his bag on the seat and reached for Alex's bag first, lifting it easily into the overhead compartment.

"You don't have to do that for me," said Alex, even as she let him take the carry-on.

"I know you are perfectly capable," Val replied, a teasing smile on his lips, "but what would people think if I made no move to help you?"

"Ah, yes," she said, finding herself smiling in return as she took her seat by the window. "I keep forgetting how self-serving and calculating you are."

Alex buckled herself in and adjusted the position of her laptop bag under the seat in front of her, watching Val discreetly to see if he was going to open any of the compartments in the armrest. She was dying to find out what was in those.

The flight attendant, a handsome woman in her fifties, came by just then and handed each of them a steaming hot washcloth. Alex took it from the metal tongs the woman was using to hold it, then looked at Val, wondering what to do with it.

Val spread his washcloth out and wiped his face and hands with the cloth, so Alex did the same, feeling slightly foolish for not having figured that out on her own.

The flight attendant came by again moments later with a bowl for them to deposit their used washcloths, and Alex reached over Val's lap to drop hers in. Relaxing back into her chair, she turned to him, deciding to own up to her ignorance. "This must be very entertaining for you."

He laughed out loud, then quickly recovered. "I don't know what you're talking about."

She rolled her eyes, smiling at his feeble attempt to deny the obvious. "You know exactly what I'm talking about. We haven't even left the ground yet, and this has already been quite the new adventure for me." Suddenly afraid that her remarks might sound ungrateful, she added, "Thanks again for bringing me with you, Val. It really means a lot to me that you would think I could help you with this very important task."

His eyes squinted briefly, and he looked down, almost shyly, before looking back over at her. "Thank you for letting me interrupt your holiday plans." His tone was confident, and his gaze was steady, making her wonder if she had misinterpreted his previous gesture as shyness.

The flight attendant came by again and asked them if they would like some champagne. Alex tried not to look too pleased as Val nodded subtly in her direction, letting her know it was okay to accept the drink.

"Sure," she replied.

The uniformed woman poured a glass of champagne and handed it to her.

"And you, sir?"

"Yes, please," Val replied.

Champagne in hand, Val turned to Alex and raised his glass. "To new adventures."

Alex raised her glass in response. "And a safe journey across the ocean."

"Cheers." They touched glasses and drank their champagne.

The drink was light and fizzy on her tongue, which was appropriate considering her overall contented state. Val was easy to get along with, and he didn't seem to mind her country bumpkin ways. Any concerns she'd had about trying to impress him, or at the very least keeping him from regretting the decision to bring her, were slowly dissipating.

A man in the row behind them coughed, and it occurred to Alex that Val had been sick at work just a few days ago.

"How do you feel?" she asked, setting down the glass of champagne. "I've been meaning to ask you."

The question must have caught Val by surprise, as it took him a moment to answer.

"Oh," he finally replied, "you mean my throat? It's all better, and whatever I had never turned into the usual congestion and runny nose I tend to get when I'm sick. I got lucky, I guess."

"That's great." She was glad he didn't have to endure ten hours on a plane feeling under the weather. "The worst is when you have to travel sick, especially with the pressure you feel in your ears as the plane gains altitude."

Val nodded, his brow crinkling slightly in thought, before smoothing again.

"Tell me something," he said, shifting his position in the seat to look at her more directly. A nervous tremor ran through her at his serious tone, and she wondered if this was how Val went about firing an employee. "Why are you working at Advance Legal doing contract attorney work? Why aren't you at a law firm or a company instead? I've seen your résumé. I know you've had an amazing academic career. And you're well-rounded—you've been in the workforce, you have business training, you speak multiple languages. Plus, you've got the intangibles—a great personality, poise, charm, wit, presence. So, what's the story?"

Alex tried not to look surprised at his question. She knew the subject was bound to come up at some point. Why had she been out of law school for five years and yet hadn't ever gotten a *real* job? What was wrong with her?

She looked down at her hands, trying to think of how to explain something she didn't really know the answer to, even though she'd spent five years wondering the same thing.

"I'm not really sure," Alex replied honestly. "I've thought about it a lot, actually, and the best answer I can come up with is that my timing was off, in the beginning, that is. I hadn't planned on practicing law here originally. I had been interviewing in Chicago and St. Louis mostly, with a couple of interviews in Dallas and one in Pittsburgh. Both of us—me and Billy—were interviewing in the same cities so that we could end up in the same place."

"Your boyfriend? He's also a lawyer?" She thought she heard the smallest hint of annoyance in Val's tone, although his face still bore a kind expression.

"Yes. We met our first year of law school and started dating a couple of months into our first semester."

"So, what happened to the plan?"

Alex chuckled half-heartedly. "Well, one of the firms he really liked in St. Louis really liked him too. The problem was that they didn't have a spot for him in their St. Louis office, so they offered him a position as an associate in a different office, here—"

"Which was a city that you hadn't even considered before," Val completed her sentence.

"That's right. I didn't think it was a big deal when it happened. But by the time I started interviewing, all the new associate spots had been taken. I took the bar exam with Billy and passed, and I thought that maybe once some of those firms had seen that I had passed the bar, they would be interested in me, but I was wrong. They would rather hold on to someone they had just hired who had failed the bar exam than give me a chance. So, I took a job doing contract work with Advance Legal just to pay the bills, thinking I would quit as soon as I found something better. Unfortunately, that something better just never came along. And the farther out from law school I got, the farther I get, the more of a hiring risk I become. Everyone's thinking 'Well, what's wrong with her? If no one else wanted to hire her, then why should we?' It's what you're thinking now, isn't it?"

He shook his head vehemently. "That's not what

I'm thinking at all. What I'm wondering is why no one in five years has seen in you what it only took me five days to see."

Alex could feel tears begin to build pressure behind her eyes. She'd always been so quick to let emotion overtake her, and what Val had just said—well, it was perhaps the nicest thing anyone had ever said to her.

She took a deep breath, willing the tears back into their respective tear ducts, and smiled. "Does Span Global need a full-time in-house attorney?"

Val gave her a wry smile. "I would hire you in a second, Alex. But it would seem we're not the most stable place to work right now."

Just then, the flight attendant came through the cabin to pick up their empty glasses as another flight attendant turned on a presentation on their individual video monitors that went through the typical pre-flight safety lecture. As a soothing female voice went on about buckling seat belts, flotation devices under the seats, and oxygen masks dropping from the ceiling, Alex closed her eyes and leaned back, trying to relax and prepare herself for what would come next.

Val was a really nice guy. Despite how successful and rich he was—and, if she were being completely honest with herself, how very good-looking—he didn't have an ego. He was confident, but not to an off-putting degree. There was a difference between confidence and conceit, and Val had none of the latter. The fact that he felt he needed her there with him to help the company get through Kurt Donovan's departure was proof that he wasn't arrogant. He was just a down-to-earth, good guy, and it was refreshing.

Alex prayed she could help him do what was

needed to see the sale go through. She knew he had faith in her, and the last thing she wanted was to let Val down.

****

The cabin attendants prepared for take-off, and the airplane began to accelerate. Alex had been quiet for several minutes, and Val couldn't help thinking it was his fault. Had he offended her with the question about contract work? He shouldn't have been so quick to ask, even though he'd been dying to know since the moment they'd met. Another minute of silence compelled him to turn in her direction. Her eyes were squeezed shut, and her hands were gripping the armrests. Did she have a fear of flying, perhaps?

As the plane began its ascent, and Val was about to ask if she was okay, Alex opened her eyes to look out the window. It was already dark outside, but the lights of the city were beautiful, and Val watched over her shoulder as those lights grew smaller and smaller, eventually disappearing.

He shifted his gaze as he saw Alex reach for the magazine that was stuffed in the pocket of the seat in front of her. Out of the corner of his eye, he saw her flip through the pages, scanning articles about travel and far-away places.

Alex turned to look at him then and grinned, catching him by surprise. "I did find some information on your company yesterday when I was studying up for this trip."

"Oh, you did?"

"I did."

"What did you learn?" Val's interest was piqued.

"I learned that you started the company eleven

years ago with a college buddy, Scott Hoover. He had an idea for a fiber optic coupling that would match up the light coming out of a laser with a fiber optic cable in a more precise way, so thinner cables could be used. Pretty cool stuff. You had just finished business school, and you convinced him to quit his job as an engineer at a Fortune 500 company and start the company with you. Kurt Donovan joined a month later. Your office was an old warehouse on Morehead Street. That's where the three of you built your first prototype, and then you hit the road to try and sell it. It took five months for you to make your first sale, but after that things just exploded for your company. You hired a bunch of people, made a bunch of these couplers, and the only problem you had was keeping up with demand."

"Well," said Val, "that wasn't the *only* problem."

"You made something out of nothing and became rich practically overnight."

Val sighed. "You know, I didn't spend a dime of what I made on myself the first three years. I was worried it wasn't real, that the business, the money, all of it, would just go away one day."

"And now?" Alex looked at him thoughtfully.

"Now I *know* it's all going to go away one day, so I want to enjoy it while it lasts."

She smiled. "Well, that's a great attitude. As long as you keep a little money tucked away in your mattress so you don't have to live on the streets if it all does go south one day."

"My mattress is actually stuffed with hundred-dollar bills. I'm surprised you knew that."

Alex laughed out loud at his deadpan delivery, and

he finally broke down and laughed with her.

"Well," she said as the laughter subsided, "I think it's pretty amazing what you've done. It's a big risk to start a company. You put everything you had into it and just hoped for the best."

"That's true," said Val, "but it's easy to take a risk when you have nothing to lose. I didn't come from money. I scraped my way through school. And when I graduated, we were in the middle of a recession. I wasn't turning down any 5- or 6-figure salaries to 'follow my dream.'"

"Regardless, I'm glad it worked out for you." Alex's voice had softened, and he could see her fiddling with the corner of the magazine in her lap. "I know I haven't known you for very long, but just seeing how much your employees love working for you, how happy everyone is, how well they treat each other, and me, it tells me you deserve every bit of the success you've had."

"Thank you," Val replied warmly. "Although I think Kurt Donovan would disagree with you."

"Kurt Donovan is an idiot," she quickly retorted. Val could see that fire in her eyes that always ignited whenever they spoke of Kurt's departure. If he were being completely honest with himself, the whole reason he had said Kurt's name just now was to see Alex's eyes light up with that inexplicable, and very gratifying, loyalty for his company. Or, as Val preferred to think of it, the loyalty she felt for him.

"I know," Val said, without really thinking, "but I like hearing you say it."

She smiled and looked down again at her magazine.

"What can I get you for dinner this evening?"

Val and Alex looked up at the same time to see the middle-aged flight attendant observing them with a pleasant expression, waiting for their responses. "Today's dinner selections are on page twelve of the in-flight magazine."

The woman waited patiently while Alex flipped to the right page and held the magazine so that she and Val could both see the selections.

Val looked over at her. "Do you know what you're getting?" Had he ended the question with the word "honey," the flight attendant would have been certain they were together, going on their honeymoon or some other romantic getaway. Oddly enough, Val warmed at the thought.

Alex nodded, looking up at the woman. "I guess I'll have the stuffed chicken breast."

"What would you like to start with? We have smoked salmon, a cheese plate, or arugula salad."

"I'll have the salad, please."

The flight attendant turned her attention to Val. "And you, sir?"

Alex moved the magazine closer to Val.

"I'll have the salad to start, as well, but I'll do the sea bass, please."

"Very good," replied the woman. "We'll be coming out with your starters shortly."

Once the flight attendant was out of earshot, Alex leaned toward Val and whispered, "I think this is the fanciest meal I have ever ordered, land, sea, or air."

Val didn't know quite how to respond, and the innocent nearness of her lips to his face didn't make the thoughts come any easier. So, he just smiled back at her, trying to think of something ordinary to say. "This flight is probably the best one in terms of food. The one back on Tuesday will be okay, but not as nice."

As they waited for the food to arrive, it occurred to Val that he had underestimated how difficult the next four days would be. True, he was very relaxed in Alex's presence, and the conversation was natural and easy, especially now that Alex had loosened up a bit. But there were moments when he was aware of her in a way that was very distracting and not exactly appropriate considering her unavailable status, their relationship as co-workers, and their purpose in visiting Israel, to begin with.

Val would just have to be careful not to cross any lines. And hopefully, Alex would stop leaning into him. He was, after all, only human.

****

Val could tell by the expression on Alex's face when she put her fork down that she had enjoyed her dinner, from the real silverware to the china to the linens to the genuinely good food. She was impressed.

They had exchanged pleasant conversation over dinner, interspersed with periods of comfortable silence. Now, as the flight attendant came by to clear away their dishes and give them their choice of dessert, it was Alex who was studying Val with a quizzical expression on her face. Val could feel her watching him as the flight attendant placed a bowl of banana pudding in front of him and a thick slice of chocolate cake in front of Alex.

When Alex looked away without saying anything, Val's curiosity got the better of him. "What were you thinking just now? I thought you were going to say something."

She fixed her eyes on him, then smiled. "You're very perceptive. I was just wondering what you were thinking, actually. You had an interesting look about you when you asked for the banana pudding. Is there a story there?"

Val wasn't sure what he had expected her reply to be, but it wasn't that.

"It seems you're the perceptive one," he answered. "I guess you could say I have a sentimental notion of banana pudding, or, more accurately, of the vanilla wafers they always use in the pudding."

He picked one up with his fingers and looked at it.

"They remind you of someone?" Alex asked, her voice soft and thoughtful.

Val put the cookie back in his pudding and wiped his fingers on the cloth napkin lying across his lap.

"Yes. My grandmother. She always had a box of them somewhere in her room. To this day I don't know how she was able to maintain such a steady supply. My grandmother couldn't drive, and she hardly ever left her room."

Alex's lips curled knowingly. "She was a special person in your life."

"She was. My grandmother lived with us for years, in our house. She never complained, never asked for anything. And my parents weren't the best of caretakers, that's for sure."

"Who else were they taking care of? Besides you and your grandmother?"

Val certainly hadn't intended on telling Alex about his family, but now that they were talking about it, it didn't seem right not to tell her.

"I'm the youngest of four. My brother, Dimitar, he's the oldest. And I have two older sisters, too. There are six years between me and my brother, three years between me and my oldest sister Gabriela, and just a year between me and Eva, my other sister."

"I didn't realize you came from a big family," remarked Alex. "It's only me and my brother in mine. I'm the oldest, but only by a couple of years."

"Do you have a good relationship with your brother?"

Alex nodded. "I do. I talk to him at least once a week. He and his wife are expecting their first child in the spring."

Val had seen all manner of smiles from Alex in the brief time he had known her, and he knew enough to detect a faint trace of sadness behind the one she gave him now.

"That's good that you're so close. It helps you in life to have the support of family. No matter what goes wrong, someone will be there to look out for you." He paused, then surprised himself by adding, "My family was never like that."

"Except for your grandmother?"

Val smiled. "Except for my grandmother."

They ate the rest of their desserts in silence. Val wondered why he had felt so comfortable talking about his family just now, with her. It was almost instinctual. He had never mentioned his grandmother or his parents or any of his mess of a family to anyone before. None of Val's girlfriends had cared enough to probe him on the topic when he had given them his typical superficial descriptions of his childhood. The only conversations that had ever come close to delving into such topics were with his niece Liza, and she already knew how dysfunctional his family was, being part of it herself.

After their desserts had been cleared away, Val opened the compartment in his armrest and took out a set of headphones. He saw Alex watch him, then do the same. She hadn't known that such treasures were hiding just within reach.

"I think my favorite part of traveling is catching up on movies," Val commented as he began scrolling through the movie titles on the screen in front of him.

"Billy and I hardly go to the movies anymore," Alex replied. "He works long hours, and I would feel weird going by myself. So, I usually just watch them at home once they're available to rent."

He was going to ask her if Billy watched the movies with her at home, but then decided that his growing dislike for the guy might seep into his speech.

Val settled on the new James Bond movie, and he could see out of the corner of his eye that Alex had chosen a period piece for herself.

For the next two hours, they watched their movies, sitting next to each other, separated by their bulky seats and armrests. Leaning back in his chair, Val couldn't really see Alex sitting there beside him, not with his eyes, at least. Still, he was very aware of Alex's presence, and something about knowing she was there, close enough to touch, was very comforting.

Instead of focusing on the movie, Val's mind began to wander toward thoughts of the young woman sitting beside him. In addition to Alex's obvious grace and beauty, there was an understated strength that was only magnified by her softness. She was professional, yet familiar; intelligent, yet innocent; sensitive, yet passionate.

Val knew all these things about her from the turn of her speech and the subtle positioning of her hands when she talked. He knew it from how she looked at him and how she looked away from him. He'd only just met Alex, really, but still Val felt as though he knew her, and everything about her drew him in closer.

Val wondered what the story was with her boyfriend. The guy sounded like an inconsiderate loser, hotshot lawyer or not. Val was sure the guy didn't deserve her.

The reasonable part of his brain tried to remind him that they were on a business trip, not an extended date, and Alex was in some form or another his employee. But even the reasonable part of him couldn't deny the technicality that Alex wasn't directly on Val's payroll. Plus, Alex wasn't a naïve little sorority girl straight out of college. And, after all, there was nothing inappropriate about two people meeting, at work or anywhere else, and hitting it off and having a good time. Just because the fate of his business depended on the success of the next few days didn't mean Val couldn't enjoy himself a little in the process.

When the movie was over, Val stood up, stretched, then made his way to the bathroom, hoping that accomplishing some of his usual nighttime routines would make it easier to get a few hours of sleep. He wasn't about to change into pajamas or anything (although looking around the cabin he saw that some people had done just that), but it wouldn't hurt to wash his face and brush his teeth.

Alex was putting away her headphones when Val got back from the restroom. Her movie was over now, too, apparently.

"Do you mind if I scoot by you to get to the bathroom before you sit down?" she asked.

"No, not at all. Go right ahead."

Val watched her walk to the bathroom, feeling a little less guilty about admiring her form than he probably should have.

He stood in the aisle until she returned, happy to stretch his legs for a few more minutes. Assuming her seat by the window once more, Alex looked down at her armrest and started pressing buttons. "I know one of these reclines the seat to a horizontal position. Oh, I think this is the one."

Her seat started to move forward, and the backrest reclined until it was flat and flush with the seat portion to form a bed.

"This is pretty cool," she remarked, smiling.

Val smiled in return. "It's not too bad, although we still won't be able to get much sleep. It'll be better than nothing, though."

Val watched as Alex pulled the blanket she had been sitting on out from under her and spread it across her legs and torso. She sat up slightly so she could see him over the partition, then said, "Well, goodnight, Val. This has been a great trip so far."

He smiled again at Alex as she lay back down and turned to face the opposite direction, toward the windows. Her words echoed his thoughts on the matter exactly.

Chapter Ten

When Val awoke a few hours later, the first thing he did was peer over the barrier separating his seat from Alex's. Her body was turned toward him now, still sleeping, and Val was struck by how beautiful her face was, even with messy hair and day-old mascara smudges under one of her eyes. She looked completely relaxed—her eyelids were closed, yet somehow they still called to mind the honey-brown eyes hiding behind them; her lips were slightly parted and were all the more inviting as a result.

He quickly sank back into his own seat, suddenly worried that Alex might open her eyes to find him studying her. After all, "creepy" wasn't exactly the vibe he was going for.

Val had no idea what time it was, or what time zone for that matter, but he knew it was morning wherever they were as the light from outside was peeking in through the tiny cracks under the window shades that had been pulled closed by all the passengers the night before. The smell of coffee and the muffled sound of drawers opening and closing let him know that the flight attendants were preparing to serve breakfast. All around him, the cabin was slowly coming to life, and before too long he heard Alex stirring beside him.

"What time is it?" Alex's voice was hoarse with sleep, and the sound of it, raw and natural, was like an aphrodisiac.

Val peered over to look at Alex again. She brushed the hair away from her face, eyelids half closed, then rubbed her eyes, opening them wider.

"How did you know I was awake?" Val asked, amused by her apparent disorientation.

"I guess I didn't. But you are."

Val reached for the remote control, which had fallen between his leg and the armrest at some point during the night, then used it to turn on his video screen. The screen flashed the local time: 7:52 a.m.

"It's almost eight," he said.

"Thanks," Alex replied, with a funny look on her face that said, "I can read, you know."

Val almost chuckled.

"So, how many hours of sleep do you think we actually got, what with the time difference and all?"

The word "we" in Alex's question struck Val as very intimate, and it warmed him to his core.

"Not much," he replied. "Four, maybe five hours, I'm not sure."

Val realized that his seat was still in a horizontal position, so he found the appropriate buttons on the armrest and moved the seat back to a semi-reclined position, where he could see Alex without as much effort. Watching him, Alex did the same.

"Do you mind if I go use the restroom before they come around with more food?"

"Of course not," Val replied, pulling his feet in so Alex could shuffle by.

"I'm sorry," she apologized, moving around him and into the aisle. She obviously didn't realize how much he enjoyed having her brush past him.

When Alex came back from the bathroom, Val took his turn, and by the time he got back to his seat the flight attendant, somehow looking fresh and well-rested, was asking Alex for her choice of breakfast.

"You got here just in time," joked Alex once the flight attendant had moved on. "I was just about to order something completely off the wall for you."

"Wow." Val laughed. "I'm getting the feeling I'm going to discover a whole new side to you over the next few days."

She threw him a tantalizing smile. "You just might."

Breakfast came and went, and soon after an announcement was made that they would be starting their descent into Munich, Germany.

They landed in Munich a little after nine-thirty in the morning, local time, and by the time they had deplaned and found their way to the business class lounge, they had just under two hours to kill before their noon flight to Tel Aviv.

Val led the way to a couple of empty seats in the back of the lounge, near the buffet of continental breakfast items, with Alex following close behind.

"Is this okay?" Val asked before sitting down.

"Sure, it's great," replied Alex, that ever-present smile on her lips. "Can't beat a spot by the food, even though I have to admit I'm not all that hungry at the moment."

"The lady at the front desk said we should start walking to the gate around eleven o'clock. We'll have to go through another security checkpoint before getting on the plane, so that might take a few minutes. I'd rather be early at the gate than rush to make our flight, though."

Alex nodded. "I totally agree. Nothing like being stranded at the airport in a foreign country. Although everyone here seems to have perfect English, which is just amazing to me."

"Yes. People in Europe, and in Israel, too, speak at least two, and often three and four languages."

As they settled into their seats, Alex turned to Val and asked, "So, do you speak any other languages?"

Val looked at her, somewhat surprised. "I do, actually." Although people sometimes speculated that he was "ethnic" because his skin was perpetually tan and his hair was practically black, people usually never bothered to ask about his background or what languages he knew.

"What do you speak?"

"Bulgarian and a little bit of Spanish. Bulgarian I learned from my grandmother, mostly, and I'm not too good. I can understand it pretty well and can speak it in a pinch, but I don't think I could read or write anything above a first-grade level. The Spanish I learned in junior high and high school, then I promptly forgot most of it. I know you have a thing for foreign languages."

Alex shook her head and laughed. "Well, I wouldn't call it a 'thing.' I took French in high school and kept it up in college, just because it was an easy elective. Italian, Spanish, and Portuguese were pretty easy to pick up on once I got good at French. You know one Romance Language, you know them all, right? And then I learned German one summer during college, trying to talk to my boyfriend's parents who were from Germany. I only dated him that one summer, though, so my German is not that good." She paused, pushing a loose strand of hair behind one ear. "So, you're Bulgarian?"

Val nodded. "My parents immigrated to the U.S. a year or so after they got married. My dad eventually brought over my grandmother and his two brothers. He had a sister who stayed in Bulgaria."

"You're first generation? That's pretty cool. Is your name Bulgarian, then? Is 'Val' short for something?"

"It is. It's short for Valentin, which I don't believe exudes masculinity, in the U.S. or in Bulgaria, so I always go by Val."

Alex laughed freely, which made Val smile. "I'll just keep calling you 'Val,' then. I wouldn't want to offend your sense of masculinity, plus I don't think I could pronounce your full name the way you just did."

Alex's gaze lingered on him for a moment longer, then she reached down to get into the laptop bag stowed between her seat and Val's. Out of the laptop bag, she withdrew a small stack of documents, a highlighter, and a pencil.

"So, you actually brought work to do?" Val asked, amused.

Alex looked up from the papers. "Of course. I thought we might have some free time, and I just want to be sure I get everything done that we need to for the due diligence with enough time to get it over to the other side."

"You know, if this thing blows up, then you won't need to finish what you're doing."

"It won't blow up," replied Alex, firmly. "I'm pretty sure everything is going to work out for you."

Val was touched by her confidence, yet again. "What makes you so sure?"

"Because you're a good guy. You should win."

"'Should' and 'will' are two very different things," Val observed.

"Not always," replied Alex, smiling again.

Neither Val nor Alex could get much work done sitting in the lounge with only a few hours of sleep in them, and their separate attempts soon converged into a singular surrender involving a series of pleasant exchanges about the very European styles and mannerisms of the people around them.

It was soon time to head to their next flight, and Val once again led the way through the busy airport toward the gate where their plane was waiting.

As anticipated, they had to pass through another security checkpoint to be able to enter the gate for their flight to Tel Aviv. Val motioned for Alex to take the spot ahead of him so he could be sure she had no problems. He watched as Alex placed her two bags on the moving conveyor belt and stepped through the large metal detectors, quietly observing how the security personnel softened when she smiled and thanked them as she passed through.

Once they were both past security and walking toward their gate, which was now in sight, Alex turned to Val with an animated look on her face. "I've never seen anything like that before! It's like a torture chamber!"

She was pointing to the glass booths positioned throughout the airport that served as totally enclosed smoking areas. Each booth was visibly filled with smoke from passengers trying to get one last hit of nicotine before boarding their planes.

Val grinned and replied, in his best cowboy impersonation, "We ain't in America anymore, little lady."

Alex laughed. They reached their gate looking like a pair of newlyweds. Or so Val imagined.

"Are they going to feed us on this flight?" asked Alex, as they stood beside a pillar waiting for boarding to begin.

"Why?" he asked, trying to suppress a grin. "Are you hungry?"

The corners of her mouth lifted in a sheepish smile. "Well, maybe a little. My body's gotten used to being fed every couple of hours from the flight over, I think."

Val chuckled. "I think we'll get something on this flight. I just can't remember if it's a full meal or a snack."

Alex ended up falling asleep as soon as the two of them were seated on the plane half an hour later, and she almost missed the distribution of food by the flight attendant (which was only a snack). But a gentle nudge from Val as the stern-looking German flight attendant approached with a cart of food brought Alex back to wakefulness so that she could select the drink and snack of her choice.

The four-hour flight to Tel Aviv seemed relatively short compared to the trans-Atlantic flight they had endured only hours before. Just the same, when Alex fell back asleep after eating a snack, Val couldn't help considering ways to "accidentally" wake her up so they could talk. Val enjoyed talking to Alex—very much. Their conversations were easy and light, and they brought him a certain amount of peace, regardless of the topic. Determining that interrupting someone's sleep was something only a two-year-old would do, and also that there was no way to do it without being found out, Val leaned back in his chair and closed his eyes, resigning himself to getting a little more rest, too.

When Val woke, he was pleasantly surprised to see Alex leaning toward him, smiling. "I was afraid the large German flight attendant over there was going to have to bring your chair back to its upright position for you. She was getting pretty annoyed after telling you twice."

Val looked over at the woman, who was indeed still glaring at him from down the aisle, and promptly adjusted his chair to the proper position. Alex chuckled next to him.

"Thanks for telling her to stand down," Val muttered. "She looks like a force to be reckoned with."

"That guy over there is still sleeping, so we might find out yet!"

****

They had a smooth landing in Tel Aviv and were able to get off the plane without too much hassle or delay, and before long, Val was leading the way through the airport to the baggage claim area. He seemed to know exactly where to go, which spots to avoid, and how best to maneuver around hapless travelers. And despite his tall frame and long stride, he somehow stayed right beside Alex so that he could amuse her with anecdotes from his past travels.

"What do we do now?" asked Alex. They had retrieved their bags from the carousel and were stuck behind a group of people they couldn't get around. Alex did her best not to hit the guy in front of her with her oversized bag as she inched forward.

"Customs is up ahead," Val replied, tilting his head up to see past a woman wearing a ridiculous hat who had positioned herself in line a few spots in front of them. "The Customs official will look at our passports and ask us some questions. We can go up together, though, and I'll tell them we're here on business and that we're visiting FiberTech. Once we're through Customs, we can make our way to the exits, where we'll look for the driver who's picking us up to take us to the hotel. Today is Saturday, the sabbath, so the airport will be pretty bare bones when it comes to personnel, as you could probably tell from all the airport shops we passed that are closed. It might take us longer than usual to get through Customs and to the exits. We'll see."

"Okay," replied Alex, taking another step. "I'll just stick with you. It's been working for me so far."

Val flashed her a smile, and Alex imagined that smile was only one weapon in a large arsenal for charming investors and customers alike. Cheeks growing warm, Alex concluded that even she couldn't avoid the effects of such a smile. Thankfully, Val's attention was drawn to the front of the line again, allowing time for the heat to dissipate.

They had to wait over twenty minutes to get through the Customs checkpoint, which Val said wasn't really too bad. As Alex tried to get her bearings again so she could help Val locate their driver, she saw Val wave in the direction of a silver-haired man holding up a sign that said SPAN GLOBAL.

"Ori!" said Val, steering them over to the older man. The way he shook the man's hand with a fond expression on his face made Alex wonder if Val knew the guy personally. Then again, Val seemed to know a lot of people, and he had a warm personality that made everyone feel like they were family.

"How are you, Ori? How is your wife?"

"Good, very good. Everyone good and healthy, thank God," the driver replied in broken English. "Come, come, I take you to the car."

They followed Ori, who was about four inches shorter than her own modest five feet five inches, out through the sliding glass doors to where several taxis were stopped, waiting for passengers. When they reached Ori's car, he popped the trunk for them and reached out to take Alex's suitcase. She felt bad making a man old enough to be her father lift the heavy bag, but refusing his help would likely be the bigger insult. So, she smiled and stepped aside, while the old man struggled to set the bag into the open trunk.

With the bags loaded, Val motioned to Alex to sit in the front seat as Ori opened the door for her. "Are you sure?" she asked, looking at Val. "There's not much legroom back there."

"Of course, I'm sure," he replied, getting into the seat behind her.

As Ori pulled out into the line of cars moving away from the terminal, he said in a thick Israeli accent, "So, Miss, this your first time in Israel?"

Alex pulled her gaze away from the scenery outside to look at the driver. "Yes. It's very exciting."

"Israel is beautiful country," Ori went on. "All you see on TV is war and fighting. You come and see what? Where is war? Nothing. Only on TV."

Though Alex would never admit it to Ori, or Val,

for that matter, she had been a little nervous to travel to a region known for civil unrest. So far, though, aside from a couple of security guards in the airport with automatic weapons tucked under their arms, she hadn't seen anything out of the ordinary and had felt quite safe.

It occurred to her that part of that sense of safety came from traveling with Val. There was something about him that was comforting and peaceful. It was most likely due to the fact that Val had been to Israel in the past and was used to getting around in this part of the world. It was almost like being with a local.

Alex turned her attention to the windows once again. At first, the scenery was mostly rural, but as the miles passed, cities rose on either side of the highway they were traveling.

"Remind me, Ori, Tel Aviv is to our left, correct?" Val leaned forward and into the gap between the two front seats as he spoke.

"You right, Mr. Val. This Tel Aviv," —Ori motioned to the left— "and this Ramat Gan." He motioned to the right. "Back there, we pass by Tel Aviv Museum of Art. Very nice. You go see if you have time."

"Thank you, Ori," replied Val. "We'll do our best."

They drove on for a few more minutes, the traffic intermittently getting heavier, then easing up again. The numerous billboards on either side of the street and the road signs all along the highway were written in Hebrew, English, and Arabic. What a unique place this was, where people could be neighbors and not even need to speak the same language. In some ways, it told of a welcoming, tolerant country that would communicate with you in your native tongue. In other ways, though, she could see how not speaking the same language, both literally and figuratively, could lead to tension and divisions.

Looking out the front window at a cluster of buildings to the left, Alex saw what looked like a college campus. "What's that?"

Ori glanced in the direction she was looking. "This Tel Aviv University. Very good school. My son study physics there."

She smiled at the pride that was obvious in the old man's voice. "He must be very smart to study physics. That's not a subject that came easily to me."

"And yet you got a degree in engineering," Val interjected, his tone playful.

"Yes, I did, but after being nearly broken by the experience I had to study law as a coping mechanism."

Val laughed at her joke, and she couldn't help grinning as she turned back to the changing landscape outside. His laughter was contagious.

As quickly as the cities had sprung up to greet them, they now receded into the ground. The concrete was replaced with fertile plots of farmland on both sides of the road.

"You see there," remarked Ori, as though reading Alex's mind. "Village of Ramat HaSharon. Those strawberries. You never eaten strawberries like that. Believe me."

"I love strawberries," said Alex.

"They have them at breakfast at your hotel. You try them."

"I can't wait," she replied, her mouth already beginning to water. Val had told her about how good the Israeli breakfasts were, and she was eager to see for herself.

They turned off the highway now and started heading west, toward the ocean. A few minutes later, Ori brought the car to a stop, presumably in front of the hotel, although the entrance was very nondescript. As Alex got out of the car, her eyes followed the white stone structure over twelve stories up, and it was only then that she saw the insignia for the hotel. The sliding glass doors from which a bell boy emerged showed no trace of commercial affiliation, looking very much like every other door along that street.

As Ori deposited the last of their bags onto the sidewalk, Val reached out to shake his hand.

"What time do you think we should leave here to be in Tel Aviv at eleven tomorrow morning?"

Ori thought for a moment. "Although not rush hour, traffic always a problem. We leave at ten, just in case. Okay?"

"That sounds good. Thank you, Ori. We'll see you tomorrow morning."

Ori smiled at him, then, looking over at Alex, called out, "Enjoy Israel, young lady."

"Thank you," she replied, breathing in the sea air. "I'm sure I will."

Chapter Eleven

For having slept only four of the last thirty-two hours, Val felt remarkably good. He stood in the shower and let the cool water come down on his head and roll off his back and shoulders.

There was a familiar anticipatory thrill building in the pit of his stomach. It was the same feeling Val always got when he was about to step into a room full of people to give a presentation. It was three parts excitement and one part fear. And Val loved it.

The problem was, he wasn't sure if that thrill had to do with the reason they were in Israel or the person traveling with him.

Val shut off the water and, pushing open the glass door, reached for the towel hanging just outside. Drying himself off, he wondered if Alex felt that same excitement. There was certainly wonder in her eyes as she stared out the taxi's windows and took in her new surroundings. And there was a note of playfulness in her tone as they had ridden the elevator up to the sixth floor and discussed when they would meet for dinner. Alex seemed pleased to be on this adventure with him, and the idea that bringing her along on a last-ditch effort to save his company could make her happy filled Val with a joy he hadn't felt in quite some time.

Rummaging through his suitcase for some clothes, he admonished himself for the sudden bout of sentimentality. Lack of sleep could really mess with a person's head.

He quickly got dressed and dialed the concierge desk downstairs. Luckily, the restaurant Val had in mind had a table available for two. Having finished his business with the concierge, Val got out his cell phone to check his emails.

The fact that it was the Saturday after Christmas meant that only fourteen emails and one voice message had come in over the last twenty-four hours. It didn't take Val long to go through each one and either respond or forward it on as a task for one of his employees to handle.

A few minutes before he was supposed to knock on Alex's door, Val stepped into the bathroom to glance at himself in the mirror. He ran a brush through his thick, dark hair and took extra care to make sure unruly spots were smoothed out with a little extra pomade. After taking one last look and giving himself a nod of approval, Val grabbed his wallet and room key off the nightstand and headed for the door.

As he walked toward Alex's room, two doors down, Val's thoughts turned to Alex's boyfriend without warning. What was his name, Billy? What kind of man was he? Did he make Alex happy? Did she love him?

Subconsciously trying to piece together a picture of Billy in his mind based on the few things Alex had told him, he knocked on Alex's door. The sight of Alex as the door opened, however, completely dispelled Val's thoughts, and all his mental faculties were redirected to the immediate and difficult task of not drooling.

"Hey," she said softly, disappearing behind the

door briefly, then reemerging with her purse and a cream-colored fleece jacket tucked under her arm. Alex's sheer white long-sleeved shirt was partially unbuttoned, revealing a lavender camisole underneath, and her dark blue jeans hugged her curves perfectly. It seemed Alex had also taken a shower, and her damp hair was pulled back and away from her face with a clip so that it cascaded in glossy waves behind her shoulders.

"You look great," Val said without thinking, as though he were there to pick her up for a date. It only took a split-second for him to recall that this was, in fact, not a date, so he quickly added, "I feel a little under-dressed."

"You're not under-dressed." Alex stepped out into the hallway and shut the door behind her. "I didn't know how cool it was going to be tonight, so I thought I would dress in layers. I'm bringing this fleece with me, too, which, as you can see, brings the whole outfit down a couple of notches." She ended with the disarming smile she always used to punctuate her sentences. She could have just told Val she was going to cut out his spleen and feed it to him, but as long as she ended with that smile, he would have happily handed her the knife and put on a bib.

They were both quiet for a few awkward moments as they got onto the elevator, but Alex quickly broke the silence. "I fell asleep after taking a shower, even though I told myself not to. Which is why my hair looks like this."

This? Was she baiting him? Her hair looked fine—more than fine. It was curly, which Val had never seen before, and he rather liked it.

"Your hair looks great." The words came out on their own. Val blamed it on the lack of sleep. "You don't like it curly?"

Alex chuckled. "It's ironic, actually. When I was a kid, my hair was *really* straight and had almost a reddish hue to it. I hated the color and the fact that it was so straight. My mom tried to curl it every once in a while, to no avail. I would have given anything for a curl or two. Then one day I hit puberty and my hair decided it was curly. Now I miss those days of no-frizz, no-need-to-brush hair. Plus, I somehow lost the red, and so now it's just plain old brown. Women—we're never happy with our hair the way it is."

Val wanted to tell her that her hair was the color of rich caramel, or maybe toasted almonds—anything but plain old brown. But thankfully, he had enough sense to keep his mouth shut this time.

They got off the elevator on the ground floor, walked past the front desk, and went down the stairs to the concierge station by the doors at street level.

"Do you need a cab, sir?" the young man opening the door for them asked politely.

"Yes, please. We're going to Tapeo."

"Right away, sir."

As the bell boy ran ahead to flag down the next taxi, Val turned to Alex. "This place I had in mind is a tapas restaurant, just a couple miles from here. Does that sound okay?"

"Sure," she replied enthusiastically. "I can't imagine that I'll find anything we eat over the next couple of days less than amazing."

The next cab pulled up to the curb, and the bell boy opened the door to the back seat for them to get in. Val tipped him quietly, then entered behind Alex.

"Tapeo, please," he said to the driver.

The driver nodded, and they pulled away from the hotel.

Less than ten minutes later, they were sitting in the restaurant at a table for two.

The restaurant was almost exactly as Val remembered it—the dark red walls rising to the high ceiling, with dark brown wooden accents, and golden light fixtures resembling old street lanterns in a row down the center of the rectangular room. The tables were covered in dark red tablecloths that matched the color of the walls.

Val and Alex sat at a table by the windows that lined one side of the restaurant, but it was dark outside, so there was not much to see.

Alex looked around the restaurant with the same wide-eyed wonder she had shown at each new stop on their journey so far. It made Val wonder if her travels had been limited to home, school, and work.

After perusing the wine list on the English version of the restaurant's menu, he decided to pull Alex out of her dream-like state. "Do you like wine?"

"I do," she replied, her lips curling into a smile.

"How about a Chianti? Should we get a bottle of that?"

Alex glanced at the menu. "I don't need to drink wine. I can just have water."

No doubt, she had seen the prices.

"Come on," he insisted. "It's not every day you have dinner in Israel. Let's live a little."

She looked at him, her brow slightly furrowed. "Are you sure?"

Val smiled. "Yes, I'm sure." He leaned in and added in a whisper, "I hear the boss signs off on reimbursement requests without even really looking at them."

A laugh escaped her rosy lips, and she relented. "Okay, but only because 'the boss' won't notice."

Val grinned and, when the waiter came around, ordered the wine. A few moments later, the waiter was back, opening the bottle in front of them. The young man poured some into Val's glass to taste, then waited for his approval. Val tried to look thoughtful as he let the wine run over his tongue, but he wasn't really much of a wine connoisseur. After the requisite amount of time, Val nodded stoically, and the waiter poured some for Alex before filling up the rest of Val's glass.

As the waiter disappeared again, Val raised his glass. "Cheers."

"*L'chaim*," she replied, touching his glass with hers.

"To life," he translated. "I'm impressed—I don't remember seeing Hebrew on your résumé."

Alex laughed. "That's about the extent of the Hebrew I know, and I owe that much to our high school production of Fiddler on the Roof."

"You are an actress, then?"

"Hardly. I was always too shy for that, although I think it would have been a lot of fun. I was in the pit orchestra. I played the oboe once upon a time."

"A musician. That's even better." Val took another sip of his wine, feeling more relaxed. Judging by how Alex was fiddling with her menu and avoiding eye contact with him, Val guessed that Alex was anything but relaxed.

"Are you nervous?" he asked, without thinking about how the question might sound. "About tomorrow, I mean. About the meeting with FiberTech."

Alex stopped playing with the corner of her menu and finally looked up at him. The light from the candle in the center of their table reflected off her hazel eyes and seemed to become one with them.

"It's kind of all hitting me now," she replied, "the purpose of our trip here. Everything that's at stake. One minute I'm looking around in awe, finding it hard to believe that I'm actually here in Israel—this seemingly mythical place—and the next minute it hits me like a ton of bricks that a bottle of wine costs more than I've ever spent on a dress or a pair of shoes, and if we don't do what we set out to do and convince FiberTech how stupid it would be to break off their deal…."

"So, it's the bottle of wine that caused all this. You'd better drink up, then. We wouldn't want to waste any of it."

Val couldn't help smiling at her reserve, and at the hint of a smile forming on Alex's lips, his own smile grew wider.

"On the flight over here, you were the one telling me that the good guys always win, and that we were the good guys," he reminded her. "Are you changing your mind?"

Alex shook her head. "No, I still think we're going to win. It's just time for me to start treating this like work instead of a vacation. Which is hard to do when you treat me like this. I'm not sure I've earned this—" she held up her glass "—yet."

The waiter came by just then and asked if they were ready to order, at which point they both hurriedly reviewed the menu and asked the waiter for recommendations. Once the orders had been placed, Alex looked back over at Val. "I don't think I've ever met anyone quite like you before."

She had a dreamy look in her eye, and Val tried hard not to allow himself to think it was anything more than a trick of the candlelight and the influence of wine.

He cleared his throat. "What do you mean?"

"I mean, with all that you have accomplished in your life—your company, wealth, even your status as one of the most eligible bachelors in the southeast—"

"I was hoping no one had read that article," he grumbled, remembering the piece from a year ago about his alleged playboy lifestyle.

"With all that, you would be justified in being a self-absorbed, arrogant, know-it-all. But you're not. You're quite the opposite, and everyone wants to do things for you as a result. People want you to succeed because you deserve it."

"Everyone except Kurt Donovan," he replied under his breath, for effect.

Alex laughed, and Val silently congratulated himself. When the laughter had faded, Alex placed her palms down on the table and leaned in. "Okay then, let's get down to business. What's the plan for tomorrow?"

"Well," replied Val, picking up his glass, "we're due at FiberTech at eleven in the morning. So, I figured we would have breakfast around nine, then have Ori drive us into Tel Aviv. It's not far from the hotel, but there can be traffic sometimes. We'll tour their facilities, then take them out to lunch. I asked Yaakov to pick a place nearby. Tomorrow night, they'll meet us at a nice restaurant in Tel Aviv with their wives around six-thirty. I've met Ayala, Gideon's wife, once before quite by chance in California. I've never met Yaakov's wife, Mara. Ayala is very into women's rights and likes to see women in positions of power. She'll most likely want to know all about you."

"She might not be so interested in me after she discovers that I've never been in a position of power," laughed Alex.

Val liked to hear her laugh. It was a sweet, light, genuine laugh, not grating in any way, but rather soothing to hear. He couldn't help smiling.

Over the course of their meal, Val talked about his company's history with FiberTech, from their very first order to his last trip to Israel a few months ago. He mentioned the emails between Gideon and Kurt and how he may have underestimated the strength of their relationship, both professionally and personally.

Alex asked questions here and there, but mostly she listened. Her eyes were focused on Val, her face reacting ever so subtly to the details he provided. Through the movement of her eyebrows, the curving of her lips, the tilt of her graceful neck, he knew they were on the same page. She understood what he was saying and was continually processing how those details would affect what she would say and do the following day.

Watching her watch him, Val again marveled at how she had been overlooked by so many employers during her time out of school. Was he the only one who saw what she was capable of?

As their plates were cleared away, the conversation turned to lighter topics. Despite the long day, neither of them was ready to leave the restaurant, so Val suggested they order some mint tea, a common after-dinner drink consisting of a sprig of mint leaves soaking in hot water, along with a couple of Israeli desserts to share.

Eager to hear her laugh, Val talked about various situations he had encountered in his travels across the globe as they sipped their tea and took turns breaking off pieces of the two desserts that had been set between them.

He told her about the time he was in Korea and was given a key to a hotel room that was already occupied by a Korean woman. The poor woman spoke no English and was terrified at the sight of Val entering her room, screaming at the top of her lungs as she pulled the covers off the bed to hide the modest floral pajamas she wore from view.

He recounted the time he had rented a car in Germany and ordered a GPS with the car, which he mistakenly set to "walking" instead of "driving." He missed every turn the stupid thing told him to take because of that setting and finally got so frustrated at the device that he tore it off the dashboard and literally threw it out the window of the moving car. He had to pay for the device, of course, but thankfully he hadn't gotten himself arrested.

Finally, when the tea was all gone and there were only crumbs left on the two dessert plates, Alex leaned back in her chair and eyed him contentedly. "I guess we should get back so we can try to get some sleep before our big day tomorrow."

Alex's soft tone and sleepy eyes brought forth images of how she would look asleep in his bed, and Val quickly picked up the mug of now-cold mint tea and threw what was left of it down his throat to clear his mind.

"Yes," he found himself grumbling. "I suppose you're right."

Chapter Twelve

The bright sun coming in through the floor-to-ceiling windows of the hotel restaurant was hopeful, and Alex figured it was a sign that their meeting with FiberTech would go well. Still, her stomach was in knots, and she wondered how she would be able to eat any of the breakfast food laid out on the various buffet tables.

"Coffee, Miss?"

Alex looked away from the windows to the smiling waitress. "Yes, thank you." Maybe the coffee would calm her nerves, even though caffeine was a stimulant. She chuckled at the absurdity of her reasoning.

As soon as the waitress stepped away, Alex saw Val approaching from the hostess stand at the front of the restaurant. He had already spotted her and was grinning.

The knots in her stomach tightened.

She was being silly, getting nervous around her boss. Val was the nicest man. Very handsome, yes, but that was nothing to get nervous about. He had never been anything less than professional and respectful toward her, despite Billy's repeated warnings that he would try to seduce her on their trip. Dinner the night before had been lovely, and Alex had enjoyed the easy conversation.

Why, then, was she a ball of nerves now?

"Good morning," said Val, pulling out a chair and sitting down. "Have you been here for a while?"

"No," Alex replied. "Just a few minutes, though I've been awake since five. When I couldn't get back to sleep, I found the gym and tried to work out. They have a nice gym on the third floor."

Alex realized she was rambling.

"Jet lag or nerves?"

"Oh, probably a little of both. Did you sleep well?"

Val shrugged. "About the same as you. I kept waking up every couple of hours, then gave up around six."

"Jet lag or nerves?" she asked, mimicking his question.

He chuckled. "A little of both for me, too."

"Hard to believe you still get nervous. Aren't you making pitches and giving presentations all the time?"

The waitress came back around with Alex's coffee, then asked Val if he would like one.

"I'll have black tea, if you have it."

The waitress nodded and left them alone once more.

"To answer your question," he began, turning back to Alex, "I still get nervous. Every time. It's not debilitating, of course, but it's just enough to keep me on my toes and force me to do a good job."

"Ah, so you're saying stress can be good."

Val gave her a lop-sided grin. "Something like that."

Pointing to the place setting in front of her, he asked, "Aren't you going to eat?"

"I don't know. I don't feel hungry, but I guess I should eat something."

Val pushed away from the table and stood. "Come on. I'll give you a tour."

Alex followed him around from one table to the next, each decked out with an amazing assortment of food. Perhaps she could eat something after all.

On the first table, there was a variety of freshly baked breads; more cheeses than she could name; different kinds of olives; and tahini, hummus, and baba ghanoush. Thankfully, all the dishes were labeled, and she recognized most of the items. On another table were several Israeli specialties and hot foods, including an Israeli egg dish called *shakshuka*, which Val explained consisted of eggs poached in a tomato and vegetable sauce. Other items included cooked salmon and herring; a bowl of what looked like refried beans called *ful medames*; Israeli salad (Val noted that as one of his favorites), which was a finely chopped salad that had tomatoes, onion, cucumbers, and bell pepper tossed in lemon juice and olive oil; and a variety of fresh vegetables. On the third table was a station where eggs were made to order and a delicious-looking selection of pastries, desserts, and fresh fruits.

For someone who didn't feel like eating anything, Alex managed to amass a sizeable portion of food by the time they returned to their table.

"This is absolutely amazing," she said, glancing at Val as he sat down. "I don't know what half this stuff is, but I felt compelled to take a little of everything so I could try it all. Turns out that's a lot of food."

"I've seen you eat—I think you can manage it," Val teased.

Alex pretended to be shocked at his comment, then laughed. "You know me well."

As they ate, Alex looked up to find Val watching her. He smiled, then looked back down at his plate. Her stomach fluttered with awareness, and she reached for her coffee, hoping it would help.

"We hadn't discussed the dress code," said Alex, putting down her mug, "but I'm assuming you're changing after breakfast?" She gestured to his zipped-up hoodie, which he wore with a pair of gym shorts.

He laughed. "Yes. While most of the employees at FiberTech wear jeans, Gideon is a little more formal. He's usually in dress pants and the crispest white shirt you can possibly imagine." He looked down at his own attire. "And I would never subject anyone to this outfit, in any case."

"Except me." Her cheeks warmed as she spoke the words.

Val's lips turned up at the corners. "Except you."

The warm timbre of Val's voice distracted Alex for a moment, but she quickly recovered and thought of her attire.

"Is this okay?" she asked, gesturing to her white silk button-down blouse and navy blue pin-striped suit jacket. She was wearing a matching skirt that went down to just above her knees and tan patent leather open-toed high-heeled shoes, though they were hidden by the table. "I can change into something more casual if you think this is too business-y." It was the nicest suit Alex owned, which is why she had chosen to wear it, but if it was going to make them stick out like sore thumbs at FiberTech…

"I wouldn't change a thing."

Again, her stomach fluttered, and again her automatic response to such fluttering was to ramble and reach for her coffee. "I guess it's better to err on the side of being overly formal than not formal enough."

Alex looked back down at her half-eaten plate, then broke off a piece of pita bread and dipped the tip of her knife in a white spread that looked like sour cream, but with a little firmer consistency. Putting it on the bread, she asked, "Do you know what this stuff is?"

"I think that's called *labaneh*, or something like that. It's basically strained yogurt." Val watched as she took a bite, waiting to see if she liked it.

Licking her upper lip where some of the *labaneh* had touched, Alex popped the rest of the piece into her mouth. "What's your verdict, Counselor?" Val asked, looking as though he was trying to suppress a smile.

"I think it's one of the best things I've tasted so far. Although this salad is really good, too, and all this bread. I'm so glad I'm not gluten-free."

"These breakfasts are my favorite thing about visiting Israel," said Val, cutting off a piece of poached egg and putting it on some bread. "The history and the sightseeing are nice, but man, you can't beat these breakfasts."

****

Ori picked them up from the hotel promptly at ten, and they rode in silence for the first several minutes after the initial pleasant exchanges with Ori. Val had insisted that Alex take the front seat again, and again Val sat directly behind her. Val took the opportunity to lean his head back against the seat and close his eyes. With the quiet noise of the engine in the background and the steady rocking of the car as it moved down the road toward their destination, he thought of the amulet, safely tucked away in the rolled-up pair of socks, which he had stowed in the laptop bag at his side prior to leaving the States. It was the first time Val had thought about the amulet since he had packed it. He had been preoccupied, he supposed, by thoughts of a certain traveling companion.

Val could hear her now in the front seat, asking Ori questions about the landmarks they passed and about growing up on an Israeli *kibbutz*—a farming commune. She had the perfect voice—just high enough to be feminine, and just low enough to be sexy. And you could always hear the smile behind her words. He had never noticed that before, that you could actually hear a smile.

As they neared Tel Aviv, the traffic got heavier, and Val heard Ori mutter a few words in Hebrew under his breath. Road rage was universal. Val chuckled inwardly.

He reached out and touched Alex's shoulder gently to get her attention. She immediately turned to him and smiled. "Hey, what's up?"

Val couldn't help smiling back. "Are you ready for this?"

"As ready as I'm going to be. I thought our conversation last night at dinner was really helpful, and I stayed up for a short while once we got back to the hotel to read a little more about Span Global's newest technology and FiberTech's vision for the future."

"I'm pretty sure that if you just say the words 'vision for the future' at any point during our meetings, we're in."

Alex laughed. "I'm sorry, I know I must sound like a total nerd. I just want to do a good job for you. I don't want you to regret choosing me for this opportunity."

"I cannot for the life of me envision a scenario where I would regret bringing you with me. Don't worry about anything. You're going to do great."

Alex smiled again, then said in a softer voice, "Thank you, Val."

She turned back around slowly to face the front, and Val leaned back in his seat once more, feeling warm and content. He couldn't help but be infatuated. It was juvenile, perhaps, but she made him feel good about himself, about the man he was. She wasn't trying to win his affection—she didn't have to. She was so different than anyone he'd had a relationship with before—different from his family, his girlfriends, his friends. Alex was just a good, sweet, kind, and humble person, and he couldn't get enough of her.

Sighing quietly, Val closed his eyes and just listened. He listened as Alex replied to a comment Ori made about the forecast for the afternoon in that sweet, unassuming way she had. He listened to the sound of her skirt rustling as she uncrossed her legs and shifted positions ever so slightly. He listened to the sound of her hair rubbing against the headrest as she turned her head to the side.

"Val, are you asleep?"

Val woke with a start, having nodded off as he was mentally going through the list of beautiful sounds Alex was making in the front seat.

The car was parked in front of an office building with the engine still running, and both Ori and Alex had their bodies turned in their seats, looking at him.

Val quickly glanced at his watch—they were twenty minutes early for their meeting.

"Ori," said Val, taking control again, "I'll give you

a call when we're finishing up with lunch, which will probably be around one or one-thirty. Does that work for you?"

"Yes, Mr. Val. You call, I come pick you up. Ten minutes, no problem."

"Okay, thank you, Ori."

They got out of the car with their laptop bags, and Ori waved as he drove off.

"What's he going to do for three hours?" asked Alex, looking at Val.

"I'm not sure. But I'm guessing he's not going far if he can be back here ten minutes after I call him."

Val looked at his watch again. "It's too early to go in there. Do you want to take a short walk to kill some time?"

"Sure," replied Alex.

They walked in silence for a minute, away from FiberTech and toward some shops down the street.

"Do you want me to carry—"

"I can carry my own computer, thank you very much." She had a teasing grin on her face, and Val couldn't help laughing at her response.

"So," she continued in that same mischievous tone, "you seem quite relaxed about this meeting with FiberTech. So much so that you can take a leisurely nap in the car on the way over here. Must be nice."

Val chuckled in reply. Alex had a familiar way of speaking with him sometimes that was very attractive. He never felt like she was trying to get something from him. Rather, he felt like Alex genuinely cared about the company. She wanted to help him. Perhaps it was because she already had a man in her life. Billy. Still, Val couldn't shake the feeling that Alex cared for him on some level. It was that uncertainty, the challenge that Alex represented, the closeness that she alluded to, that made her so sweetly seductive. There was no way anyone could do that on purpose.

They walked for a few blocks, commenting on the things they saw along the way, then circled back to FiberTech's building. They entered the lobby eight minutes before their eleven o'clock meeting, but Val figured that was close enough. The receptionist called Yaakov, and a few minutes later a man in his late thirties walked into the main lobby where Val and Alex were sitting and waiting.

"Yaakov, how are you!"

The two men shook hands warmly as they exchanged greetings. Then Val turned to Alex, who was standing next to him with her hands together, a warm smile lighting up her face.

"Yaakov, I'd like to introduce you to Alex Weaver. She is the attorney who has been going through all the document requests from FiberTech's counsel and has been interfacing with them on the acquisition."

Alex stretched a hand toward Yaakov, who took it gladly in his own. "Very nice to meet you, Yaakov," she said, shaking his hand. "Val has told me a lot about you."

"Has he? All good, I hope."

"Of course!" she replied, eliciting a chuckle from Yaakov.

So far, so good.

"She's much easier on the eyes than Kurt Donovan, isn't she?" Yaakov addressed the comment to Val, still looking at Alex. Val hadn't warned Alex about this particular aspect of Israeli culture—very open and direct statements about people's physical attributes, even the people they worked with. It was an HR nightmare for many Israeli companies that opened offices in the US, including FiberTech.

Alex didn't blush, look away, or act offended. Instead, her smile only grew wider as she said, "I've never met Kurt Donovan, but I'll take that as a compliment."

Yaakov let out a belly laugh. "As well you should, Miss Weaver—as well you should!"

Yaakov turned back to Val and patted his arm in a friendly gesture. "Come, I've booked us a conference room down the hall. Why don't we deposit your things in there? Then we can go grab Gideon and take a tour of the office before heading to lunch. How does that sound?"

"Sounds perfect," replied Val.

The three of them went through some glass doors off the reception area and down a bright hallway to a conference room with glass walls. Val placed his laptop bag on the long wooden table in the center of the room, and Alex came up beside him and did the same. Then they followed Yaakov back out of the room and continued down the hall to an open area filled with cubicles. Several people looked up from their computers and acknowledged them with a polite smile or nod before getting back to work.

At the far end of the room was an office enclosed by more glass walls. The placard by the door read "Gideon Krantz." Yaakov knocked on the closed door, and Gideon turned away from his computer and motioned them in.

Yaakov opened the door and entered, with Val and

Alex following him. Gideon smiled broadly as he stood up to shake hands with them. He was a tall man, standing almost a foot taller than Yaakov and a few inches taller than Val. The top of his head was bald, with a crown of shortly-cropped brown hair surrounding it. He looked a little older than the forty-nine years Val knew him to be.

"It's good to see you, Val. And it's good to meet you, Alex. How was the flight yesterday?"

"It wasn't bad at all," answered Val. "It's long, but we had no problems with the connection."

"That's good," replied Gideon. "The flight to the West Coast is terrible. I always try to stop in New York for a couple of nights when I go to Silicon Valley. My sister and brother-in-law live in Brooklyn, so it's good to break up the flight that way."

Gideon moved toward the door. "I thought you might like to see the new data center where we test the equipment. We can start there, then go to the Engineering floor where you can see some of the new projects we are working on. That should take about forty-five minutes to an hour, then Yaakov can take you to lunch. Unfortunately, I have a call at noon that I must take, so I won't be joining you. But Ayala and I are very excited to have dinner with you all tonight. She even has a new dress for the occasion."

Val could tell that both Gideon and Yaakov were proud of the new data center. Alex was quick to pick up on that feeling, as well, and very skillfully encouraged it. As Yaakov described the different equipment on the racks and explained the system of cables, devices, and corresponding connections, Alex listened attentively, nodding at the right times and asking intelligent questions that prompted Yaakov and Gideon to further elaborate on their accomplishments with pride.

By the time they got to the Engineering floor, which consisted of another open area with white boards on every wall and couches in the middle surrounded by an array of cubicles, Gideon was speaking almost exclusively to Alex, and Yaakov had dropped back to engage Val in a separate conversation.

"She's something, your Alex Weaver," he said to Val, well out of earshot. "Why haven't you ever brought her to visit us? We could have avoided this whole mess had you brought her instead of Kurt Donovan."

"She only just started working for me earlier this month," replied Val, watching Alex's hands as they moved gracefully to emphasize the points she was making to Gideon.

"Really? Well, she seems to know a lot about our business, and yours. And all of that knowledge comes in a very attractive package."

Val looked at Yaakov to assess his last statement. He hadn't meant it in a lewd way, Val could see that, and his initial defensive posture softened a bit.

"I hadn't noticed," Val finally replied.

A quiet laugh rumbled out of Yaakov. "This is why I trust you, Val. Because you are a terrible liar."

After saying goodbye to Gideon and retrieving their bags from the conference room, the three of them walked across the street to an Italian restaurant for lunch.

"This is Italian food, with an Israeli twist," said Yaakov as they were seated at a small table by the window. Yaakov and the waiter exchanged a few words in Hebrew, and the waiter handed Val and Alex an English version of the menu.

"I'm beginning to wonder if the English version has all the same items as the Hebrew version," said Alex with a teasing smile as she opened the menu and scanned the selections.

Yaakov chuckled as he gestured for the waiter to bring over a basket of bread. "The items are the same, Ms. Weaver, but I'm not sure about the prices."

When they had all placed their orders, Yaakov turned his attention to Alex once more. "Val tells me you just joined his company a few weeks ago. Are you just out of school, then?"

Alex looked surprised before breaking out into a grin. "Oh no, I've been done with school for years."

It was Yaakov's turn now to be surprised. "I don't believe it. How old are you?"

Upon hearing that, Val's human resources instincts kicked in. "Yaakov, we don't ask questions like that in the U.S.," he said, smiling to make the statement less of a reprimand.

"That's okay," replied Alex, good-naturedly. "I'm thirty-two."

Val could almost hear Yaakov's jaw hit the table. "Impossible. You look twenty-five or twenty-six, maybe twenty-seven at most."

"Well, thank you," said Alex, taking a sip of water. Then, turning to Val, she added, "You know, I'm really starting to like the Israeli custom of saying what you think, political correctness be damned."

Yaakov laughed and slapped his hand on the table. "You know, it does work well when you are talking to an intelligent and beautiful woman. But not so well when the woman is, well, not so intelligent or beautiful."

This time, Val could see the color in Alex's cheeks rise slightly, and she only smiled in response.

"Are you bringing your wife to dinner tonight, Yaakov?" asked Val, trying to steer the conversation in a different direction.

"Oh yes," Yaakov replied. "She will enjoy very much meeting Alex. Plus, the restaurant you picked for tonight is new and is getting great reviews. Mara has been bugging me for weeks to try it, so she is very excited about tonight."

Without Gideon at lunch, the atmosphere seemed a little more relaxed and casual to Val. Alex had an amazing ability to ask personal questions in a way that was not at all intrusive but rather came off as genuine interest, and Val could see Yaakov's ego swell with each exchange. From his educational background to his decision to return to Israel after living and working in the States for eight years after college, to how he met his wife, Alex managed to get more information out of Yaakov than Val had been able to extract in the previous six visits.

On the drive back to the hotel, Val had wanted to have a debrief with Alex, but Alex's position in the front seat, coupled with Val's recent paranoia about talking business in front of people, even harmless Ori, made him reluctant to have that conversation right then and there.

Alex was quiet as they entered the hotel and ascended the steps from the street level to the lobby area. At the top of the stairs, she finally turned to face Val, excitement sparkling in her eyes. "So, how do you think it went?"

From the look on her face, Val could tell Alex had been biting her tongue for the past half hour, trying to keep herself from asking that question in front of Ori. Val grinned with equal excitement. "I don't think it could have gone any better. What did you think?"

A relieved smile spread across Alex's face. "I was thinking the same thing. They seem to like and respect you and Span Global. And I think it meant a lot to them that you came all this way just to see them for a day."

Val nodded as they walked past the lobby area to the elevators. "It helps to have that personal touch. But I think you're leaving out a very important aspect of the meeting."

Alex gave him a puzzled look. "What do you mean?"

"I mean," he replied, enjoying the intrigue, "you left out the part about *you* doing great. You handled yourself really well, even in some awkward, politically incorrect situations."

Alex laughed as the elevator doors opened and they got on. "They meant no harm. It's just a cultural thing, I think."

"Yeah. I've heard stories from my lawyer about some of her clients who are based in Israel and decide to open up shop in the States. They go through all this employment law training, telling them what they can and can't say to their employees, both male and female, and those companies still run into trouble very often. Which of course my lawyer doesn't mind one bit since she gets paid by the hour."

"Damn lawyers," Alex replied sarcastically, the corner of her mouth raised in a smile.

They got off the elevators on the sixth floor, and Val felt a twinge of disappointment that her hotel room was so close to the elevators. He walked Alex to her room, and she turned to look at him before reaching into her bag for the room key.

"So, what's the plan now?" Alex asked. "What time is dinner?"

"I've made reservations for seven o'clock at a restaurant back in Tel Aviv called Jewel. We should give ourselves forty-five minutes to get there since I'm not sure what traffic will look like at that time of day. Ori doesn't drive in the evenings, so we'll have to take a taxi. Let's say we meet at ten after six to walk down. I'll come by your room and pick you up, does that work?"

"We don't need to meet beforehand to talk about anything?" she asked, surprising him.

Wishing there actually was a legitimate reason for them to meet, Val responded with a slightly dejected, "I don't think so."

"Okay," said Alex. "I guess I'll keep going through the files I brought with me until I have to get ready. I can probably get a good chunk of it knocked out in the next few hours."

"All right," Val replied, smiling, "but don't work too hard. I need you in top form for tonight, when we go in for the kill."

Alex threw him a heart-breakingly beautiful smile in return. "Don't worry. I'll be ready."

Chapter Thirteen

Alex looked out her hotel room window at the blue sky beyond and tried to focus her thoughts. Accordion files and manila folders were scattered on the desk in front of her, as well as on an extra chair nearby and on the edge of the bed. There was a lot left to go through, but her mind kept wandering.

Instead of thinking about Span Global's tax returns from 2018, she kept replaying scenes from their tour of FiberTech and the lunch with Yaakov in her mind. It had gone well—much better than Alex could have reasonably hoped it would go. She had understood what Gideon's main concerns were, had seen what the man valued in his organization, and had said just enough to help him realize that she and Val—Span Global—shared his company's values and concerns.

She had done a good job. And Val had noticed.

Val. He was so good at what he did. He was easy to talk to and trustworthy, and he knew how to navigate a conversation, even when the topics got uncomfortable or bordered on inappropriate. Val just always knew what to say and what to do. And it made him that much more attractive.

Alex amended her last thought—she wasn't attracted to Val. Not in a romantic sense, in any case. She was learning a lot from him, that was for sure, but she didn't want to date him or anything like that. She had Billy, and Billy loved her. She didn't need anything else.

At the thought of Billy, Alex reached for her laptop, which was sitting off to the side on another small pile of folders, and logged into her personal email account. Still no messages. Even with the time difference, her boyfriend was certainly awake by now, probably already at the office. Hadn't Billy gotten the email Alex had sent yesterday after checking into the hotel? And the email she sent later, just before falling asleep?

Alex reached for her phone. Maybe Billy was in meetings this morning. He often had meetings with clients or with the partners managing the cases. He probably hadn't had time to look at Alex's messages, let alone respond. She had told him she was shutting off her phone while she was in Israel to avoid having to pay for international cell service. Could Billy have forgotten and been trying to call or text her?

She set the inactive phone down. Billy would email her when he was out of his meetings. It wasn't like he was mad at her. He wasn't avoiding her on purpose. They had made up before Alex left on Friday afternoon. He had kissed her and told her he loved her. He had told her to be safe. Alex had smiled and kissed him back, though she still hurt from the emotions she'd spent on Christmas Day thinking he was finally going to propose. Billy hadn't noticed that, though. As far as Billy was concerned, it was business as usual and she had gotten over her little outburst.

Sighing, Alex picked up the next file and opened it. Vendor contracts from Q2 2018.

Billy would email her when he could. Until then,

she wasn't going to worry about it. She would do her job, learn as much as she could from watching and listening to Val, and maybe even relax and enjoy herself.

And hopefully, get through a few more files.

****

The next four hours went by at a snail's pace for Val. He laid down on the bed with his computer and answered a few emails, but unfortunately, that didn't take nearly as much time as he had hoped it would. Then Val reviewed some proposals for new products and a marketing report. Still, the clock had only moved forward by an hour and a half.

Restless, Val grabbed the hotel key off the dresser and went downstairs to the lobby. Across from the check-in desk were some glass doors that led out to the beach. Val pushed open the doors and went outside. The afternoon sun felt good, and the sound of the water lapping gently onto the sand had a calming effect.

As he walked down the stone path that ran parallel to the beach, Val wondered what Alex was doing. He could picture Alex sitting at the desk in the little living room of her hotel suite, her lovely neck bent over some documents she was reviewing. Was she still wearing that white silk shirt and tight skirt? Or had she changed into something more comfortable?

It was almost four-thirty when Val got back to his room, a little sweaty from the long walk in the Mediterranean sun. Shrugging out of the fleece he was wearing and kicking off his shoes, Val made his way to the bedroom, where he tugged his t-shirt up and over his head in one swift move. He tossed the shirt onto a pile of dirty clothes, then pulled off his jeans and hung them up.

Before shucking his socks and boxers and stepping into the shower, he answered a couple more emails that had come in during his walk.

Val tried his hardest to take a slow shower. Once done, he just stood there under the steady stream of almost-too-hot water, head down, eyes closed. He'd taken countless showers as a kid, and those had been so different—always hurried, with Val constantly worried one of his siblings would barge in and scold him for taking too long. And there was never any hot water left by the time it was his turn to shower, and he had to dry himself off with his brother's used, damp towel. But the thing Val had always relished about his few minutes in the shower, even back then, was the peace. The sound of the water drowned out all other sounds. He couldn't hear his parents fighting. He couldn't hear his siblings yelling. It was just him, and he could pretend there was no one to bother him, even if only for those few precious minutes.

Val turned off the shower and dried himself with an extravagantly thick towel. Stepping into the bedroom with the towel wrapped around his waist, he turned on the television to distract himself while he got dressed.

He had been dressed and ready for almost twenty minutes, standing in front of the television in his dress pants and crisp white shirt to avoid any wrinkles while attempting to work out the plot from the actors' actions and the few Hebrew words he could understand, when he decided it was time to go.

He turned off the TV and placed the remote on the nightstand by the bed. Then, grabbing his blazer and tucking his room key and wallet in his pocket, Val headed out the door.

Past girlfriends had lectured him about the evils of showing up too early to pick up your date, but he doubted Alex would mind that much. She was too good-natured. Plus, he reminded himself, Alex was his co-worker—most definitely not his date. As Val approached her room, he could hear the muffled sound of a television show in the background. Alex had probably been killing time, just like him. Taking a steadying breath, Val knocked three times on her door. A couple of seconds later, the door opened.

Alex was wearing a simple black dress with short sleeves and a neckline that dipped deliciously low. A small silver buckle connected two strips of black material above the plunging neckline, which emphasized the delicate bones in her neck and made a necklace unnecessary. The dress went down to her knees, hugging her hips in a most flattering manner. The strappy black heels on her feet made her legs look like they went on for miles.

This is not a date, Val reminded himself weakly.

Resisting another urge to look Alex up and down, Val focused on her beautiful hazel eyes, which seemed even larger and more seductive as a result of the eye makeup she had applied. Her hair hung in loose curls about her face, completing the picture of her beauty.

"Hi, Val," she said softly.

"Hi, Alex. You look great." It was as much as he would allow himself to say about how truly amazing she looked.

"Thanks." Alex's smile was hesitant. "I have a problem. Well, more of a slight wardrobe malfunction. Is it okay if you come in for a minute?"

All of Val's Human Resources alarms sounded at the prospect of entering Alex's room. It was a damn foolish thing for any man to enter the hotel room of a female employee or coworker—it screamed sexual harassment lawsuit, or worse. But Alex had asked so innocently, and she had already moved out of the way to let him enter. He stepped into the room without even having answered her question.

At the sound of the door clicking shut, Alex looked at him somewhat timidly. A rosy blush spread across her cheeks before she even said anything.

"I'm really sorry to put you in this position, but the zipper on my dress is stuck. I can't move it up or down, and I don't have another dress to wear. Do you think you could see if you can move it? I'm really sorry…"

Alex turned her back to him, and Val could see the silver zipper was only halfway closed, sitting stubbornly just high enough to cover the clasp of her bra.

Oh, good Lord. He moved in closer to investigate the cause of the problem.

"I'm just going to pull the dress away from you a little so I can maybe see if it's stuck on something," said Val, his voice lower than intended. His hands moved toward her, and he took gentle hold of each side of the unzipped dress and tried to flip the zipper out, so he could see the inside seam. The knuckles of Val's thumbs brushed the smooth skin of Alex's back in the process, sending every nerve in his body into high alert.

"It looks like there are a few threads stuck in here. I'm going to try to back it up and see if that gets them out."

"Okay," she replied quietly.

Val grasped the unzipped ends at the top together with his left hand, the backs of his fingers resting on Alex's warm skin. With his right hand, Val took hold of the zipper and applied two firm tugs. On the second tug, the material came free, and the zipper moved down to just past her satiny black bra. Val swallowed hard. The sight of her exposed skin contrasting with the material of her bra and the warmth emanating from her body was almost too much for him to resist, but he gritted his teeth and moved the black threads that had caused this whole mess out of the way, grazing more skin in the process. He then gently pulled the zipper all the way to the top.

His mission accomplished, Val quickly stepped away before he could give in to the overwhelming urge to unzip the dress once more and plant kisses all over Alex's exquisite back.

"Good, now we don't have to cancel the dinner," Val joked, trying to bring himself back to reality.

"I'm so sorry," she repeated, turning to face Val and clasping her hands together. "Thank you for fixing it. My mother's right, you get what you pay for. And I got this off the clearance rack."

The color in Alex's cheeks remained, but she smiled now and moved toward the stool in the kitchenette area to grab her shawl and purse.

Val took the hint and opened the door to the hallway, simultaneously relieved and disappointed to be out of there.

****

As they waited in awkward silence for the elevator, Alex concluded it was difficult to find a normal topic of conversation after making your boss fix the zipper of your dress while wearing it. She tried not to emphasize her embarrassed state by fidgeting, so instead Alex stood as still as a statue, clutching her purse demurely at her waist.

In contrast, Val seemed totally at ease as he stood next to her with his hands in the pockets of his charcoal gray pants and the top two buttons of his smooth white dress shirt casually undone. As the elevator doors slid open, Val remarked on the weather forecast for the evening, and Alex replied. After a few similarly cautious exchanges, however, their normal easy flow of conversation resumed as they tried to anticipate what the mood might be at dinner with the wives present.

Unfortunately, as Alex settled in the back seat of the taxi and reached for the seat belt, her hand brushed Val's as he reached for his own.

"Oh," she gasped, drawing her hand back as though she'd been scalded. "Sorry."

"You're fine," he replied, cool as a cucumber. "Did you find yours?"

Checking to make sure his hand was safely back in his lap after hearing the click of his seat belt, Alex groped the crease in the seat for hers once more. "Got it," she answered, drawing the belt across her chest.

Then she folded her hands in her lap and stared straight ahead.

She was being ridiculous; she knew that. Completely ridiculous. Val had helped her zip up her dress—big deal. So what if his warm hands had touched her skin? So what if she had felt his breath on her neck? So what that she was acutely aware of his physical presence beside her, that each time he shifted his body, she felt the energy of that movement travel from him to her, like the ripples in a pond?

Val was a seriously attractive man—it was a factually objective observation. It was quite normal, then, that her skin would have tingled at his touch, as innocent as it was. He had been a complete gentleman with her, and neither of them had done anything wrong. And Alex certainly wasn't replaying the three minutes Val had spent in her room, fixing her zipper, over and over again in her mind.

"You're quiet."

Val's deep, low voice startled Alex into looking at him, and she prayed she wouldn't blush.

"Billy hasn't answered any of my emails," she blurted out, even though Billy was the farthest thing from her mind. "I mean, he hadn't, the last time I checked."

"Oh," Val replied. "Did you try calling him?"

"I shut my phone off. I don't want to pay the extra fee every day for having international cell service."

One side of his mouth lifted in a half-smile. "I think that since your boss made you go to Israel with him, he would certainly pay any extra cell charges that were incurred."

"I know," she sighed, "but there's no reason to pay for something I don't need. Billy's probably just caught up in back-to-back meetings. He'll email me when he has a few minutes. I'm not worried about it."

"You could just use my phone to call him," Val suggested.

"It's okay, really. But thank you."

Val shrugged, raising his eyebrows.

Alex turned her head to stare out the darkened window as she exhaled a slow breath. It was going to be a long night.

****

They were the first to arrive at the restaurant by design. After checking in with the hostess, they went back outside to stand on a picturesque stone patio and wait for the rest of their party. It had been dark for a while, and it was somewhat hypnotic watching the lights from the cars as they went by and listening to the accompanying hum of their motors. Alex stood near him, leaning against the metal railing, and each time the breeze picked up, Val's lungs filled with her scent. He knew it was just the hotel shampoo, but still, the smell of tangerine was intoxicating when it was coming from her body.

When their guests arrived a few minutes later, Val watched out of the corner of his eye as Alex shook hands with Gideon and Yaakov and warmly welcomed their wives. Alex was more talkative now, more relaxed than she'd been in the cab ride over. She had been worried about her boyfriend, apparently. Even from across the globe, this boyfriend of hers was irritating.

At the table, Val and Alex exchanged looks as he silently assessed the most strategic places to sit in an effort to include everyone in the conversation. With another glance in Alex's direction, Val moved to sit at one end of the table, with Yaakov on one side of him and Yaakov's wife, Mara, on the other. Gideon's wife Ayala, who was a talkative redhead, was already in the middle of telling Mara and Alex the story of her life, so she sat down next to Mara. Alex, rather than sit at the other end of the table across from Val, sat down opposite Ayala, next to Yaakov, leaving Gideon to sit at the end of the table opposite Val.

Val made a mental note to thank her for so naturally allowing Gideon to have the other power position.

Throughout their dinner, Val found himself captivated by how charming and at ease Alex seemed. She had the charismatic demeanor of a diplomat, constantly wearing a warm, inviting smile and always knowing the perfect moment to deliver a witty comment, inspiring laughter, or emphasizing the importance of what someone had said.

At one point during their meal, Alex caught Val looking at her, and the curve of her lips changed from the polite smile of a hostess to the knowing grin of a confidante or co-conspirator. The acknowledgement that they were working together to seal this deal, even though it was in the form of an almost imperceivable change in the curve of her lips and the subtlest raising of her eyebrows, brought him such joy and comfort that for a few moments, Val couldn't look away.

As the desserts were cleared and Val was signing the check, he again stole a glance in her direction. This time he found Yaakov, who was sitting beside her, leaning in to tell her something meant only for her ears. Val felt a jealous sting, which caused him to furrow his brow. Then, realizing the absurdity of the feeling, he quickly looked back down at the check in front of him.

The party stood up in unison, and Val turned first to Mara and held out his hand.

"Handshakes are for suspicious strangers," replied Mara, hugging him.

Across the table, Val saw Alex embrace Gideon before turning to Yaakov, who seemed more than eager to receive the same treatment.

Although the men did not embrace each other, Gideon shook Val's hand with both of his and delivered an encouraging smile, even as he held Val back from the rest of the group to speak more privately.

"Val, it will not come as a surprise to you that I was greatly disturbed to hear Kurt was leaving to join Pierce."

"Yes," Val nodded, "I know, and believe me, I understand."

"But the fact that you came here to Israel to give me your assurances in person, and the fact that I can see for myself you are more than capable of attracting the best talent to work for you—" At this, he gestured toward Alex several steps ahead of them. "—well, that speaks volumes. I now give you my personal assurances that when the board meets in two weeks to take the final vote, I will recommend to them that they proceed with the acquisition of Span Global. There are no guarantees, of course, that they will vote in accordance with my recommendation, but I can't remember the last time they did not on a matter of such importance."

Val had not expected to have such positive feedback as instant gratification for their efforts. The best he had hoped for was his own and Alex's assessment of how the meetings had gone. Val shook hands with Gideon once more, thanking him.

Gideon and Ayala got into one car, and Yaakov and Mara got into another. Val and Alex stood back and waved as they drove off. It would be a few more minutes before the cab they had called from the restaurant arrived. As soon as their guests were out of the parking lot, Alex turned to Val with a huge smile on her face.

"Well, how do you think it went?" she asked, her excitement obvious.

"How do *you* think it went?" Val asked back, mirroring her expression.

"I think it went as well as it could possibly go," Alex replied. "I think they really like you, and, more than that, they trust you. Gideon mentioned more than once how much he appreciated us coming all the way out here for one day of meetings with them."

"Yes," said Val, still smiling. He enjoyed seeing her so happy and animated.

"You look like you know something I don't know. What are you hiding from me?"

Val's smile grew larger as the cab they were waiting for pulled up to the curb.

"I'll tell you in the cab," he said finally, giving in under the weight of her stare.

They got into the cab, and Val leaned forward in his seat to ask the driver to take them back to the Ritz. When he relaxed into his seat once more and looked over at Alex, the impatient look she gave him made him laugh out loud.

"You're making me want to drag this out even longer," he teased.

Alex hit his arm playfully with the back of her hand. "We're in the cab—now tell me!"

"Okay, okay. As we were leaving the restaurant, Gideon told me he would recommend to the board that they proceed with the acquisition of Span Global."

"Oh my gosh! That's great!" squealed Alex, clapping her hands. "You did it! You won—you beat Kurt Donovan at his own game."

"We can't declare victory yet, Alex. The board votes in two weeks, and they can vote however they wish. Nothing obligates them to follow Gideon's recommendation. It's just that—a recommendation."

"So, they could still vote against the acquisition? Is that likely?"

Val paused, letting his own enthusiasm take over for a moment. "Well, although it is definitely possible for them to vote contrary to Gideon's recommendation, Gideon said that they've never done that. They've always gone with what he recommends."

Alex's face lit up once more. "That's so wonderful, Val. I'm so happy for you. Even though I know you won't know for sure for a couple of weeks, I think we're in the best position we could possibly be in, given the circumstances. And chances are you're going to get some really good news in two weeks."

"We'll just have to wait and see, I guess."

They were both quiet for a few moments. Alex turned her head slightly to look out the window. Then she turned back toward him and said, with a mischievous grin, "I noticed Mara was pretty eager to hug you goodbye."

Val chuckled. "Really? Is that what you noticed? Because I noticed that her husband was even more eager to hug you goodbye."

She laughed. "It would seem the Israelis are a very warm people."

"Yes, especially when it comes to embracing attractive young women under socially acceptable settings. I was rather jealous of our friend Yaakov."

This last comment had come out of his mouth unfiltered, and Val immediately knew he had crossed a line by insinuating that he, too, wanted to hug Alex. Especially since he wanted to do much more than hug her.

To Val's surprise, she smiled coyly at him. "The night is young. You may get your chance yet."

While Val was still pondering, somewhat in shock, what exactly Alex meant by her statement, she clasped her hands together and looked at him conspiratorially. "I think we should do something to celebrate our success tonight. Don't you?"

"I think that's a great idea. What do you have in mind?"

"Nothing in particular," she replied. "There's a trendy-looking bar in the lobby of the hotel. We can start there."

When they arrived at the hotel, they agreed to go upstairs and change into more comfortable clothes, then meet back downstairs in the lobby. As Val unbuttoned his shirt and pulled a dark blue sweater on over his t-shirt, he felt almost giddy. He couldn't remember the last time he looked forward to seeing anyone, or doing anything. It was borderline ridiculous, the sense of anticipation growing in the pit of his stomach.

As he passed by Alex's hotel room to go back down to the lobby, Val wondered if Alex had managed to get her dress unzipped. He pictured Alex standing there again, with her back to him, lifting her hair away from the zipper to give him access. He imagined slowly pulling down the zipper, down past her bra, and further down, to the small of her back, the fabric gently falling away to reveal soft, smooth skin.

Shaking his head, he tried to erase the enticing images from his mind. If he was going to get through the evening without committing every violation in the Span Global Employee Manual, he had to have a clear head and an iron will. He couldn't make any more mistakes.

Chapter Fourteen

Alex's heart was already beating faster than it should have been when she saw Val round the corner. Somehow, the man managed to look just as good in jeans and a sweater as he did in dress pants and a tailored white shirt.

He smiled as he approached, and Alex's heart beat faster still.

Taking a quick breath, Alex told herself that being in an exotic location and finished with meetings that had gone very well was doing a number on her.

When Val was a few steps away, Alex stood up, nervously tugging at the hem of her snug brown sweater.

"Hey," she said softly, remembering to smile.

"Hey yourself," Val replied in a voice as smooth as satin.

"Shall we get a seat at the bar?" he added, gesturing to the area behind him. "There are plenty of seats to choose from."

"I noticed." She laughed, looking over to where a man sat at the long counter, drinking alone.

Alex followed Val to the corner of the bar counter and sat. The bartender, who looked rather lonely having only the one guy to serve, came over immediately to give them a drink menu.

They ordered their drinks, and a minute later, they

were touching their glasses together before taking the first sips.

"I know I keep saying this," Alex began, after a few minutes of silence, "but I'm really happy to be here. It's been such an amazing trip for me, in every way."

"Good," replied Val, setting his glass down. "I'm glad to hear that."

There was more she wanted to say, to convey how much she appreciated this assignment, but there was no way to say it without sounding pathetic. The truth was that the last couple of weeks working on the project for Span Global had been the most fulfilling of her legal career. It made her feel that she was part of something important and, more than that, it made her feel like a real lawyer. She felt as though Val *needed* her, but for the life of her, she couldn't figure out why he would.

"You know," she said, gathering the courage to look at him, "I'm still not really sure why you brought me in the first place. You work with such a talented team."

Val didn't answer right away, and Alex worried she had said something wrong.

"I brought you," he finally replied with clear and articulated words, "because I couldn't imagine bringing anyone else. I went through all the engineers, all the sales folks, everyone who works for me, and I couldn't pick out a single person who I thought would make as good an impression on Gideon Krantz as you would, as you clearly did. Alex, you put more effort into learning about the company, and serving the company, in the past two weeks than some people put into their whole careers. And even more importantly than that, you have this unique talent to connect with people, to make them feel important and at ease. I saw it at lunch today with Yaakov and at dinner tonight with Gideon. It's amazing, and to be honest, I've never seen anything quite like it."

His words rendered Alex speechless, and she felt her eyes begin to mist. Refusing to get all teary-eyed in front of Val, Alex took a long, slow sip from her glass before looking at him again.

"Thank you," she said, finally, her voice cracking ever so slightly with emotion. "No one's ever said anything like that to me before, and I can't tell you how good it makes me feel."

Val continued to look at her, as though he had more to say. Without thinking, she leaned forward in her seat, toward him, toward the words he had yet to speak.

"Alex…" He sighed. "I know you've had a tough time getting a job since you graduated from law school. But your difficulties were all due to circumstances, and other people's stupidity and short-sightedness. They had nothing to do with you, with who you are, or what you have to offer. You are an incredibly intelligent woman, you're kind and passionate, and you take ownership of everything you touch and make it better. You're a person I can trust, a person whose opinion I value, and that's pretty rare these days, for me at least."

They looked at each other for a moment, and a dozen responses crossed Alex's mind. She wanted Val to know how much his words meant to her and how much she admired what he'd done with his company. She wanted to convey, in some small way, what a good man he was, to tell him how peaceful it made her feel to just sit with him and have a conversation about anything. Unsure how to say those things without making Val think she had romantic notions, Alex just smiled shyly and looked away. Draining the last of her drink, she put the glass down with a quiet clink. Then she looked at Val again. "Do you want to take a walk or something?"

****

Val nodded as his stomach moved up into his throat, then back down again. "Sure."

He gestured for the check, and Alex didn't even challenge him as he paid for both their drinks. Then he followed her out of the large glass doors that led out to the beach, trying to keep his breathing steady.

The air outside was cool but refreshingly welcome. They walked for a couple of minutes in silence, turning right onto the concrete path that extended along the beach in front of them.

"This is beautiful," said Alex finally, breaking the stillness between them. She was looking out to the gentle waves that lapped the shore with a calm rhythm, like a slow heartbeat. The moon above was almost full and cast a pale light on her face, making her look otherworldly.

"Yes, beautiful," he replied, looking only at her.

Alex turned her head slowly back toward him, seeming to catch his meaning, then looked away, out onto the ocean once more.

They walked along for a few minutes without speaking, the sound of the waves filling the space between them. Keeping her eyes on the path ahead of her, Alex asked, "So, what do you do for fun, Val? In your spare time? Or do you have any?"

He laughed. "I'm sure you have just as little spare time as I do. I like to read, and I like sports. College football is my favorite, with play-off baseball a close second."

"Do you go out with friends?"

He didn't answer right away, but she made no move to modify or retract her question. Unable to justify any other option, Val decided on the truth.

"I've never been very good at making friends. As a child, I had no one, and I suppose I never learned how."

Even as he said this, Val thought of the classmates who had bullied him relentlessly. He spoke with an accent back then, and his clothes were always well-worn hand-me-downs. Everything about Val was different, from his clothes to his unkempt hair to the food he ate at lunch to the lunchbox he brought the food in. Nothing about Val had conveyed familiarity or attracted friendship. And though his speech, his clothes, and his status had changed over time, that part had remained the same.

"Now," he continued, "well, most of the 'friends' I have are for convenience, more so than actual companionship."

Alex was quiet for a moment. "I think people talk about 'friends' without knowing what that word actually means. I'll bet the vast majority of people, if they knew what true friendship looked like, would realize they don't have any friends, either."

"That's a nice thing for you to say," replied Val, a lump forming in his throat. He didn't want to say anything else, bewildered by the effect her words had on him, afraid that his voice would betray his emotions.

"It's true," Alex went on, her expression somber. "I

think that's why so many people get married to the wrong person and end up getting divorced. They just want someone to fill the loneliness, and they don't realize until it's too late that it's the wrong person."

"And misery is worse than loneliness?"

A smile played on her rose lips. "Only slightly." She paused, then added more seriously, "You've never been married, have you?"

"No, I haven't."

"And you're not in a relationship right now?"

"How do you know I'm not in a relationship?" Sensing her sudden hesitation, Val tried to suppress a smile.

"Well, you've never mentioned a girlfriend. I guess I just assumed…"

"You're right." He chuckled. "I'm not. I broke up with my latest fling just before Christmas."

"Your latest 'fling'? So, you really *are* a playboy, then. The magazine articles are true?" The tone of her voice was playful now, and it was clear Alex was teasing him.

He laughed again. "Not exactly. It's just that, looking back, I don't know why I ever decided to go out with her, other than because she asked, and she seemed, well—"

"Gorgeous?" Alex finished his sentence for him.

He nodded, chagrinned. "I'll be honest, yes."

"I like honesty," she added softly. "So, why haven't you ever been married? You're, what, thirty-three, thirty-four years old?"

"I'm actually thirty-six."

"Is it for the same reason, then, the 'no-friends' thing?"

Val tried to assess the history of his love life in ten seconds or less so he could provide her with an accurate root cause for his bachelorhood. "I'm not sure I would want to subject any woman to a lifetime sentence of having me as a husband."

Alex stopped walking abruptly, causing Val to also stop, then turned to face him. "You're kidding, right?"

Laughing at her incredulity, Val shook his head and started walking again. "I am not kidding. I told you, I don't know how to make friends. I sure as hell wouldn't know how to be a good husband. I'm not 'family-man' material. It's not in my blood. I suppose I've always known that on some level, and so I've never selected my female companions with wedding bells in mind. Or at least that's what my niece has told me based on her one psych class in college."

"Your parents are divorced?"

"No," Val replied, "they were married until the day my father died. But they despised each other every minute of it. They were just plain nasty to each other. Each one blamed the other for their own shortcomings. It was toxic. I hated it."

He breathed in the salty air, the solid thuds of their footsteps in perfect cadence reverberating off the sandy concrete. With each passing moment, he felt tranquility slowly settle into him again.

"I'm one hundred percent certain that you would never be like them, Val, if you ever decided to get married."

He raised his eyes to her, admiringly. "How can you be so sure?"

"Well, if you are able to recognize the mistakes your parents made, then I don't see how you would make the same mistakes yourself."

"I suppose I would just make a bunch of new mistakes. The result would be the same, though."

Alex was silent for a moment, her lips pursed in thought. "You know, just because our parents are a certain way doesn't mean that we will be the same. I mean, look at me—my parents met in high school, got married at the end of their senior year, and have been madly in love ever since. I, on the other hand, have been 'living in sin' with my boyfriend for over five years, with no indication that he's ever going to propose."

"'Living in sin'? I didn't know they still called it that." Val smiled at her, hoping she would recognize that he was teasing, not judging. He was the last person in the world to judge her for living with a man she wasn't married to. Val was no saint himself, and despite what he had told her earlier about the tabloids and his love life, at least half of the stories were based on truth.

"The proverbial 'they' may not call it that, but my very Catholic mother does. She is in a constant state of denial over it. She never comes over to visit me. I always have to go to my parents' house to see them. And when I bring Billy along, she's almost surprised to see him, like she's remembering all over again how I've shamed myself by 'being his wife' without being his wife. That's her phrase, too."

"She's full of phrases, I see."

"Yeah. I know she loves me, but I also know I'm a disappointment to her for how I've handled my life." Alex paused to take in a slow breath. "Sometimes I wish things were like they were a hundred years ago. There was an order to things back then, you know? Boy meets girl, boy proposes to girl, boy and girl get married, boy and girl have sex for the first time, boy and girl raise a family together. It was simpler. No choices to make, no disappointments."

Val nodded. "It's true, it is simpler to have a path already set for you. And it works well if it's the right path. But sometimes in your scenario, for example, the girl doesn't love the boy but is forced to marry him anyway, and that doesn't turn out so well."

"I know," she replied. "You're right." Alex's voice carried a heavy note of sadness, and Val's first instinct was to take that sadness away somehow. He wanted to wrap his arms around her and make her forget all about that dolt of a boyfriend who hadn't proposed.

But he couldn't. Instead, he tried to comfort her with words. "I'll let you in on a little secret."

Alex looked at him with wide eyes, her eyebrows raised in curiosity.

"Men have an innate fear of commitment. It's as though committing to a woman for the rest of your life is acknowledgement that one day your life will end, that you are mortal and you will, in fact, die someday."

Her lips turned up at the corners, encouraging Val to continue.

"I'm serious," he went on. "Sometimes a man just needs a little nudge to get him over his inborn fear. Have you ever tried proposing to him?"

Alex looked away again, and the smile was gone. "Whenever I bring it up, Billy gets upset. He asks me why just being together isn't enough for me. He doesn't think we need a piece of paper to prove we love each other. But to me, it's not just a piece of paper. It's a promise, a seal of approval. And I don't know why just being together, without anything more, *is* enough for him."

She gave an ironic laugh and added, "You know, I had myself convinced he was going to propose to me on Christmas Day. I had discovered a black velvet box that I was sure was a ring, and I'd heard him on the phone talking to someone about 'availability' and 'taking him through the process.' Do you want to know what I got from him for Christmas?"

"I'm guessing it wasn't a ring."

Alex shook her head. "Nope. Inside the box was this lovely pair of earrings"—she raised her hair to display the diamond studs on her perfectly apportioned ears— "and inside the envelope he gave me minutes later, after I had my first hysterical breakdown, was a gym membership. It includes a weekly session with my own personal trainer, though, so that's nice."

"Ouch," replied Val. "Men can be real idiots, I'll be the first one to admit it." It was then that he remembered how quiet Alex had been on the drive to the airport. "There was something off about you when I picked you up a couple of nights ago, or whenever it was that we left the States. Was that why?"

Alex looked at him again, this time trying to read him. "Could you really tell there was something bothering me?"

"I knew you weren't your usual happy self. I just thought you were nervous about the trip."

"Huh."

They had walked quite a distance together, and now Alex wrapped her arms around herself. She was cold.

"Let's head back," said Val, stopping. "It's getting

a little chilly out here."

"Yeah, it is."

They started walking back toward the hotel. The breeze felt stronger and cooler. Out of the corner of his eye, Val saw Alex tuck her hands under her crossed arms for warmth.

Neither of them spoke, and there was no one else out walking. Only the sound of the waves gently rolling onto the shore, punctuated by the soft shuffle of their feet against the pavement, filled the air around them.

Unable to resist the growing urge to be closer to her, and against all his better judgment, Val slowly raised his arm and brought his hand down to rest on Alex's shoulder, squeezing gently. "Are you okay?" he asked, keeping his hand where it had landed.

To his surprise, Alex stopped walking and turned to face him. The light of the moon reflected on her beautiful face, and Val realized he was in big trouble. Her large, hazel eyes were focused on his, and it took every ounce of willpower for him not to draw her closer and press his lips to hers. To distract himself, he began talking.

"I just don't like seeing you sad about this, or anything. I mean, I wish there was something I could do to help. The only thing I can say is that I know everything will work out for you. Because these things we think are problems, sometimes aren't as big or as bad as we might think they are in the moment. And things have a way of becoming clearer, with time."

He had no clue what he was saying, and kissing her was sounding more and more like a good idea to him. Val had both his hands on her shoulders, holding her at arm's length, still trying desperately not to pull her to him. He realized with a combination of horror and intense desire that his hands were now moving up and down along her arms, warming them, and in the process feeling as much of Alex's body beneath his fingers as the thick sweater she wore allowed.

"I love him," she said, her gaze unwavering, and for a moment Val desperately wanted to pretend she had said, "I love *you*."

Alex took a step toward him and wrapped her arms around him. His own hands left her arms and moved to her back, holding her close. Alex—being at least six inches shorter than Val—turned her head to one side and placed it on his chest, as though trying to hear his heart beat, which shouldn't have been difficult considering it was about to burst through his chest. Without thinking, he brought his head down to the top of her head and allowed himself to place a single kiss upon her hair.

The smell of her hair was intoxicating, like tangerines and wildflowers. He brought a hand up and rested it gently against the back of Alex's head, his fingers burrowing into her soft hair, pressing her closer to him.

"I'm sorry," she said, but made no move to separate from his embrace.

"What on earth are you sorry for?" Val replied softly into her hair.

"We're supposed to be celebrating. I'm kind of a buzz killer."

Slowly, Alex lifted her head from his chest and turned to look at him.

Val seriously considered kissing her again. She looked so vulnerable, so sad, and so completely at his mercy. It would have been easy to make her his, at least for tonight, and he so desperately wanted to. But what would happen tomorrow, when she woke up and found Val at her side, not Billy? Alex would hate herself for betraying the bastard Billy, and she would resent Val for being the catalyst for her sin. She would never look at Val the same way again. She would never look at him the way she was looking at him now, with appreciation, need, and perhaps a little admiration, a little bit of love?

Whatever small regard she held him in, he couldn't poison it. Because even if that regard was all he would ever have, he was grateful for it.

Against the screaming protest of every inch of his body, Val gently moved her so there was some space between them now. He hoped the sheer disappointment he felt at their separation was not apparent on his face as he said, "You're not a buzz killer. We all need to vent sometimes. Unfortunately for you, I'm the only one around at the moment, so you're stuck venting to me. But I'm happy to be the one if it makes you feel even a little bit better." Then, almost against his own will, he added, "Everybody needs a friend to talk to sometimes."

Alex smiled at him, and even though it was a sad kind of smile, it lifted him and made him proud of his Herculean display of self-control.

"You're a good man," said Alex, almost in a whisper. "And I think you grossly understated your abilities in the friendship department. I just hope I can be the friend to you that you have been to me."

"You already have been."

He placed his arm around her as they began

walking back to the hotel. Alex leaned into him as they walked, and he held her closer in response. Was this how friends walked side-by-side on a chilly evening by the ocean in the moonlight? Val didn't care. He had done nothing wrong, and neither had she. At least not yet.

Chapter Fifteen

Alex felt herself blushing as she entered the breakfast area the next morning and immediately glimpsed Val sitting at a table in the center of the room. Instinctively, she lowered her eyes, the memory of Val's arms around her vivid in her mind despite her best efforts to displace such thoughts. He had been so kind to her the night before, listening patiently, offering comfort. It was no wonder Alex had been overcome with tender feelings. The fact that Val had reciprocated her impromptu embrace only showed how compassionate and understanding he was.

Shaking off the sentimental thoughts, Alex looked up to find Val's eyes on her. He smiled warmly as she approached.

"You beat me this morning," she said, proud of herself for making it to the table under Val's gaze without stumbling. The exotic location and spirit of romance and adventure that seemed to permeate this place had made Alex very silly. And the fact that her boyfriend still hadn't emailed her didn't help matters. She had sent Billy another email that morning, in case something had happened to the earlier message. It was the middle of the night for him right now, though, and he wouldn't see the email for another four hours, at least.

"I didn't think it was right to make you wait for me

two mornings in a row," said Val.

"You didn't have to wait for me to get your food," she said, hoping he couldn't read her thoughts in her expression.

"I'm in no hurry. But now that you're here, what do you say? Are you hungry?" Val pushed his chair away from the table and stood up.

"Starving, as usual." She chuckled, following him toward the buffet.

****

Val had wondered what Alex would be like this morning, after all that had transpired the previous evening. Would she be distant, embarrassed, or more cautious? So far, though, all he could detect was a sparkle of excitement in her eyes, and he relaxed a little.

As he stood near Alex at the omelet station, Val couldn't help quietly admiring the flattering jeans and burnt orange t-shirt she was wearing. Her hair was in a casual ponytail this morning, and already several strands had fallen free from her hair tie to hang down on either side of her face. A pair of large-framed brown and black speckled sunglasses sat on top of her head, completing her beautiful tourist look. Val had arranged for a tour guide to pick them up and drive them around to various spots of religious and historical significance in the area, and although Val had seen many of the sights on past trips, he was eager to spend the day exploring with Alex.

When they were both sitting at the table again, Val talked about the plan for the day. He continued to watch for any signs that something had changed between them from the previous evening's walk. On the one hand, he was afraid of things becoming awkward between them, and on the other hopeful that she might start seeing him in a different light. As they sat there, eating and talking, Alex looked him in the eyes, laughed at his little jokes, and even accepted a piece of the pastry sitting on his plate when he asked if she wanted to try it. As far as Val could tell, their walk on the beach the night before hadn't changed a thing.

They met their tour guide at a quarter to ten just outside the hotel. His name was Ben, and he greeted each of them with a heartfelt handshake and a small bow in front of a pale yellow Volkswagen van that was to serve as their tour bus.

Both Ben and his VW looked like they had been plucked from the set of an old movie about archeologists on the hunt for the tomb of King Tut. The tour guide's coarse dark locks were streaked with silver, making Val guess the man was in his sixties. Ben's skin was tan and leathery, and he wore a short-sleeved white polo shirt with all three buttons undone.

The van was clean and smelled of cinnamon, compliments of the oversized air freshener hanging from the rearview mirror alongside a bead necklace. There was room enough for seven or eight people to sit comfortably in the back of the van, but Val had requested a private tour. Val and Alex sat in the two bucket seats closest to the front so they could hear Ben talk, and it was apparent from the outset that Ben liked to talk.

As Ben pulled out onto the road, he briefly discussed his own personal beliefs. He was not a religious man, he explained, but he knew a lot about religion from a historical perspective. He knew the

Bible cover to cover, Old Testament and New, and knew Israel like the back of his hand. It didn't matter whether they were pilgrims on a spiritual journey or avid historians—his job was to tell them the documented historical facts about the places they were about to visit.

Their first stop was the old city of Jerusalem, which was about an hour's drive from the hotel. "The Old City of Jerusalem is a magical city," began Ben in his heavy Israeli accent as they entered the suburbs of the Old City and made their way slowly through the stop-and-go traffic. "With its towering stone walls and sacred buildings, it has been considered the center of the world for all of history. It is a holy place for three major religions—the Jews, the Christians, and the Muslims. It is enchanting and colorful; conflicted and holy; dynamic and constant. It has seen war and peace; love and hate; death and resurrection."

Ben's attempt to be a dramatic narrator caused Alex to look at Val with a smirk.

Unnoticing, Ben beeped twice and shook his head at the car that had cut him off as they approached another light. Then he went on with his poetic discourse.

"The Christian Quarter is a common destination for tourists of all faiths and no faith. It has more than forty churches, monasteries, and hostels for Christian pilgrims. The Church of the Holy Sepulchre is the heart of the Christian Quarter and is believed to be the site where Jesus Christ was crucified and buried.

"The Christian Quarter also holds the marketplace, called *souq* in Arabic, which is one of the Old City's most popular tourist attractions. There you can purchase pottery, candles, souvenirs, clothing, jewelry, rugs, food—many, many things. But if you decide to buy something, you must bargain for it. You cannot pay the original price. Bargaining is expected."

Ben didn't wait for any response from his captive audience. He simply kept on talking.

"And then there is the Jewish Quarter, which is the main residential area for Jews in the Old City. This is where the Wailing Wall is located. The Wailing Wall was part of the Temple, and people write their prayers on a piece of paper and leave it at the wall for God to grant.

"There are many important archeological sites in the Jewish Quarter. The Cardo, for example, is a typical Roman street that was built in the 6th century."

At this point, Ben made a left turn from the right lane, maneuvering himself across two lanes of traffic by sticking his hand out of the window and making generous use of his horn.

"Finally, there is the Muslim Quarter, which is the largest quarter in the Old City. The Muslim Quarter has churches, mosques, and Jewish homes and Yeshivas. There are of course many important religious sites for Muslims in the Muslim Quarter, such as the Dome of the Rock on Mount Moria, which is a holy place for the Jews as well."

They had come to another stoplight, and Ben looked over his shoulder at Val and Alex. "So, where would you like to visit?" he asked. "After Jerusalem, we will be heading north to the next site Mr. Val has requested on this tour, which is about a two-hour drive, so we may have time for one or two of the Quarters. Which would you be interested in?"

Amulet

Val looked at Alex, making it clear it was her decision. When she responded only by looking back at him, he said, "I've seen a lot of this stuff on my other visits. You choose."

Alex looked back at Ben's face in the rearview mirror. "I guess I would like to see the Jewish Quarter and the Christian Quarter, if we can't see all of them."

"Very good," replied Ben, making a right-hand turn when the light turned green. "We will go to the Jewish Quarter first, then I will drive you to another gate to enter the Christian Quarter. There an alley that connects the two quarters, but it is narrow and winding, with many dark corners for people with ill intentions to hide in. Just last week, a man was stabbed to death in that alley. This is why I will drive you to another gate to enter the Christian Quarter. Don't worry, you will be safe in the open spaces."

Alex looked over at Val again and raised her eyebrows. He shrugged his shoulders nonchalantly in response, eliciting a smile from her in return.

Once he had parked, Ben took two scraps of paper and a pen and handed them to Alex and Val. "Write down your prayer, then roll it up and stick it in one of the cracks along the Wall. And remember, Jews believe the Wall to be a very holy place—they believe the Divine Presence is in the Wall. When you approach, you will see that there is a men's section and a women's section. Young lady, you may want to cover your head with your scarf. And when you leave the Wall, you should both back away until you are a reasonable distance from the Wall, for you do not turn your back on God."

"You're not coming with us?" Alex asked.

"No, young lady. I will stay here with the car. When you come back, I will take you to the Christian Quarter."

Val and Alex found their way to the gate for entry into the Jewish Quarter, and the metal detectors and soldiers in charge of security at the gate were a comforting sight to Val. Despite his unconcerned response to Ben's little story about the stabbing, he questioned if it had been a good idea to take Alex away from the safety of the quiet beach town of Herzliya to bring her to a place so close to the conflict of the West Bank.

Inside the gate, they made their way to the Wall. Before parting for their respective sections of the Wall, Val touched Alex's arm. "I'll meet you right back here when you're done, okay?"

She nodded, a sweet smile on her lips. "Don't worry. I'll be okay. See you in a few minutes."

Their separation troubled Val. The fact that he couldn't see the women's section from where he stood at the Wall in the men's section was even more troubling. As a result, his prayer was short, and soon he was back at their rendezvous point, watching as the most beautiful woman in the crowd, wearing a cream-colored fleece and a beige scarf on her head, slowly backed away from the Wall and finally turned to walk toward him.

Later, when they were finished with the Jewish Quarter and were heading back to Ben's van, Alex asked, "Are you religious, Val?"

He took his time in answering. "I believe in God, but I'm not sure I'm what you would call 'religious.' I don't go to church unless it's for a wedding or a funeral, but I have been known to pray every once in a while. I did just now."

Although Alex did not respond in words, the graceful tilt of her head and quiet footsteps beside him conveyed that she heard and understood exactly what he meant, how he felt. And in that silent connection, Val felt the need to say more.

"My grandmother was religious. Eastern Orthodox Christianity is the predominant religion in Bulgaria, and that's what she was. The closest Orthodox church was forty minutes away from our house, and I remember how upset my grandmother was when my father stopped taking her to church, a couple of months after she moved in with us. But she continued to pray, every day, for my parents, my aunts and uncles, me and my brother and sisters. She had this morning ritual, where she prayed as she got dressed, washed her face, brushed her hair, and got ready for the day. It took her maybe fifteen or twenty minutes, and she would not respond to any distractions during her prayers, even the incessant attempts of a mischievous nine-year-old to divert her attention."

Here, Val chuckled, remembering how he used to tug on her sleeve, ask her questions, sing out loud, and do countless other things that would have annoyed even the most saintly of individuals, all without the slightest acknowledgement by his grandmother until her prayers were over.

"My grandmother was also very superstitious," he continued, "which I always found to be an amusing combination, although some people might say that there is a fine line between religion and superstition, if there is a line at all. She gave me all sorts of advice and directives about how to 'avoid the Evil Eye.' From spitting over my left shoulder when someone complimented me to wearing underwear with holes in it on the day of a big test, she was adamant that I steer clear of anyone's envy or ill wishes. Little did she know that no one envied me growing up."

He looked over at Alex and found her grinning at him. "Do you still spit over your left shoulder and wear porous underwear?" she asked teasingly.

Val nodded, a little embarrassed to be admitting to something he had never told anyone. "Old habits die hard," he replied, "and in the end, you never really know."

At his confession, Alex laughed out loud. "I guess you're right about that. And it's worked for you so far. I wouldn't do anything different. Just remind me not to give you any more compliments." She leaned in and added with a whisper, "Especially if I'm standing to your left."

He laughed with her, reveling in their playful exchange and the closeness he felt telling her bits and pieces of his strange childhood.

They took their time touring the Christian Quarter. The sun had warmed up the air from earlier in the day, and Alex had unzipped her fleece and loosened her scarf. Val could see the wonder in her eyes as they made their way down one of the stone pathways that led to the Church of the Holy Sepulchre. The shops that lined the pathway on both sides were like caves, hewn from the same-color stone. Eager merchants called out to passersby in whatever language they thought would be most effective, and Val watched as Alex made eye contact with several of them and politely declined.

"Do you want to look at any souvenirs?" asked Val when they had passed over a dozen vendors.

"I'm not really into the bargaining thing," she replied. "It makes me a little uncomfortable."

"That's just because you're not used to it. You probably feel like you're trying to cheat them out of their profits, but it's not like that at all. It's a dance, and if you do it right, both parties feel like they got something out of it. Pick a vendor and I'll show you."

"Are you sure?"

He nodded. "I promise, it'll be exhilarating."

They walked past a couple more shops before Alex motioned toward a vendor of religious souvenirs. "I think my mom would like a rosary from the Holy Land."

"The perfect gift for a very Catholic mother," Val teased, eliciting a grin. "Let's go in."

Ten minutes later, Alex and Val walked out, each of them carrying a bag.

"That was amazing, Val. You were so good at that. And you're right, nobody was upset, and the guy was actually happy because we ended up buying more than just this rosary."

"And at half the original price." Val looked over at her bright, smiling face. He liked impressing her.

"So, what are you going to do with that big wooden crucifix you bought?" she asked.

"I'm going to give it to my niece with instructions to display it prominently in her dorm room. Nothing works better to deter college boys with lustful thoughts than the sight of a cross."

Alex laughed. "I never knew college boys were so much like vampires, but, in a way, it actually makes sense."

By the time they had finished touring the Church of the Holy Sepulchre and made their way back to the mini-bus, where Ben was patiently waiting, it was almost one o'clock. "We go to Cana next, right, Mr. Val?"

"That sounds good, thank you, Ben."

Cana was a city to the north of Jerusalem, an hour and forty-five minutes away, but the time passed quickly with Val and Alex talking comfortably about the people and places they had seen together. During the pauses in their conversation, Ben was quick to interject with interesting facts about the various landmarks they passed along the way.

As they got closer to Cana, Ben went into dramatic narrator mode again to give his audience some context for what they were about to see.

"As you may know, it was at a wedding in Cana where, according to the Gospel of John, Jesus performed his first public miracle when he turned water into wine at the request of his mother Mary. What you may not know is that there is much speculation as to where the biblical Cana is truly located. Five places are suggested as the location of the Cana mentioned in the Bible. One of these is Qana, Lebanon, also known as Qana al-Jalil, which, as it is in Lebanon, is obviously not where we are going today."

At this, Alex chuckled under her breath. Val looked at her and agreed with a smile of his own.

"Another candidate is the Arab town of Kafr Kanna in Israel, which is about seven kilometers northeast of Nazareth. Still, another potential location is the old and now-ruined town of Khirbet Kana, also in

Israel, which overlooks the Beit Netofa Valley from the north and is about nine kilometers north of Kafr Kanna. Khirbet Kana has long been recognized as the true location of the wedding at Cana, and recent archaeological discoveries have supported this theory.

"The fourth candidate is a city just north of Kafr Kanna that was more recently excavated by a female Israeli archaeologist, a place called Karm er-Rasm. Although she is convinced this site is the true Cana, most scholars do not agree with her.

"Finally, we have our last candidate, Ain Qana in Israel, which means 'the spring of Cana,' located a couple of kilometers north of Nazareth."

When Ben paused, Alex asked the million-dollar question, "So which Cana are we going to?"

"An excellent question, young lady. We will be visiting Kafr Kanna, also known as Cana of Galilee. I will take you to the center of the city where the Greek Orthodox Church of St. George was built in the late 19th century at the place where some believe Jesus performed his miracle. At the very least, it will be interesting for you to see an Arab village, and even if it is not the exact spot where the miracle at the wedding occurred, it is close enough."

Parking was not readily available at the center of the village, but that didn't seem to bother Ben. He simply turned on his flashers and stopped the car by the side of a busy road. Alex looked at Val with wide eyes, as though saying, "We're not supposed to be parked here," and he shrugged, chuckling quietly at her reaction.

The two of them walked along the road Ben indicated, up an incline, to a stone plaza between the entrance to two churches, which were situated along adjacent sides of the busy plaza.

Alex leaned closer to Val. Distracted by her nearness and an overwhelming urge to turn his head and kiss her, Val focused his efforts on staring down at the cobblestone path as she spoke. "I thought Ben only mentioned one church, a Greek Orthodox Church. This looks like two churches, doesn't it?"

The church straight ahead of them was a pale-yellow stone structure with three arches at the entrance. Above the entrance were more arches, with a statue of Jesus under the middle arch and angels on either side. On the roof were perched two more angels and another statue, which looked like Mary.

Putting some space between himself and temptation, Val turned to a European-looking man who happened to be walking past and asked if the man knew what they were looking at. Luckily, the man understood English and quickly answered that the church with the arches was the Catholic Wedding Church, and the church on their right with a green dome was the Orthodox Church of St. George.

"Something for everybody," quipped Alex when the man had gone on his way.

After they had toured the churches, they followed a path behind the seminary that was connected to the rear of the Orthodox church. At the end of the path, they found a hidden garden, which was a welcome surprise. They spent a few minutes wandering amongst the different blooms before continuing to some shops selling more souvenirs.

"Look at this," Alex called quietly to Val, who was a few steps away from her. They were in one of the shops, and Alex was holding up a bottle of wine labeled "Cana Wedding Wine."

The shopkeeper, an old Arab woman who had been watching them from behind the counter, came over with a small tray and two plastic shot glasses filled with wine.

"You try some?" she asked in broken English.

"Thank you," replied Alex, taking one. Val did the same.

The wine was a little sweet for Val's taste, but Alex seemed to enjoy it, and the old woman looked like she could use a sale. Val put his empty cup back on the old woman's tray and turned to Alex. "Should we get a bottle of this stuff?"

"Sure," she answered, without any mention of who would pay or splitting the cost.

In the warmth of Alex's simple acquiescence, Val didn't feel like bargaining with the old lady and paid her the price that was marked on the bottle, considering the over-priced purchase an act of charity.

As they headed back to the mini-van, or the spot where Val hoped Ben was still waiting with the mini-van, Alex asked Val if he knew what time it was. Val glanced at his watch. "It's almost three-thirty. Are you hungry?"

She laughed shyly. "Am I that predictable?"

"No," he smiled, "I'm hungry, too. I saw a food vendor across the street from where Ben parked the van. Let's see if we can grab something there and eat it in the van on our way to the last stop."

"Sounds like a plan."

Val was relieved to see the van in the same location they had left it an hour ago. They told Ben about their plan to get something to eat, then jaywalked across two lanes of traffic to the hole-in-the-wall restaurant Val had noticed earlier.

The smell of fresh bread made his stomach growl in more urgent demand, and he watched as a teenager removed large, freshly-baked loaves of pita bread from the huge clay wood-fired oven in the wall behind the counter where they would be placing their order.

Val ordered two of the large loaves with labaneh yogurt spread and a thyme and sesame seed topping, along with a small bag of black olives. Back at the van, Ben had arranged a homemade wooden table between the two bucket seats and handed Val and Alex each a bottle of water as they stepped into the vehicle. When they were seated and buckled in, Ben started the van and pulled out into traffic.

Val watched as Alex opened the wrapper for her sandwich, folded the round loaf in half, then tore it down the middle. She placed one of the halves onto a paper towel and said, "Are you hungry, Ben? There's some here for you, if you are."

Val was annoyed with himself for having forgotten about Ben and, at the same time, touched by Alex's thoughtfulness. She was a very caring person, always thinking of others and their feelings, but never made a big show of it.

As Ben reached a hand back, taking her up on her offer, Val wondered if it were possible for a person to be *too* caring, *too* empathetic. After all, here she was now, hungry, with only half a sandwich to eat.

Val tore off a quarter of his sandwich and quietly placed it on Alex's wrapper, which she had laid out on the makeshift wooden table.

"You don't have to…"

"Just take it," Val said, a little more gruffly than he had intended. "It's a big sandwich, I can't eat it all."

Alex nodded, smiling, and he knew she appreciated the gesture.

"So, what's next on our whirlwind tour, Ben?" Alex asked, turning her attention to the driver who was unaware of the exchange between Val and Alex.

"Next, we go to Mount Precipice, our last stop today. It is only a short drive from here, about half an hour. Mount Precipice is located about two kilometers south of Nazareth, the hometown of Jesus. It is believed to be the site of the Rejection of Jesus by his people, who did not accept Him as Messiah and tried to push him from the mountain."

Ben took another bite of the bread before continuing. "You may recall the following from the Gospel of Luke, where Luke describes what happened when Jesus addressed the people in the synagogue and told them that the scripture he had been reading to them had just been fulfilled in their presence. Jesus said to them, 'I tell you the truth, no prophet is accepted in his hometown. I assure you that there were many widows in Israel in Elijah's time, when the sky was shut for three and a half years and there was a severe famine throughout the land. Yet Elijah was not sent to any of them, but to a widow in Zarephath in the region of Sidon. And there were many in Israel with leprosy in the time of Elisha the prophet, yet not one of them was cleansed—only Naaman the Syrian.'"

"How does he remember all this stuff?" Alex asked Val under her breath, causing him to chuckle softly.

Ben paused, and Alex straightened up, as though

she had just been caught passing notes in class. But Ben simply took a long breath, then continued. "Luke tells us that 'All the people in the synagogue were furious when they heard this. They got up, drove him out of the town, and took him to the brow of the hill on which the town was built, in order to throw him down the cliff. But he walked right through the crowd and went on his way.' This hill that Luke describes is believed to be Mount Precipice."

Alex nodded quietly, obviously trying to behave herself.

"I was uncertain when you added Cana to the stops for today, Mr. Val, that we would be able to make it to Mount Precipice before sundown. But it looks like we will make it after all."

As the driver uttered the words, Val instinctively glanced at Alex to see if the full meaning of what the driver divulged had registered with her, but her expression remained the same, and he wasn't sure one way or the other.

"What time is sunset?" Alex asked.

"Today, the sun sets at four forty-five. We will be there about twenty minutes before, which should give us time to go up the mountain and see the buildings of Nazareth in the last of the day's light."

When they pulled into the parking lot at the base of the mountain half an hour later, the desert air was cooling down significantly, and Val and Alex both put on their fleeces as they stepped out of the van.

Ben led them up the mountain slowly, showing his age more with each step, and Val understood now why he had not accompanied them on any of their other on-foot sightseeing. At the top of the mountain, Ben pointed out the city of Nazareth down below, with its own religious and historical sites that they would not have time to visit, as well as some of the other significant landmarks they could see from their vantage point, including Mount Tabor in the distance, which was believed to be the site of the Transfiguration of Jesus (according to Ben).

With the history lesson over, Ben motioned for the two of them to find a spot to watch the sunset, while he began to make his way back down to the van. "The climb down is more difficult for me," he explained, "and I have seen the sun set over this land many times."

When Ben was out of earshot, Alex leaned over to speak to Val. "Poor Ben. He doesn't seem to be doing very well. I guess I didn't realize that earlier in the day."

"Neither did I," replied Val.

They found a spot near the edge of the hill and stood near each other in silence as the sky turned all manner of beautiful colors to honor the setting sun. Val wasn't sure if he had swayed, or perhaps it had been her, but their shoulders touched at one point, then remained there in contact, passing warmth between their two bodies.

"Are you cold?" he whispered, finally, as the sun kissed the earth.

"Yes," she whispered back, which made him wonder if she were challenging him to do something about it.

Val wanted very much to wrap his arms around her in reply, but then she added, "I don't mind the cold right now, though. It makes the night more memorable, somehow."

They stood there, shoulders touching, for a while after the sun had dipped out of sight. As darkness fell around them, Val realized how much he had enjoyed the last few days with Alex. It pained him to think about going back to the stark contrast of his everyday life. Waking up alone in his condo. Eating breakfast and lunch, and sometimes dinner, alone at his desk. Arriving at work before the sun rose in the morning and leaving after the sun had set on most days. How could he go back to that solitary existence?

It was true, he would see Alex at work for at least a couple more weeks, but then she would be gone, and he would have no one.

"Should we head back?"

Alex was looking at him, a concerned expression on her face. Val shook off his gloom and smiled at her. "Yes. Hopefully Ben made it back to the van all right."

It was another hour and a half drive to get back to the hotel from Mount Precipice, but, at Ben's suggestion, they stopped at a roadside restaurant half an hour outside Herzliya to have dessert and tea instead of dinner after their late lunch.

By the time Ben dropped them off at the hotel, it was almost eight o'clock. Val didn't want the evening to be over just yet, but he realized he had spent almost twelve hours straight with Alex. He didn't want to overstay his welcome.

As they walked through the hotel lobby on the way to the elevators, Alex slowed down and touched his arm. "Val?"

Val stopped and turned to look at her.

"Do you think they would give us wine glasses at the bar? I'd hate to get stuck in customs because we were trying to smuggle a single bottle of wine in our luggage." The corners of her mouth turned up in a sweetly devilish smile as she patted the bag she was holding with the bottle of wine they had bought from Cana.

Relieved that he wouldn't have to say goodnight to Alex just yet, Val grinned unabashedly. "I'm pretty sure they can find a way to accommodate us."

****

A few minutes later, Alex was sitting comfortably beside Val on one of the couches in the lobby, sipping the wine he had poured out into the two glasses the bartender had provided.

"I can't believe it's back to reality tomorrow," she said as Val poured her a second glass. Though she didn't say it, the thought of their adventure ending the next day had prompted her to suggest prolonging the evening. Their day together had been perfect in every way, and Alex just wasn't ready for it to end.

"Well," replied Val, touching the rim of his glass with an outstretched finger, "first it will be an incredibly long flight, then a long layover in Newark, then another shorter flight, and *then* back to reality."

Alex laughed. "True. Nothing like a full day of arduous travel to help you transition back to the real world."

The real world. It seemed so far away in that moment. Her car, her townhouse. Billy. She hadn't thought about Billy all day, and now, sitting with Val and reminiscing about their sightseeing, Alex wasn't sure she wanted to think about him—at least, not quite yet. She wanted to linger just a little while longer in this dream-like place of new sights, sounds, and tastes—this world that Val had brought her to and shown her, where there were no complications or stress. Where she had a friend who seemed to genuinely care about her and how she felt.

Looking up from her glass, Alex found Val watching her, and heat immediately rushed into her cheeks. Despite her first instinct to look down again, she had to ask the question she had been pondering since that afternoon.

"What did Ben mean when he said that he wasn't sure we would make it to Mount Precipice when you added Cana to the tour? Were we not supposed to go to Cana today?"

It seemed that Val stopped breathing for a second. He didn't answer, at first, but then finally chuckled and shook his head from side to side slowly, as though she had caught him in a grand scheme.

"No, Cana was not originally on the schedule."

"Did you add it because of our conversation last night? Because of what I told you about wanting to get married?"

It was what she'd thought when Ben mentioned the timing of their stops. But if that were true, if Val had added a stop just because of what she was going through with Billy and what she wanted in her life...

"Yes," he replied simply. "I thought it would be meaningful for you. I thought you would like it."

"I did. It was perfect. The whole day with you was perfect. It was the trip of a lifetime. Thank you for that. Thank you for all of it."

Val nodded, saying nothing, but there was something in his eyes that made her think that, perhaps, he wanted to thank her, too. Maybe it was meaningful for him, as well.

Alex sipped what was left of her wine, conscious of Val's nearness, wondering what he was thinking. But as she tipped the last drop from her glass, he still said nothing, and she couldn't find the right words to ask what his silence meant.

Val was quiet as they rode the elevator together, and when she ventured to glance at his face, the hint of melancholy in his expression made her heart squeeze. The sound of the elevator doors sliding open when they reached their floor jarred her from her contemplative state, and Val gestured for her to step off the elevator before him.

Alex stopped at the door to her room and withdrew the room key from her back pocket as Val came up behind her.

Suddenly wary of the fluttery feeling in her stomach, Alex unlocked the door and gripped the handle to push it open. Seconds passed as she paused, her hand unmoving, and the door locked again with a click.

She found herself turning away from the door and boldly looked into Val's eyes. The confusion and, quite possibly, panic she saw written on Val's face made her smile and, oddly enough, gave her courage.

"Thank you again for a wonderful day, Val."

Whether it was due to the wine or the look in his eyes, the tenderness Alex felt for Val overwhelmed her, and she reached up to hug him. Without hesitation, he leaned in to wrap his arms around her, his strong arms holding her, making her feel both protected and powerful. They held each other for longer than was necessary, but neither of them seemed inclined to let the other go. With her eyes closed, she felt his chest rise and fall against hers, and without effort, their breathing fell into sync.

Finally, after what could have been one minute later or ten, Alex slowly released her hold on Val and felt him do the same. As she withdrew, Alex turned her head and brushed her lips against his cheek.

It was an innocent gesture, like the kisses she had given her brother at least a hundred times before, and she told herself she merely wanted to convey how much she cared for Val, as a friend. But then Val's hand slid into hers, and of their own accord, her fingers spread apart, weaving with his.

Val bent his head toward her, and Alex froze, watching as his lips drew closer to her cheek. As he placed a chaste kiss just under her cheekbone, she closed her eyes and sucked in a quiet breath.

His lips lingered on her skin, and when she heard him whisper her name, felt his breath on her neck as he spoke the word, Alex realized with equal parts exhilaration and dread that she had made a terrible mistake.

Chapter Sixteen

At the sound of her intake of breath, Val came undone.

"Alex," he whispered, his cheek still against hers.

Her fingers tightened around his, and before he could consider the situation rationally, his other hand moved around her waist to the small of her back, and he pulled her gently closer.

Slowly, Val placed another kiss on Alex's cheek, and then another, and another, each one lower than the last until he had reached her collarbone. The scent of her hair was intoxicating, and he could do nothing but continue to kiss her soft, warm skin under its influence.

Her head rolled away from him as she sighed, and his trail of kisses continued from her collarbone down until he reached the neckline of her shirt. He wanted to keep going, shirt or no shirt, to feel the swell of her curves with his lips, but conscious thought took over once more, and he paused, considering.

"Val?" she breathed.

He straightened as her free hand clutched at the fabric of his sweater. It took only a moment to realize that Alex was not pushing him away with that hand. She was holding him there, in place, with her. And when her lips parted in an unspoken question, Val answered by lowering his mouth to hers.

Her lips were sweeter than he had imagined, the

taste of wine combined with her citrus scent overpowering his senses. She met his kiss with fervor, as though she had wanted to kiss him just as much as he had wanted to kiss her.

Alex tilted her head to the side, sighing her contentment as the kiss deepened, and Val moved his hand from her back to grasp her waist. As he continued to kiss her, he stepped forward slowly, moving them together until her back was against the door to her room.

At the contact of her body with the door, Alex gasped, breaking their kiss and opening her eyes. Instinctively, Val released her and took a step back.

They stood there, staring at each other for at least a minute, and Val couldn't help lowering his gaze from her wide, hazel eyes that drove him crazy, to her slightly parted lips that made him even crazier.

"I'm sorry," she breathed, finally turning away from him and fumbling with her back pocket as she tried to pull out her room key again.

Saying nothing, he watched as Alex hurriedly opened the door and went inside, pulling it shut behind her.

His head falling under the weight of disappointment and uncertainty, Val turned and walked the few feet to his room. The click of a door down the hall behind him caused his gaze to snap back up, and for a moment Val's imagination got the better of him as he thought he heard her footsteps approaching. But when he looked over his shoulder, the hall was empty. She hadn't changed her mind.

With a resigned sigh, Val opened his door and entered, accepting the solitude of his own, darkened room as the door swung shut behind him.

****

What had she just done?

Alex collapsed onto the bed and curled up in a ball, knees tucked close to her chest, eyes closed.

She had let him kiss her. No, she had encouraged him to kiss her. She had kissed him back. She had held his hand, tilted her head so he could cover her neck with kisses, and grasped at his sweater when she thought he might retreat.

And she had enjoyed every second of it.

She hadn't thought of Billy, waiting for her halfway across the world. She had pushed him out of her mind completely. Because the person consuming her thoughts was Val.

Groaning with self-loathing, Alex forced herself to sit up.

She was still thinking about Val. In fact, she couldn't get him out of her head.

Val was, after all, a very attractive man. It wasn't just that he was physically attractive, though. He had also been kind to Alex, right from the start. Kind and thoughtful and smart—so smart. He had accomplished so much. But there was another side to him, too—a loneliness, a vulnerability that made him that much more endearing. She had wanted to take care of him. From the first time Val told her about Kurt leaving the company, to his request for her to come with him to Israel, Alex had wanted to help him, to support him, and solve his problems.

She shook her head, at the same time getting up off the bed and moving into the bathroom. Turning on the light, Alex looked in the mirror, disgusted with herself.

She had betrayed Billy. She had betrayed Billy's trust.

And she would have to tell him.

She contemplated calling her boyfriend right then and there, international cellular charges be damned, but Billy was still at work. What if he was in the middle of a meeting? What if there was something important going on at work? Alex couldn't just disrupt Billy's day with the news that she'd just kissed her boss, and she certainly couldn't do it over the phone.

No, she'd have to wait one more day. She would tell Billy tomorrow night, at home.

And hopefully, he would forgive her.

****

Early the next morning, as Val stood waiting for Alex by one of the couches in the lobby where they had shared the bottle of wine the night before, he replayed their goodnight kiss in his mind for the thousandth time. He had hardly slept at all that night, remembering the feel of her chest pressed against him, her mouth moving in sync with his, her body in his hands. In that moment, Alex was his and his alone, just as Val was hers. There was no Billy, no Employee Manual, no dysfunctional families or secrets or shortcomings. Alex had felt something for him; she cared about him. She wouldn't have responded to him as she had if that were not true.

But that was last night. It was a new day, and nothing could change a person's mind as quickly as a sunrise.

Val had no doubt that Alex had stayed awake all night thinking about that kiss, too. The question was, what would her conclusion be? Val did not regret his actions; did she? Was she angry with him for having kissed her? Was she riddled with guilt at having enjoyed it?

Almost as though he could sense her approach, Val looked up just as Alex came around the corner from the elevators. She smiled politely at him from a distance, then went straight to the desk to check out. Val's heart sank.

When she was done, she came over to stand next to him.

"Good morning, Alex," said Val as she arranged the strap on her carry-on. He knew she was trying to avoid looking at him.

"Good morning, Val," she replied, gazing intently at her luggage.

Val had gone over what he would say to her that morning at least a hundred times. He was going to admit how he felt about her, why she should be with him and not Billy, why their kiss the night before was not a mistake, but an opportunity.

As he watched her start digging in her purse for something, he realized a speech would be completely pointless. Her hazel eyes continued to avoid him, even after she found the slip of paper she had apparently been seeking. Without so much as a glance, Alex directed her attention to the handle of the larger suitcase and started pulling on the old airline tag that was still attached.

"You're not going to talk to me?" Val's tone was soft and calm, a stark contrast to the tumultuous storm he felt inside.

His words had the desired effect—she stopped messing with her suitcase and turned to face him.

"I'm not upset with you," said Alex, her tone matching his.

"I know. But you are upset."

She closed her eyes and shook her head. "I'm sorry about what happened. I lost my head, and I put you in a bad position. I hope you don't think less of me…"

"Think less of you? Because I kissed you? I don't understand, what makes you think I would think less of you?"

"I shouldn't have acted the way I did. I have a boyfriend, and it wasn't right. I think it's just that we've spent a lot of time together on this trip, and the familiarity, combined with the wine and just the atmosphere of this place—well, I'm just sorry to end it on a bad note. Can we just agree not to talk about it?"

Was that what Alex really thought of their kiss? That it had ruined the perfect time they had spent together? Val couldn't help shaking his head in disbelief.

"I guess I'm just saying," she began again, "that I hope I haven't ruined our relationship. I think of you as a very good friend, and I don't want that to change."

"You haven't done anything. I don't know why you're taking all the blame."

Blame—now he was beginning to sound like her. They hadn't done anything wrong. It had only been a kiss. The fact that Val wanted more, well, that wasn't wrong either. Not if Alex was with a boyfriend she wasn't supposed to be with. Not if she was supposed to be with him.

"In any case," she added, looking Val in the eyes for the first time, "can we still be friends? Can we forget what happened?"

Disappointment filled him, displacing the air in his lungs, making him almost gasp for breath. Rallying,

Val forced himself to smile. He would never forget what had happened between them. He wanted more than Alex's friendship—he wanted her love. But he knew she could not, or would not, give that to him.

"Of course. Friends," he replied, defeated.

Alex held out her hand in the gesture of a handshake, and Val let out a quiet sigh as he took it.

"All right," he said, reluctantly separating from the brief platonic contact of skin on skin, "Ori is probably already waiting for us outside, so we should get going."

They rode in awkward silence to the airport, to the point that even Ori likely wondered what had transpired between the two co-workers over the past few days.

Their flight was on time, and, aside from a slight delay when Alex, of all people, was selected at random for a more thorough screening as they passed through the security checkpoint, there were no surprises.

Over the course of the twelve-and-a-half-hour flight from Tel Aviv to Newark, Alex relaxed a little, and the conversation between the two of them gradually grew more comfortable. But she made a point to pull out a stack of documents and her laptop as soon as it was permissible to do so, making the unnecessary excuse that she had not done anywhere near the amount of work she had intended to do during their time in Israel.

When they deplaned in Newark, they followed the line of fellow passengers to claim their bags and go through U.S. Customs. Val took the opportunity as they were standing around, waiting for the baggage carrousel to start spitting out the bags from their flight, to turn on his cell phone so he could check emails and voice messages. Although he excused himself and took a few steps away from Alex as he did so, Val observed her out of the corner of his eye, the recollection of her frank denial of their connection and the knowledge that his time with her was coming to an end causing an ever-increasing tightness in his chest.

Alex took out her phone and turned it on. She stared at it impatiently, no doubt waiting for it to find a signal and download any voice messages she had missed during their time in Israel. Flicking a finger across the screen, she navigated to a particular message, then held the phone up to her ear to listen. Val watched as the blood drained from her face and her whole body stiffened.

Something was wrong.

In a split-second Val was at her side, not caring whether it was obvious he had been observing her the whole time.

"What is it? What's wrong?" He placed a hand on Alex's arm to steady her. She looked so frail, as though she could hardly stand.

Oblivious to the buzz that announced the arrival of their bags at the carousel, Alex lowered the phone from her ear and looked up at Val, slowly, her eyes beginning to water and her lower lip trembling slightly.

"Billy, he's in the hospital. He was mugged on the way to his car Sunday night. They, they left me messages, the hospital did, but I didn't have my phone turned on...."

Val knew what Alex was thinking—while she was sightseeing, eating pastries, and making out with Val outside her hotel room, her faithful boyfriend Billy was being attacked by ruthless thugs. Suddenly, Val's self-pity turned into self-loathing. Had he not lost control of himself the night before, Alex would not have felt the added burden of her guilt now as she tried to grasp what had happened to Billy.

"I was upset because he hadn't replied to my emails," she added, tears streaking down her cheek.

"Listen, there's nothing you could have done had you gotten the hospital's messages. The flights were all booked on Monday, remember? This was the earliest we could have come home. You didn't do anything wrong."

She nodded absently, and he racked his brain for something he could do or say to bring her some comfort.

"What condition is he in? Did they say?"

"They just said he's in the ICU. That's bad, isn't it?"

Alex looked at him with such vulnerability that he wanted to gather her in his arms and protect her from the world.

"Not necessarily. Sometimes it's just a temporary thing, while they wait for something to stabilize. It could even be that they didn't have a regular room available and they're just waiting for one to open up."

Val had absolutely no idea if anything he was saying was true.

"I think your bag just went by, and there's mine," he said, glancing over at the baggage carousel. "Just stay here for a second and I'll go grab them. Then we'll figure out what to do. Everything is going to be okay, Alex."

Again, she nodded, her face still pale and expressionless. Looking up, Val noticed their bags going around the next turn, away from them. He pushed his way through the groups of people gathered around the baggage carousel and grabbed their bags before they were out of reach, then made his way back to Alex, dragging the bags behind him.

"Come on," he said, nudging her arm. "Let's get in the line for Customs. It's getting longer the more we wait."

Alex took her bag, and Val was about to insist that she let him handle the bags when he realized that with one hand now free, he could hold her arm and gently guide her past the crowds of people to where they needed to be.

As they stood in line, moving forward ever so slowly, Alex called the hospital to see if she could get more details about Billy's condition. Val tried to pick up on what was going on based on the questions she was asking, but for the most part, he was in the dark until Alex hung up the phone.

"Billy's going to be okay," she said, a smile fighting its way to brighten her still-pale face. "He has a concussion, and his kneecaps were shattered. I guess one of the guys that robbed him ended up hitting him over the head with the butt of his gun, and that caused Billy to lose consciousness and fall onto his knees. One of his knees was hurt worse than the other one and is going to require surgery, which is scheduled for tomorrow morning. But he's going to heal. It will take time, but he'll heal."

Her voice trailed off, then she looked back at Val. "Billy could have been shot with that gun, Val. He could have been killed."

"You can't think about that," Val quickly replied. "The important thing is that he wasn't hurt any more than he was."

Once they got through Customs, they checked with the airline to see if there were any earlier flights home, but there weren't—they would have to wait for the flight that evening at nine-twenty. They checked their bags again and resigned themselves to waiting it out.

Having done all they could, and feeling better knowing Billy's condition was stable, Alex seemed to relax a little. They found a Spanish restaurant near their gate and had dinner, then spent the next two hours in the first-class lounge until they could finally board their plane.

It was after eleven-thirty when their flight finally landed, and they quickly and quietly deplaned and made their way to the baggage claim area.

Alex called the hospital again from the car as they drove out of the parking lot and onto the highway, heading toward the city.

"They said he's sleeping right now, but that I can see him," she said to Val, getting off the phone. "Would you mind—"

"Of course not," Val quickly responded. "I'm already headed in that direction. I figured that's where you'd want to go."

They drove along in silence, Alex checking her phone nervously every couple of minutes. It was as though she thought the hospital could have called and left her another message without the phone even ringing.

Val couldn't help feeling bad that Alex's boyfriend had gotten jumped by criminals. The guy was in for a long recovery, and his knees would probably never be the same again. Still, the selfish part of Val was annoyed, angry even, at having this be how his few days with Alex ended. Yesterday they were seeing the sights and enjoying each other's company, so much so that the day ended with them kissing, right or wrong. And now all of it was tainted, their whole time together overshadowed by this event. He couldn't help blaming Alex's boyfriend for that, as unreasonable as it might be.

Val pulled into the parking garage at Presbyterian Hospital, and Alex fixed her gaze on him as he put the car in park and shut off the engine. It seemed as though she wanted to say something, but instead, she opened her door and stepped out. By the time he had gotten out, she was already at the back of the car, waiting for Val to open the trunk.

"We can leave your bags here for now," Val suggested.

"No, that's okay," Alex replied, her voice shaky. "I'm going to spend the night here, if they let me, so I should probably have my stuff with me."

Having no good reason why she shouldn't take the bags and spend the night in the hospital with her injured boyfriend, Val pulled the luggage out of the trunk.

They walked in silence, and when they got inside to the front desk, Alex asked for directions to her boyfriend's room in the ICU. The reception area was quiet this time of night, and there was only one man sitting on a couch in the corner, half asleep, aside from the attendant at the desk and a janitor on the other side. The attendant's voice as she explained how to get to the ICU seemed unnecessarily loud in contrast, and Val was glad when she was done talking.

Alex took a few steps in the direction the attendant

Amulet

had pointed, then stopped to look at Val. "I think you should go," she said softly, almost as though she were afraid she would hurt his feelings. "It's late, and I know you must be tired. You should go home and get some sleep."

"You're tired, too." Val wasn't ready to leave her side just yet.

"Yes, but I'll be okay. I'll crash on a couch in Billy's room or something, so I'm there when he wakes up. If they have the surgery tomorrow morning, like they said they would, I'd like to be with him for that. Is it okay if I'm late coming in?"

"You know you don't have to ask me that," Val replied gently, resisting the urge to tuck a loose strand of hair behind her ear.

"Thank you, Val, for everything you've done for me. You don't know how much I appreciate it."

"I'm the one who should be thanking you. I think you might have saved my company."

He gave her a lopsided grin. He wanted to kiss her again, to the point that he didn't even care anymore whether it was appropriate or whether it would make her feel guilty. But then her lips turned up in a smile, and it made him feel like he'd won some small victory, even without the kiss.

She stretched her hand out toward him, and, thinking for a moment that Alex was reaching for him, Val's heart nearly leapt out of his chest. But, instead of his hand, her fingers wrapped around the handle of her suitcase.

"Be careful driving home," she said softly. Then Alex turned and walked away, the sound of the squeaky wheels on her roller bag echoing down the empty hall and getting fainter as she moved farther away.

****

It was a test of Alex's will not to turn around and look at Val as she walked toward the ICU—almost as difficult as telling him she felt nothing more than friendship for him that morning when they were leaving the hotel in Israel.

She did the math quickly in her head—it had been around twenty-four hours ago when she had looked Val almost in the eye and told him they should forget about their kiss. He had been gracious about the whole thing. He'd even tried to tell her it was his fault, not hers. But she knew that wasn't true. She had wanted to kiss him—wanted him to kiss her. It was why she'd hugged him, why she'd reached up and kissed his cheek, even if she hadn't realized it at the time.

She was not so innocent.

Alex got off the elevator and saw a sign for the ICU down the hall. Hurrying to the double doors under the sign, she pressed a large square button to open them, then almost ran into the nurse on duty.

Despite the woman's silent glare as Alex explained who she was and who she was there to see, the nurse showed her to Billy's room without much fuss.

"He was sleeping a few minutes ago when I was doing my rounds," the nurse whispered as she opened the door. "He'll be happy to see you when he wakes up."

Alex looked at her in surprise. "What do you mean?"

The nurse shook her head with a "bless your heart" expression on her face. "Poor boy's been asking about you since he got here."

After pulling a pillow and a blanket out of a closet and putting them on the chair near Billy's bed, the nurse quietly left the room.

"Oh, Billy," whispered Alex, leaving her bags by the door and slowly approaching the bedside. "What did they do to you?"

Billy's blond hair looked oily and stuck to his skin around his temples and forehead, and an oxygen mask had been placed over his nose and mouth. An I.V. was stuck in his arm, and the skin near the I.V. was bruised and discolored, evidencing prior attempts to get at one of his blood vessels.

Alex resisted the urge to touch him as tears welled up and began to fall. She didn't want to wake him. He needed to rest.

Glancing at the outline of Billy's legs under the blankets, she wondered what his knees looked like. He had suffered so much in just a few days, all while she was in Israel enjoying herself with Val...

Closing her eyes, Alex shook her head. She couldn't think about that right now. Somehow, thoughts of Val and the kiss they'd shared had to be pushed out of her mind. She had been giddy with the success of their meetings, enchanted with the sights and sounds of an ancient world, and in the company of a very kind, very handsome man. The kiss had been a mistake. It was as simple as that. It hadn't meant anything.

Alex knew she would have to tell Billy what had happened. Not now, though—she couldn't tell him while he was going through all of this. He had to get through surgery, begin his rehab, and start getting better. Then she would tell him. Billy would understand. He would forgive her. Maybe they would even be stronger as a result.

For now, though, they had to focus on Billy getting better. She would help him. She would take care of him. And he would be all right.

Everything would be all right.

Chapter Seventeen

For the first time in eleven years, Val did not feel like going to work when his alarm clock woke him up the next morning. He silenced the annoying ringing and rolled over in bed, closing his eyes in an attempt to go back to sleep. After all, he'd only slept for five hours, as it was well after one in the morning by the time he had gotten into bed the night before. Not to mention the jet lag.

He thought about Alex and wondered if she had gotten any sleep in her boyfriend's hospital room. Even lying in a hospital bed with a bashed-in head and two shattered knees, her boyfriend was one lucky bastard. Billy had won. The guy hadn't even known there was a competition, but he'd still won.

Val should have admitted defeat at the baggage carousel at Newark Airport. It had been readily apparent from the expression on Alex's face when she'd heard the message from the hospital which man had her heart. And it wasn't Val. She had told him to go, dismissed him in as kind a way as possible, but it was a dismissal just the same. She had chosen Billy, and there was simply no place for Val.

Val didn't belong with Alex. He belonged in his clean, quiet, lonely condo in his clean, quiet, lonely bed. Why had he thought it could be any different?

Just as Val was drifting off to sleep once more, the

ringing of his phone woke him again. At first, he thought he'd accidentally snoozed the alarm, but it took only a couple of seconds for Val to realize the phone was actually ringing. Someone was calling him.

The display on the phone was very bright against the darkness of the room, and he squinted to see who was calling. Val didn't recognize the number, but in the back of his mind, he wondered if it could be the hospital or some other number Alex might use to call him.

He cleared his throat and answered the phone.

"Hello?"

"Val? Is that you?"

Val immediately sat up in bed at the sound of his sister Gabby's voice.

"Gabby?"

"Yes, it's me. Are you at work?" His sister's tone carried a note of disgust, as though the fact that Val got up and went to work every day was offensive.

"No, not yet."

Val couldn't remember the last time Gabby had called him. He wondered what could have caused her to do so now. Then he thought of his niece Liza, and a chill ran up his spine.

"Is everything okay?" he finally asked, wishing she would just tell him what was going on.

Gabby laughed unpleasantly in response. "Of course. Everything is great. I lead a charmed life, as you know. I have a shitty job, and I have three kids to take care of with the shitty salary I get from my shitty job because I have a fucking bastard of an ex-husband who won't pay shit for child support. So yeah, everything is just fucking fantastic. Thanks for asking."

Amulet

Val heard the tremor in her voice, and he knew there was more. His sister didn't cry easily—she was anything but fragile. Something was very wrong.

"Gabby," he said softly, "tell me what's happened."

He heard his sister take a short breath on the other end of the line before it came out.

"It's Liza, Val. She's sick, very sick. My baby, my baby girl…"

At this, his sister began to sob uncontrollably, and Val felt as though his heart had just been pierced through with a knife.

"What do you mean?" he asked frantically. "I just saw her last week and she was fine—what's wrong with her? What is it?"

"It's cancer, Val. Fucking cancer! She's so young, she's just a baby. How can this happen to her?"

Val's head was spinning. Cancer? Liza?

"What kind of cancer? Has she seen a doctor?"

"Of course, she's fucking seen a doctor! How do you think we know it's cancer?"

"Well, tell me what you know then. There has to be more. People don't just get diagnosed with 'cancer.' What kind of cancer is it? Where is it? How bad is it? What's the treatment?"

"There is no treatment, Val. It's terminal, and she doesn't have long. It started with headaches when she first got back to school in August. At first, she thought it was just the stress of starting the new semester, with new classes and all that. But she went to see the doctor on campus, and she sent her to get some tests, and that's when we found out. It was in her blood, spreading everywhere. My poor baby…"

Again, his sister's voice trailed off as her words became sobs.

"Gabby, there has to be something we can do. People survive cancer all the time. She's young, she's strong. We can get her in to see a good doctor, and I'm sure there's a clinical study or—"

"She doesn't need a fucking clinical study! What she needs is a miracle!"

Val was quiet as he thought through all the options. He knew an oncologist at the Mayo Clinic. He could call him up and see if they could get Liza in to—

"Did you hear what I said, Val? She needs a *miracle*. You know where we can find a miracle, don't you?"

Gabby's voice had changed. She had regained control, and she knew exactly what she was doing.

"How do you know about Baba's amulet?" Val asked after a long pause.

The sound of her condescending laughter was grating on his nerves. "Everybody knows about Grandma's 'amulet'! After Dad wrapped his car around a tree driving home from the bar that night, I went to see him at the hospital. He was on a lot of meds, slipping in and out of consciousness. Mom was there, and Eva and Dimitar. You were stuck at school because of that blizzard and never made it to see him before he died, do you remember?"

Val remembered. It was his first semester of college. He had gotten a scholarship to a school three hours away from home in the most rural part of the state, and that freak snowstorm the first week of October had felled trees everywhere because most of them still had their leaves. All the roads were blocked, and by the time they were finally passable, his father was already dead. Val had barely made it to the funeral.

"It was only a few months after Grandma died," she continued. "You remember, don't you? And all Dad could talk about every time he woke up was that damned necklace. He said it was magic. He said if only his mother had given it to him before she died, this wouldn't have happened to him."

Gabby laughed again, as though she found it amusing that she had Val's full attention.

"Mom tore the house apart after Dad died, looking for that fucking thing. She said it had to be there somewhere, in Grandma's room or maybe hidden somewhere else in the house, but she couldn't find it. Then we wondered if maybe Grandma had given it to somebody before she died. If she hadn't given it to Dad, then maybe one of her other kids. Uncle Jeko, or Aunt Sophie, maybe. But as the years passed, it became very clear who had all the 'luck' in our family. She gave it to you, didn't she? You got it, you little shit. She always felt sorry for you because you were such a little pussy, and so she gave it to you. And you used it to get everything your little heart desired."

She was quiet now, no longer rueful, but just sad.

"Mom said she asked Dad how the amulet worked, just before he died, and he told her what his grandmother had told him about it when he was a kid, about how his mother, our grandmother, was pregnant with him when she got sick, about how her mother gave her the amulet and how she wished for her health and the health of the baby. She got better and had Dad. I guess it makes sense—she gave you the amulet, then bit the dust, and so did Dad. That's how it works, right?

You get one wish, but when you give the amulet away, the wish goes away too. Grandma didn't think about Dad dying when she gave that thing to you, did she? She didn't realize that he was part of the same wish, that she was killing him to help you."

"You don't actually believe that, do you?" Val tried hard not to let his own guilt seep into his words. He had stayed awake many nights after his father's accident, wondering if he was to blame for his father's death. His father had driven drunk so many times before—why had his luck run out? How could it have been a coincidence?

"Of course I believe it, just the same as you do. But it doesn't matter, Val. What matters is that you have something that can help Liza. You can make her better. All you have to do is give me the amulet and—"

"Wait a second," Val interrupted her. "Why should I give you the amulet? You're not the one who's sick. She is."

"I know, Val," she replied, as though she were explaining something to a four-year-old, "but Liza doesn't believe. I do. I will wish for her health. I'm her mother. No matter what you may think of me, you must know I love her more than anything. I'll make the wish for her. It's the only way to be sure the wish isn't wasted."

Val was silent. He knew that giving the amulet to his sister, to anyone, would mean the end of everything he had accomplished. His company would fold. His money would evaporate. His popularity would disappear. But none of that mattered to him when Liza's life hung in the balance.

Mistaking his silence for reluctance, Gabby chimed

in again: "You've had your good luck, Val. Isn't it about time someone else had a turn?"

Val was annoyed that she would think he could put his own comfort and well-being above the life of his niece, but he told himself that she simply didn't have the capacity to understand him. She never did.

"I will give it up for her, Gabby. I'll come today and give it to you."

He could hear his sister breathe a sigh of relief on the other end of the line. "Oh, thank God. Thank you, Val. Thank you."

"I'll be at your house around ten. Will you be there?"

"Yes, Val, I'll be here. I'll see you then."

It took Val only a few minutes to throw on some clothes and prepare for the three-hour drive to his sister's house. Glancing at his watch, he decided it was too early to call Judy to let her know he was back from Israel but wouldn't be coming to the office. He would just have to call her from the car.

He grabbed a granola bar from the cupboard and a bottle of water from the fridge, then went over to the suitcase and laptop bag that still stood by the front door, exactly where he had deposited them the night before. Reaching into the side pocket of the laptop bag, Val fished around the bottom until he found the sock that held the black velvet bag with the amulet in it. He pulled the velvet bag out of the sock, then opened it and took out the amulet. Satisfied, he tucked everything back into place and slung the laptop bag over his shoulder. Then he stepped out of the condo, locking the door behind him.

It was New Year's Eve, and it had been exactly one

week since Liza's visit on Christmas Eve. She had looked so healthy to him, so vibrant. She was bubbly and talkative. There had been no mention of headaches, and she didn't seem to be in any pain. How could Liza be as sick as her mother said she was?

As Val pulled out of the parking garage, he went over the dinnertime conversation with Liza from that night, trying to recall exactly how his niece's face had looked as they had talked about school and boyfriends, and even Val's love life. Val would never have guessed in a million years that there was something not right with her. Never.

He wished he had someone to talk to about this. No, not just "someone." Val wanted to pick up the phone and call Alex. He wanted to tell her what was happening. He wanted her sympathy, her reassuring smile. He wanted to hear her say that everything would be all right. But he knew he couldn't call her. Even if Val hadn't kissed her and put their relationship in the most awkward place possible, Alex had her own stuff to deal with right now and didn't need Val to pile on.

As Val approached a red light and slowed to a stop, he glanced over at the laptop bag he'd set on the seat next to him. Everything would be all right, he reminded himself. He had the amulet, and the amulet could make Liza better. She was going to be okay.

The light turned green, and Val moved into the right lane, taking the ramp onto the highway, going north. He accelerated to match the flow of traffic, which seemed heavy for the morning before a holiday.

Yes, everything was going to work out. He would give the amulet to his sister, and she would make a wish for Liza's health. Then Liza would get better. Not only that, she would never again have any health problems. She would remain healthy for the rest of her life.

It was only then that the flaw in their plan occurred to him. The power of the amulet, the wish that it granted, lasted only as long as the person who made the wish held on to it. As soon as the amulet changed hands, as soon as there was another owner, the previous wish went away. It was gone. It had happened to his grandmother and her mother, and it would soon happen to him.

The same would also happen to Liza someday. Sure, she would be fine as long as his sister had the amulet, but once his sister died, the amulet would change hands, and that wish for Liza's health would evaporate. Liza would get sick again. She would die.

Who knew how many years Val's sister had left in her life? Gabby was almost forty, which was young by most standards, but she was still older than Liza. And she didn't live an easy life. She smoked, she drank, she took risks. Gabby lived hard, and once that hard living caught up with her, Liza's fate would be sealed. The amulet was unforgiving in its adherence to the rules.

There was only one way to ensure that Liza would be healthy for the rest of her life. Liza had to make the wish. Val had to give the amulet to her, not his sister.

His sister had been adamant that Liza could not make the wish because Liza didn't believe, but Val could talk to her, tell her the stories his grandmother had told him. He could make her believe. Besides, when people were sick, when they knew they were dying, they would believe anything that promised them a second chance. They would turn to God after a lifetime of not praying; they would put their faith in an experimental drug; they would make a wish on an ugly old necklace.

Without another thought, Val took the next exit, then turned to cross over the highway and took the ramp to get back on, going in the opposite direction.

He reached into the side pocket of the laptop bag and grabbed his cell phone.

"Call Liza," he said into the phone.

The phone rang a couple of times before Liza picked up.

"Hi, Uncle Val. What's up?"

The sound of Liza's voice was both reassuring and heartbreaking. Images of his niece as a baby, a curious toddler, a precocious pre-teen, and a sassy teenager flashed before Val's eyes, all in the span of five seconds. How could she be taken away from them now, when her life was just beginning?

"Hi, Liza," he said, hearing the trembling in his own voice.

"Uncle Val, you don't sound good. What's going on?"

He couldn't bring himself to say anything about her illness.

"Nothing, Liza. Everything is fine. I think you said something last week about spending New Year's on campus with some friends. Are you there, at school right now?"

"Yeah, I got back last night. Jen is having a party tonight. I'm helping her set up."

"Would it be all right if I come see you today? I can't stay long. I…I…"

He looked at the laptop bag and remembered that, by some stroke of luck, he had put the cross he had bought in Jerusalem for Liza in one of its zippered compartments when he had packed for the flight home.

"I wanted to drop off something I bought for you while I was in Israel. Can you see me for half an hour? I should be there around eleven."

"Oh. Yeah, sure, Uncle Val. Just give me a call when you're getting close and I'll go back to my apartment. Do you even know my address?"

"No—that's one of the reasons I thought I'd call first."

Liza laughed, as though she didn't have a care in the world. "I'll text it to you. Maybe we can have lunch together while you're here. I'm glad you're coming. It's been like, what, one whole week since I last saw my favorite uncle?" She laughed again, a bright, cheerful laugh, and Val couldn't imagine what the world would be like without that sound.

"Great," he finally managed to say. "I'll see you soon. Bye, Liza."

"Bye, Uncle Val."

He put the phone in the cup holder beside him, and his foot pressed harder on the gas pedal.

Chapter Eighteen

At around eight-thirty, Val called Judy and explained that he wouldn't be at work because he had some family business to attend to. It was his practice to dismiss his employees at noon on New Year's Eve, so he asked Judy to make the announcement this year in his place.

"Is everything okay?" Judy asked for the third time at the end of the call.

"Yes," Val replied confidently. "Everything is going to be fine."

Val checked the voice messages on his work phone later in the morning to find that Alex had called. She said they had operated on Billy's knee that morning and everything had gone well, but that Billy had asked her to stay with him and keep him company. She apologized profusely for not going to work and assured Val that she would continue reviewing the documents she had with her, that she was still on track to finish and turn everything over to the other side by the following Monday, when the documents were due.

Val dialed her cell phone number when he had finished listening to her message, but Alex didn't answer, so he left a short message telling her it was completely fine for her not to be at work, that his employees were all going home at lunchtime anyway for New Year's Eve, and that he hoped everything continued to go well for Billy. He wanted to say more, to tell her he was on his way to visit Liza, and why. He wanted to confess that he couldn't wait to see her on Friday when everyone was back at work, but he was no fool. Pushing down those feelings, Val simply wished Alex a Happy New Year and hung up, recognizing fully how much he missed her already.

At ten-fifteen, Val's phone rang, and his pulse quickened at the thought it might be Alex. A glance at the phone confirmed it was his sister, and he let the call roll over to voicemail. Liza's college was about an hour farther than his sister's house, in the opposite direction. It was only a few minutes past the time he should have arrived at his sister's, but Gabby was already wondering why he hadn't shown up yet, no doubt.

He resolved to call her after he had talked to Liza to explain the change in plan, but until then he had no desire to defend his decision. Gabby would just have to wait.

When his sister called again five minutes later, he shut off his ringer.

About an hour later, Val was knocking on the door to Liza's apartment. There was a knot in his stomach the size of a grapefruit, and his mouth was dry, despite the bottle of water he had drank in almost one gulp right after he had parked the car.

Liza opened the door, and he exhaled. After the call he had received from Gabby, Val thought he would be looking at a pale, sallow, fragile-looking girl with hollow cheeks and a tired expression. That was not the girl who answered the door. The girl who answered was his Liza—bright, vibrant, confident Liza—and Val chided himself for having expected anything less.

"Hi, Uncle Val!" she greeted cheerfully, throwing her arms around him just as she had done a week ago.

"Hi, Liza." He hugged her back a little harder and a little longer than usual.

"Uncle Val," —she laughed— "something is definitely up with you. Come in and you can unload your problems on me."

"You still think you can solve the world's problems just because you took one semester of psychology?" Val was trying to tease her, but his heart wasn't in it, and he knew she could hear it in his voice.

He followed Liza into the small apartment she shared with one of her friends. The front door opened into a twelve-by-twelve living space, where the two girls had crammed a sofa and an armchair in front of a television that must have been at least ten years old. The walls were a dingy white, the carpet a neutral beige.

Unashamed of her humble surroundings, Liza glided over to the couch and almost jumped into a sitting position at one end, patting the couch cushion next to her in a signal to Val to take a seat.

Val walked over and slowly sat down beside her. Then he just stared, taking in her dark brown curls and big, beautiful eyes. Her cheeks were a healthy pink, and the whites of her eyes were whiter than his. There wasn't a hint of sickness or frailty in the girl who sat beside him, but instead of finding comfort in that, it made him feel a stronger sense of anger at the unfairness of life.

"Uncle Val, you're starting to creep me out."

He shook his head to come back to the present and then laughed nervously. "Sorry, Liza. There's a lot of stuff going on. I guess I'm just distracted."

Liza raised her eyebrows into two gracefully doubting arches, then sighed. "All right. So, you said you had something for me? Maybe we can start with that?"

"Yes, yes I do," replied Val, happy to have something to do to avoid the conversation he knew he had to start, eventually.

He unzipped the side pocket of his laptop bag and, pushing aside the sock with the amulet, lifted out a brown paper bag and handed it to Liza.

"Sorry, I didn't have a chance to wrap it."

Liza took the package from him, visibly surprised that he actually did have something to give her.

"This is so sweet of you, Uncle Val! You didn't have to get me anything—"

As she took the rather large crucifix out of the bag, she grinned. "Wow. I think this is the biggest cross I have ever seen. Umm, thank you?"

"You're welcome," replied Val, enjoying her reaction to the very religious gift. "I thought it might be nice to have a symbol of your virtue and chastity somewhere in your apartment." He turned to look at the wall directly opposite the front door. "Like maybe right there."

"Yes." Her smile widened. "Nothing says 'come in and make yourself at home' better than a cross with a very large and life-like Jesus nailed to it. I think there's actually drops of blood coming out of the wounds in his hands and feet."

"Perfect," replied Val, smiling comfortably now.

Liza hugged him, and he felt an overwhelming sense of gratitude for being part of her life. "Seriously,

Uncle Val, I do like it. Thank you for thinking of me. And I will put it right on that wall back there, just so that I think of you every time I come home after a long day of classes."

As she pulled away from him, he stroked her hair and her cheek, just as he used to do when she was a child, and his eyes filled with tears.

"Uncle Val, seriously, what the hell is going on? What's wrong with you? You're acting as if you're never going to see me again. What is it?"

"Oh, Liza," he began, hesitating for a second. He took in a slow breath, then let it out. "I know. I know about what's going on, with you. And I'm so, so sorry."

Val took her in his arms again, wishing he could take the disease away from her and into himself, hoping that the amulet would work, even if it was just this one last time.

Liza pushed him away and almost shouted in response, "What? What are you talking about? Tell me!"

"You!" exclaimed Val. "Your sickness, your... cancer." He hated saying that word, as though saying it fed it, gave it life. "Your mother called me and told me. Don't be upset with her. I'm glad she did. Because I can help you, Liza. Everything's going to be all right, but you have to trust me. You have to believe what I'm going to tell you."

At this, Liza stood up and walked to the small window near the front door. Then she turned around to look back at Val, her mouth open, as though she were trying to find the right words to express exactly what she was thinking.

In the end, Liza simply stood there, shaking her

head, her mouth still open, ready to speak.

"I can't believe she would sink that low."

"Liza, it's not your mother's fault. She loves you, she's just trying to—"

"My mother loves nobody but herself, Uncle Val. Don't you understand? Don't you see what she's doing? I'm not sick, Uncle Val. There's absolutely nothing wrong with me. I'm fine. She's been dying to get that necklace from you for as long as I can remember, and she finally figured it out. She finally found a way to take it from you."

Val stared at her in disbelief. "You know about the amulet?"

"Of course I know about the amulet, Uncle Val. Everyone knows about the amulet. That's all she ever talks about when she gets drunk with Grandma and Aunt Eva and Uncle Dimitar. 'Why did Baba have to give the amulet to Uncle Val? Why him, why not us? When will it be our turn?' Every Christmas, every Easter, every birthday. It's shameful, Uncle Val, which is why I never mentioned it to you. They're horrible, horrible people, the whole lot of them."

Val couldn't believe what he was hearing. Was that the real reason they never asked him to family gatherings? So that they could sit around and talk about how lucky Val was to have the amulet? Had his sister been trying to devise a plan to get the amulet from him for all those years? Could he have been that stupid? That gullible?

As Val reviewed the facts in his head, it began to make sense. Gabby had been adamant that he give the amulet to her, not to Liza. She had been sparing on the details of the disease, saying only that Liza had had headaches and that the doctors had said it was cancer. She hadn't even told him where the cancer was. She had just said it was everywhere. Gabby had lied about all of it, right down to the pretend sobbing and the feigned relief she had expressed when he had agreed to hand over the amulet. No, he told himself. She had been genuinely relieved when he had agreed—relieved that she would be getting the amulet soon.

"I'm an idiot," was all Val could say. "I fell for her whole act. She sobbed on the phone, Liza. She actually sobbed."

"I'm sure she's been practicing," replied Liza sarcastically.

"But, Liza," —Val squeezed her shoulder, overcome with emotion— "I'm so glad you're okay. It's been killing me to think that someone so good, so sweet, whose life is full of such promise, could be—"

"All right, Uncle Val, don't start up again. I'm fine, okay? Everything is fine. My mom was just being herself. She's always blamed her problems on everyone around her, never on herself. Like I said, she's been talking about how lucky you were that your grandma gave you that necklace for as long as I can remember. And it's always the worst at Christmas. She gets completely drunk and starts lamenting all the things she could have done with that thing. I hate it, it's so pathetic."

Val looked at Liza and heard his sister's words again: "You've had your good luck, Val. Isn't it about time someone else had a turn?"

Maybe his sister was right. Maybe it was time for someone else to have a turn. Maybe it could be Liza's turn. If anyone deserved to have a wish granted, it was his niece. Val had already been prepared to turn over the amulet to Liza to ensure she would be healthy and have a good, long life ahead of her. He had been willing to give up all his success for Liza. For Val, nothing had changed. How much better would it be to give Liza the amulet now, knowing she could use it for whatever she wanted, her whole life ahead of her regardless of what she chose to wish for?

"Liza," he said, reaching into his laptop bag and pulling out the balled-up socks, "I want you to have this."

"You want me to have your socks, Uncle Val?" she replied with a questioning look.

"No," he answered, unfolding the socks and pulling out the black velvet bag. He uncinched the bag and reached in, taking out the amulet and laying it on the palm of his other hand. "I want you to have the amulet. The amulet that your mother has wanted all this time. The amulet that has given me so much success and comfort in my life, things I would never have been able to achieve on my own."

"I don't think you're giving yourself enough credit, Uncle Val. Nothing has been handed to you. You've worked hard for everything you've gotten. You've deserved all of it."

Val sighed. "The amulet is real. Its power is real. I want you to have it. Please, you deserve it." He held the amulet out to her, and she took it. She held it up by the chain to examine it, then looked at Val and smiled.

"I appreciate your offer, I really do. I've heard the stories, about you, about your grandma, about her mother. Maybe it's true that the amulet grants everyone a wish, maybe it's not. I honestly don't know. What I do know is that I don't want it. I don't want to live my life thinking that the good stuff I've gotten was because of an old necklace I have hidden away in a rolled-up pair of socks."

She put the amulet back in Val's still outstretched hand, and he closed his fingers around it reflexively.

Val didn't say anything in response, because Liza was right. He had always assumed that every good thing in his life had happened because of the amulet. Every test he'd aced in college, every contract he'd won, every decision that went his way—he always chalked it up to good luck, the luck the amulet gave him. But even sitting there, listening to Liza describe him and what he had accomplished, Val still couldn't deny the fact that the amulet had come through for him. It had power, he was sure of it because he had felt it. He knew it was real.

"Are you sure, Liza? I'm not saying you'd have to rely on it. It could just be your backup, your escape clause. Please, Liza, take it. Everyone can use a little good luck."

Liza smiled again, and for some reason that smile made Val think of his grandmother. "Uncle Val, you can keep the amulet. You'll find someone else you can give it to. I just don't need it. I'm going to make my own luck."

Val finally broke into a smile of his own and put the amulet back into its bag, then folded the bag back into the socks. "If anyone can make their own luck, Liza, it's you."

Chapter Nineteen

Val had a lot to think about on the drive home. Liza had explicitly instructed him not to call her mother or confront her about the lie. Liza's exact words were "Leave her to me." And Val had no doubt that Liza could handle her. She had handled her mother like no one else could for the past twenty years.

With Liza safe and sound and his sister in good hands, Val's thoughts turned inward. He thought about his life and everything he had done, all the things he had accomplished. To the outside observer, he was living the dream. His was a rags-to-riches story. Val had started from nothing, spent all he had to get an education, connected with the right people, and built a booming business. He lived in the lap of luxury, enjoyed his work, was loved by his employees, and was handsome and charming to boot. Every eligible woman he met (and some of the ineligible ones) wanted to date him, and practically every man who had heard or read about him wanted to be him. Val was, as his sister had put it, a very lucky man.

But even with the amulet still firmly in his possession, Val did not feel lucky. He was grateful for his wealth and position, yes, but something was lacking. He had always felt it, though up until the last few days, he could never pinpoint exactly what it was.

Now he knew.

Val thought of Alex and remembered how it felt to be with her. Her smile had made him whole. Her company had made him feel special, more worthy somehow. She had confided in him, teased him, laughed with him, and he had never felt more alive in his life. He had never felt more loved.

But, he reminded himself, she was not "in love" with him. Although she may have cared for him as a fellow human being, her heart belonged to her boyfriend. And that made her boyfriend the luckiest man alive.

Val sighed, taking a hand off the steering wheel to rub the back of his neck, where a headache was starting to form. Alex deserved to be happy. She deserved to have everything her heart desired. She deserved a good job with excellent pay doing the things she had been trained to do, the things she was born to do. And she deserved to have the man of her choice, completely and unequivocally, which in her eyes meant she deserved to have him as her husband. If the man Alex had chosen was Billy, then so be it.

By the end of the following week, they would have an answer from FiberTech. Whatever their decision, Alex's work at Span Global would be complete, and her time there would be over. She would go back to her staffing firm for a new assignment. The thought of Alex leaving was terrifying—Val couldn't imagine not being able to stop by her office on his way to the break room, not surprising her in the file room while she attempted to move heavy boxes off the shelves. He'd grown used to eating meals with her, stealing glances, and sharing inside jokes.

And now he couldn't imagine his world without

her.

Yet that was exactly where Val's world was headed, and there was nothing he could do about it. He didn't have the legal work to support a full-time attorney, or else he would have hired her in a second. He could have hired her anyway and paid her an excellent salary, regardless of the amount of work, but he knew she would not feel fulfilled sitting around twiddling her thumbs to pass the time.

As Val processed the situation, a solution began to take shape in his mind. It was true, *he* couldn't hire Alex at Span Global, but that didn't mean he couldn't find another job for her, one that would satisfy her intellect and make use of her legal and professional skills. Alex's problem wasn't that she had any lack of qualifications, education, or presence. It was just that nobody knew how good she was. The fact that she hadn't gotten a job straight out of law school put a huge red flag on any application she sent out. Nobody wanted to take a chance on her, regardless of her stellar résumé.

All she needed was an advocate, someone who would vouch for her.

Val grabbed his cell phone from the cup holder, eyes still focused on the road. "Call Sarah Mahoney."

He put the phone on speaker and set it back down, listening to it ring on the other end of the line once, then twice.

"Hello, this is Sarah Mahoney," came the answer just before the third ring.

"Sarah, hey, this is Val Nikolov. How are you?"

"Val, hi. I'm good, how are you? Aren't you supposed to be in Israel?"

Sarah Mahoney worked for Farber and McCraw, one of the larger corporate law firms in the city. Val had met Sarah at a seminar during the first year of Span Global's operations when she was still a young associate rising up the ranks at her firm. Now she was a partner with associates of her own.

"I was in Israel," Val answered her question, "but I just got back last night."

"How did it go?"

Val could hear Sarah typing in the background, but he had grown used to the fact that she was very good at multitasking. Besides that, Sarah rarely charged him for the time they spent on the phone.

"As well as it could. Hey, listen, I have a favor to ask of you, if you can swing it."

At that, she stopped typing. "What do you need?"

"Well, it's not really something for me. I've had a contract attorney working for me for the past few weeks. She's done a phenomenal job and has an excellent work ethic. And she has an impressive résumé."

"Why is she doing contract work?" countered Sarah.

"She had a unique set of circumstances coming out of law school, and her timing was off for getting a full-time position as an attorney."

"I see," Val's lawyer replied. He knew what Sarah was thinking.

"Look, I'm not asking you to hire her. I'm just asking you to bring her in and talk to her. Look at her résumé. Ask her questions. Listen to her answers. She will impress you, I'm sure of it."

Sarah sighed. "We're not hiring right now, and

besides that, I've got to be honest with you Val. Hiring contract attorneys as full-time associates hasn't really worked out well for us in the past."

"Sarah," Val replied, trying not to plead, "I'm just asking you to consider her. It will take only half an hour of your time. You can even bill me for it."

"I'm not going to bill you for interviewing a candidate, Val." Sarah was quiet for a few seconds before he heard her exhale again. "Oh, all right, shoot me her résumé, and I'll give her a call for a phone interview. If I like her, we'll bring her in to meet some of the other attorneys here."

"Thank you, Sarah, really. Thank you. You've always been good to me. I'll see if I can't find more clients to throw your way."

Sarah chuckled as she started typing again. "Thanks, Val. I'll be looking out for your email, okay?"

"I'll send it to you tonight."

Val was about to say goodbye when he thought of something else.

"Sarah, one more thing. Don't tell her why you're talking to her. I mean, don't tell her that I recommended her for a position with you. Just say you were going through the résumés you had on file, or something like that."

"Val, I'm not going to lie."

Val couldn't help smiling to himself. "I'm sure you can find a way to avoid telling the truth without lying. You are a lawyer, after all."

Chapter Twenty

Alex woke up on Thursday morning with a crick in her neck and something jabbing her left thigh. Shifting her body to a semi-reclined position, she pushed the blanket off to the side of the couch she had slept on for the past two nights.

"Good morning, Sleepyhead."

She looked up to find Billy sitting up in the hospital bed with a plate of bacon, toast, and overcooked scrambled eggs in front of him. It was the first time she'd seen him without the oxygen mask covering his face, the first time he'd spoken to her since she'd left for Israel almost a week before.

"Billy!"

She got up off the couch and went to stand by his bed. "Billy, you're sitting up. You're eating." Her throat was thick with emotion, and she reached over to smooth away the hair that had fallen across his forehead. "How are you feeling?"

"Like I got hit by a truck. But I'll live. And the doctor came by a little earlier and said my knees look as well as can be expected. So, that's good news."

"I slept through the doctor's visit?" Alex couldn't believe she had missed the opportunity to talk with his doctor. She had so many questions about Billy's recovery and the next steps.

"Don't worry. She'll be back around this afternoon.

Oh, hey, Happy New Year."

Alex had almost forgotten—it was New Year's Day.

"Happy New Year, Billy."

She leaned down to kiss him on the forehead.

"Do you want something to eat?" Billy motioned to the toast on the side of his plate.

"Not right now. You eat it. You need your strength if you're going to get better."

Alex glanced at her watch. It was after nine already. She still couldn't believe she'd slept so late.

"Your phone was buzzing a little while ago," said Billy, picking up a piece of bacon. "I don't know who would be emailing you on New Year's Day. Even the partners I work with don't send emails on New Year's."

Curious, Alex found her phone on the little table near the couch and scrolled through her emails.

"Do you know someone named Sarah Mahoney at Farber and McCraw?"

Billy thought for a moment before shaking his head. "I've heard of the firm, but not the attorney. It's a boutique firm with a good reputation for doing corporate law, transactional-type stuff. Why? Is that who sent the email?"

Alex sat down on the couch and read the email for a second time before answering.

"She wants to do a phone interview. With me."

Billy dropped his bacon and clapped his hands together. "That's great, Lex! You didn't tell me you sent your résumé out again."

"I didn't."

In fact, Alex couldn't remember ever reaching out to this firm, even when she had first moved to the area and was sending around her résumé to any law firm with an email address.

"Well, you know how these things work. Someone else you'd sent your résumé to probably forwarded it to them. In any case, it doesn't matter. You got a phone interview! So, when is it?"

"Today at four in the afternoon." She was still dumbfounded.

"Wow, they must mean business if they're interviewing you on New Year's. Hey, Lex?"

She looked up from the phone to find Billy staring at her with a peculiar expression.

"Yeah?"

"You're not nervous, are you?"

She wasn't nervous. She was petrified.

"A little," she fibbed.

"Come here."

He pushed his food tray off to the side and patted the bed. Alex sat down, careful not to touch him. She knew he was sore all over.

Billy reached for her hand. "You've got nothing to worry about, Lex. You're really smart, and you're good at talking to people. Just ask her a bunch of questions about herself, her career, how she got to where she is, that kind of thing. People love to talk about themselves. You'll do great."

Smiling, she put her other hand on top of his and patted it twice before leaning over to kiss his cheek. "Thanks, Billy. I know it'll be fine."

As her boyfriend started telling stories about his experience interviewing law school students for positions with his firm, Alex's mind wandered. She hadn't asked Val what his plans were for New Year's.

He'd told her that everyone got to leave work at lunchtime on New Year's Eve, but she had no idea what Val's plans were. Did he have fancy parties to go to? Or did he opt for a quiet evening at home? And what about today? He liked sports—would he spend the day watching football? Or would he be catching up on all the work he had missed while they were in Israel?

Suddenly, Alex wanted to know. She wanted to hear all about Val's day yesterday and everything he was going to do today. She wanted to know what Val was doing right now—where he was, who he was with, what he was thinking. And she wanted to tell him about the interview, get his advice, listen to his encouragement.

Remembering where she was, Alex looked over at Billy, who was still giving her interviewing tips. He hadn't noticed her daydreaming. Or maybe he had attributed her strange behavior to nerves.

When he paused between stories, she asked, "Are your parents coming today?"

Billy nodded. "Should be here around eleven. Why?"

"I was just thinking maybe I should head home after lunch. Get cleaned up, do some laundry, maybe take a nap before the call with this lawyer at four. I can come back to see you for dinner, but then I should probably try to get a good night's sleep tonight. I have to go to work tomorrow."

She hoped he wouldn't ask her to spend the night on the couch here with him. She needed some time alone, to think.

"Sure, Lex. That's a good idea. The way the doctor was talking this morning, I'll probably be released by tomorrow night, anyway. It won't be too much longer now. This will be over soon."

Alex nodded.

She had a lot of thinking to do.

****

Val got up on Friday morning, ready to go to work. What he felt as he put on his clothes and arranged his hair with his fingers bordered on excitement. He left his condo a few minutes ahead of schedule.

At the office, Val worked with the door open most of the morning, even as he made a few phone calls, hoping it would somehow encourage a visit from a certain young contract attorney.

It was a little after ten in the morning when the subject of his thoughts appeared in his doorway, wearing a very flattering pink silk blouse and a dark gray pin-striped skirt that stopped just above her lovely knees.

"Hi, Alex," he said, smiling.

"Hi, Val," she replied, her smile a little more guarded than the one he was used to seeing. "Do you have a couple of minutes to talk?"

"Of course."

Alex made no move to enter, so Val had to gesture for her to come in. He wondered if Sarah Mahoney had already contacted her, despite the holiday yesterday. He would have been impressed if that were the case.

Alex took two steps into the office. "Do you mind if I shut the door?"

"Not at all, please do." One of Val's favorite fantasies involved a beautiful woman coming into his office, shutting the door quietly, and proceeding to seduce him. More recently, the woman in his fantasies bore a striking resemblance to Alex Weaver.

"How's Billy doing?" Val forced himself to say her boyfriend's name, taking great pains not to look or sound annoyed.

"Oh," Alex replied, sounding a little surprised, "he's doing great, better than expected, actually. If nothing changes during the day today, I should be able to take Billy home tonight. He'll have to go to physical therapy a few times a week starting on Monday, and there are exercises he has to do at home, but things should be almost back to normal in a few weeks. He's not supposed to go to work next week, but his firm has been very understanding and supportive about the whole thing, and he'll be able to work from home some, so we're lucky we don't have to deal with those types of issues."

She paused, lowering her eyes for a moment before capturing his gaze once more. "You've been great, too, letting me take off on Wednesday. I really appreciate that I could be with Billy before and after his surgery."

"Please," Val replied, starting to grow irritated at how long he had to sit there and hear her talk about Billy and how she was going to take good care of him, and how much she loved him. "Please," he began again, with more control this time, "don't even mention it. I'm glad things are going well."

He said no more, wanting to give Alex a chance to tell him whatever it was she had come to say, as she thankfully hadn't come to talk about Billy. When she remained standing an unreasonable distance from where Val sat at his desk, clearly avoiding direct eye contact, Val couldn't help prompting her. "Please, Alex, sit down. What's on your mind?"

She took a few more steps forward to one of the two black leather chairs in front of his desk and sat down without a word.

Then she took a breath and finally looked at him. "A strange thing happened yesterday morning. I got an email from a law firm in town, Farber and McCraw. Do you know them?"

Val cleared his throat. "I've heard of them. On the small side, specializing in corporate law if I'm not mistaken. I think they have a bigger office on the West Coast, and maybe another office somewhere in the northeast, too."

"Well," Alex continued, her eyes lighting up, "the email asked if I would have a phone interview with a lawyer named Sarah Mahoney at four o'clock in the afternoon, so I replied and said yes. When I talked to her, Ms. Mahoney said she had seen my résumé and wanted to discuss a possible position as an associate with her firm. We spoke for almost half an hour on the phone."

Alex was grinning now, and Val knew the interview had gone well. Alex had won Sarah over, just as he knew she would.

"That's great news, Alex." He wanted to hug her, to kiss her smiling mouth. "What happened at the end of the call? What did she say?"

"It's so crazy, Val—she wants me to come in on Monday morning for a real interview. She says there may be a spot for me in their transactional group, and she wants me to meet some other folks on that team. I can't imagine anything will come of it, but it's still so nice to just be asked to come in for an interview—"

"Why would you say that?" Val interrupted. "Of

course something will come of it. Law firms don't waste their time interviewing candidates they don't like. Even if they don't have a position for you, maybe they know someone else who does. That's how these things happen."

Val thought there was something more Alex wanted to say, but after waiting a moment he felt compelled to fill the silence again.

"So what time is the interview on Monday?"

"Nine-thirty," she replied. "I'm supposed to meet with five sets of interviewers, and then a couple of their newer associates will take me to lunch."

Val watched as Alex took in a quiet breath, then let it out in a sigh. "It's sad," she said softly, "here I am, a thirty-two-year-old woman, not a kid fresh out of college, and I'm nervous just thinking about going in and talking to these people to try and convince them to give me a job. I'm going to be a mess on Monday morning."

"No, you're not," Val replied, moved by her vulnerability. How she felt was such a stark contrast to how she carried herself. He had seen Alex engage people from all walks of life with ease and grace over the past week, from old Israeli cab drivers to politically incorrect executives. How could she possibly be doubting herself now?

He stood up and walked around the desk to sit in the chair next to hers. "Don't think of it as trying to convince them to give you a job," he said, looking her in the eyes. "Just think of it as allowing them to find out for themselves how valuable you could be to their firm. I know you, and I know you'll be fine."

She smiled a perfect smile for him. "Thank you,

Val. I think that's just what I needed to hear."

Val wanted to pat her arm or touch her face. He would have been happy just shaking her hand. But she stood up and quickly retreated a few steps toward the door.

"Alex?" said Val, standing up.

She turned to look at him. "Yes?"

"Take your time getting ready on Monday morning, and don't come here before your interview. Just promise you'll come by and let me know how it went, after you get back from lunch with them."

She smiled again. "Thanks. And I promise, I'll let you know how it goes."

Driving home from work that night, Val was determined not to spend the weekend alone. Very briefly, he considered giving one of his ex-girlfriends a call, but going through the list of women in his head made him remember why he broke up with each of them, and he quickly decided there were other ways to avoid loneliness.

By the time he pulled into the parking garage of his condo, Val had settled on inviting a few guys over on Sunday to watch football. There were at least two good games he wouldn't mind watching, and with football playing in the background, he wouldn't need to engage in too much conversation. People would just be there, filling the space around him with motion and sound. And, really, that was all Val needed.

Later that evening, Val made calls to four guys he knew, and each of them accepted without hesitation. Val was certain at least a couple of them already had plans, but an invitation to the luxury condo of one of the most successful men in the city took priority over all other engagements, at least in their minds.

Val went grocery shopping on Saturday morning, against his housekeeper's wishes, and bought some food and supplies he thought he might need for the next day. Then he spent the earlier part of the evening rearranging the furniture in the oversized living room at least twice to get the right configuration for the event.

Val's housekeeper arrived to start preparing hors d'oeuvres for the party around nine-thirty on Sunday morning, and by noon all the guests had arrived and were sampling the wonderful cheese and vegetable dips Val's housekeeper had made.

Everyone seemed to be having a good time, and the food his housekeeper kept bringing out was amazing. Val was pleased he had succeeded in filling the space around him, but it had brought him no peace. He still felt lacking, restless, and empty. His "friends," if that's what he could call them, knew nothing about Val, really. Oh, they knew where he worked, his high position, his annual income, and who he was or wasn't dating at any given time, but they didn't know who he was. And it wasn't that Val wanted to keep who he was a mystery or hide his soul from anyone. It was just that they'd never cared to ask.

Val stood in the doorway to the kitchen, looking into the living room at the four men gathered around the large coffee table laden with food in front of the even larger wall-mounted, curved screen television. His friends were talking over each other—this one about how his wife and kids were coming back in a few days from spending a month in France over the holiday break; that one about the car he just bought. Another one was talking about a charity auction he would be organizing over Valentine's Day weekend, and the one pretending to be listening chimed in with a story about how he met his supermodel girlfriend at a charity auction.

In the end, it was all just noise, and Val realized he was just as lonely in the noise as he was in the silence of his own solitude. He felt it so acutely now, this loneliness he had lived with all his life, and he knew exactly why: Alex.

She had cut through his loneliness from the moment he first set eyes on her. She knew him, saw him, and cared for him.

Yes, Alex cared for him, she felt something for him. That had to be true, regardless of her boyfriend, regardless of what she told him after their kiss.

That kiss—Val remembered every detail. The softness of her lips, the warmth of her mouth, the feel of her body in his hands. She wouldn't have felt that way in his arms if there was nothing in her heart for him, would she?

At work the following day, he spent all morning glancing at the clock. He had spent a restless night, tossing and turning, willing the sun to rise so that he could leave for work—so that he could see Alex.

She had said she would tell him how her interview had gone, and she kept her word. After an excruciatingly long morning, just as Val was checking the time again at two o'clock, Alex appeared in his doorway.

Almost sensing her presence, Val looked up to see her radiant face, her hand raised in a fist, about to knock on the open door. And he knew just by looking at her how the interview had gone. Standing up, he motioned her in.

"I gather by the look on your face that the interview went well?" Alex stepped into his office and closed the door, her smile widening.

"They called me as I was driving back over here to offer me the job—Val, they liked me!"

"Of course they liked you," he replied softly, his words full of meaning. "How could they not?"

"Oh, Val," she said, coming toward him. Had Val not been standing behind a huge oak desk, he would certainly not have been able to resist taking her in his arms. He sat back down in his chair, gripping the armrests as a precautionary measure.

Alex stopped between the two leather chairs, then sat down rather abruptly in one. Leaning forward in her seat, she continued, "I really don't know how this happened, Val. Last week I couldn't get a firm to even respond to my application, and today I get an on-the-spot offer—from a firm I hadn't even contacted. It's just so hard to believe."

"So, does that mean you've accepted?"

"No," she replied quickly. "I wanted to talk to you first."

"Oh? Why? Is there something wrong with the offer? What's the starting salary?"

"No, no," she replied, "it has nothing to do with that. I just, well, I don't want to leave you hanging. You hired me to do a job, and I don't want to leave before it's done, you know?"

"When are they asking you to start?"

She paused before answering. "Next Monday."

Monday—that was only a week away. The imminence of Alex's departure struck him with an immediate sense of loss.

Val swallowed down the lump forming in his throat. "That should be fine, I would think. I saw the email you sent on Friday with the last of the summaries. The other side hasn't come back with any other questions on the due diligence that I've seen. Is that right?"

"Yes, that's right."

"Then I would say your work here is done, wouldn't you?" His words came out more tersely than Val had intended, so he quickly added, "What I mean is that according to Gideon, the Board of FiberTech is having their big meeting to take the final vote on the acquisition on Sunday morning their time, and the end of their workweek is Thursday, around ten a.m. our time. So really, as long as you stay until lunchtime on Thursday, we'll be able to answer any last-minute questions they might have."

When Alex didn't say anything, Val spoke again. "Alex, this is your time now. Your turn. Your job."

She smiled a dazzlingly happy smile. "That's how I felt when I was there interviewing. I felt like I belonged there."

Yes, she belonged there. Not here. Not with him.

"You'll be bored here this week with nothing to do. You don't really have to finish out the week here if you don't want to. I can call or email you if the other side comes back with questions." Even as he made the offer, Val hoped she wouldn't take him up on it.

"No. If you don't mind, I would like to finish my week here."

"Of course," he nodded, relieved. "Whatever you want to do."

She smiled, a little hesitantly, and he realized how callous his response must have sounded.

Val stood up, the lump in his throat growing larger. "Then that's that. I'll let your agency know that you will have completed your work here by Friday, but I'll let you tell them about your new employment. Big things are going to happen for you, Alex. I can just feel it."

She nodded, her eyes bright. "I hope you're right."

Alex stood up and leaned across the desk to shake hands with him. The touch of her hand in his brought him back to that kiss in front of her hotel room, and he closed his eyes, then quickly opened them, hoping she hadn't noticed.

"Thank you, Val, for everything," said Alex, smiling sweetly, her hand still in Val's.

"No," he said quickly. "Thank you. In fact, I'd like to thank you properly by taking you out to lunch on Friday. As a show of the company's appreciation for all you've done. Would you let me do that?"

"Of course," she replied, gently withdrawing her hand from his.

"Great, I'll have Judy set something up and put it on our calendars."

As Alex turned to leave the office, she looked back at Val with a cheerful grin. "I still don't really understand how this is happening. I mean, it's like you're my lucky charm or something!"

She let out a breathy chuckle, then added, "Now if only there was something to be done to get the rest of my life in order." Her eyes lingered on him, the curve of her brow heavy with something bordering on melancholy, and his face felt warm under her gaze. Val searched for something to say and was about to utter her name, just to make her stay a moment longer, when she quickly turned around and walked away.

Alex had called him her lucky charm. Her amulet. But that last look she had given him left Val wondering. He had gotten her an interview, which had led to a job. But there was still sadness behind her smile. Her joy was not complete. He knew she still didn't have what her heart wanted most of all. She was still Billy's girlfriend—not his wife.

No, he was not her amulet, but at that moment Val realized that more than anything else, that was exactly what he wanted to be. He wanted to do everything in his power to see that Alex got the one thing she desired most, the one thing she had always wanted but could never have. Val wanted to fill the void in her life, see her happy—truly happy—as the wife of the man she loved. It was not just because Val loved her that he wanted to do this, but because he knew it would help him fill the void in his own life.

And the only way Alex would get the thing she wanted most was to give her the amulet.

Val had to admit, the timing wasn't great. He was less than a week away from hearing FiberTech's answer on the acquisition, and he knew without a doubt that if he gave away the amulet, the deal would not go through. But in that moment, the thought of losing the deal, losing his company, losing everything he had worked hard to get, meant less than nothing to him. When compared to the thought of Alex never knowing the joy of having the one thing she wanted more than anything else, living the rest of his life in peaceful squalor seemed the much more desirable fate.

Amulet

Val walked over to the door and shut it. Then he started pacing, walking from the door to the wall of windows on the opposite side, then back to the door again.

He thought about his grandmother then, about getting the amulet from her. He was eighteen years old when she gave him the amulet, eighteen years ago. Val thought he knew what he wanted back then. He was sure of it. Would he have made the same decision if he received the amulet today? Would he ask the amulet for success? Or was there something else that was his heart's true desire, something more important than all the money he had, all the people who knew him, all the things he had accomplished?

He knew the answer, of course. It was easy. It was love. He wanted to be loved, to be with the woman he loved. Knowing that Alex's love could have made him complete made Val stronger in his resolve that Billy's love, as her husband, would complete her. And that made Val want, more than anything else, for Alex to be happy. With or without him.

He would give Alex the amulet; that much was settled. Now the question was how to do it. How would Val give her the amulet and have her make the wish? He only had until Friday with her, and that wasn't enough time to ease her into the whole story of the amulet and have her believe it. Even if, somehow, Val did have the time to tell Alex the story and present the evidence, it would be hard for her to believe. Liza had heard the story her whole life, apparently, and even she didn't really believe it.

No, it was better to find another way to get Alex to make the wish. Maybe all he had to do was ask her to make the wish. She would do it if Val asked, he knew she would. That was her nature.

And that gave Val an idea.

He stopped pacing. Dashing to the door, Val opened it and stepped out of his office.

Seeing that his secretary had returned from lunch, Val immediately walked over to her desk.

"Judy, I need your help."

Chapter Twenty-One

Val got the package Judy ordered for him on Wednesday. He took it home that night and opened it, careful not to destroy the box. The box was the whole reason he had ordered the Tenth Anniversary watch from Span Global's supplier of branded products. It was a silver cardboard box with the words Span Global printed on the lid, and inside was a black velvet box with a matching cushion, around which was positioned the watch.

Sitting at the marble island in the kitchen, Val took the watch out and placed it aside. Then he reached for the amulet and carefully arranged the chain around the cushion, making sure the stone was prominently displayed at the top as he closed the velvet box and placed it back into the bigger silver one, finally covering it with the Span Global imprinted lid.

He was looking forward to having lunch with Alex on Friday. Ever since they had parted ways at the hospital the week before, Val had only talked to her twice, when she had come to his office to tell him about the interview and then later, when she told him about the job offer. Other than that, he had only seen her in passing.

Each time they met, Val would smile and ask her how Billy was doing. Her response would be short, he would nod in acknowledgement, and they would go about their business.

Val would focus his gaze on something nearby as she walked away, like the Exit sign overhead, or the coffee maker, studying it intently until she was out of sight. It was the only way he could keep himself from touching her arm, drawing her close, bringing his cheek to rest against hers, telling her—showing her—how he felt.

When Friday came, he was relieved and afraid at the same time. Val knew that when the day was over he would never see her again. The logical part of his brain knew that the pain of being so close to her and yet unable to be with her as he was in Israel would go away eventually. That persistent longing would fade with time, but knowledge was a poor consolation. The thought that did console him was that Alex would have his amulet, and with it, she would finally get what she wanted. Perhaps more importantly, in Val's mind, at least, was that the amulet carried a part of him now, and by having the amulet with her always, Alex would have him with her, always. Even when she married another man, bore his children, and grew old with him, Val would still be with her in some small way.

They had agreed to meet for lunch a quarter before noon, and Alex appeared at Val's open door right on time. At the sight of her, his heart caught in his throat. He was sure she looked more beautiful that day than on any other day he had seen her. Did she have to wear her hair down, today of all days, with that shade of green in her blouse that made the specks in her eyes sparkle, and that particular skirt that accentuated all her curves?

He collected himself, stood up, and smiled graciously. "Are you ready to go?"

"I am if you are," she replied, smiling in return, and for a moment, it felt as though they were back in Israel.

He took her to a Thai restaurant a couple of blocks away, and they were seated at a table by the front windows overlooking the main thoroughfare. They were both quiet as they looked over their menus, but once the waiter had taken their orders and menus, they had no choice but to look at each other and try to make conversation.

Val asked about her new job and if she had seen her new office. Alex asked if Val had heard anything from FiberTech. Reluctantly, Val asked Alex how Billy was doing. Even more reluctantly, Val sat there and listened as Alex told him.

By the time their meals were set before them, though, they had started to settle into a comfortable back-and-forth. Val made Alex laugh just as she was taking a swallow of her water, almost causing her to spit it out all over her food. After that, they forgot how awkward they were being and started enjoying each other's company. It was not exactly the same as it had been when they were together in Israel, but it was close enough.

When the waiter brought the check forty minutes later, Val remembered the purpose of their lunch. He paid for the meal, then reached into his coat pocket to find the box with the amulet.

Alex was thanking him for lunch when she stopped mid-sentence and stared at the package he was placing on the table in front of her. He had wrapped the silver box in white wrapping paper and used some leftover silver ribbon from Christmas to tie a neat bow around it.

"Is that for me?" Alex asked, pointing to the box.

"It is," he replied.

"You've done so much for me—I can't possibly take more from you."

"I'm not asking you to take anything from me," he replied, too quickly. "This is a present from the company, from Span Global. It's a 'thank you' for traveling with me to visit FiberTech and for working around the clock to finish the due diligence." Seeing the skeptical look on her face, he added, "All employees get something when they leave. Here, please open it. And then I'll tell you what you have to do with it."

The lines of doubt around her eyes relaxed somewhat, and she reached for the package. Carefully, she pulled off the ribbon and tore the wrapping at the seams to get to the silver box inside. She looked at him again, her eyebrows pulled together in a question.

"Go ahead, open it," he replied, "so I can tell you about it."

She lifted off the cover, then cracked open the velvet box inside. Seeing the necklace, Alex looked at Val again, her lips parted in surprise. She carefully picked up the small pillow, cradling it in her hands, and gently unwound the necklace. When she had succeeded, she placed the pillow back in the box and held the necklace in her palm, studying it.

"It's beautiful," said Alex finally, her eyes moving from the necklace to Val's face once more. "I've never seen anything like this. Is this stone turquoise? I can't believe your company gives all of its departing employees a necklace like this."

"Well," he replied, smiling in anticipation of what

he was about to say, "perhaps not all of our employees. I can assure you that Kurt Donovan didn't receive a parting gift."

Alex chuckled. Then she unclasped the chain and put it around her neck. Seeing that she was having trouble securing the clasp, Val stood up and moved to stand behind her chair, taking the chain from between her fingers. Silently acquiescing to receive his help, Alex moved her hair to one side, exposing the delicate skin of her neck in the process. Shaking off images of unzipping and zipping her dress in her hotel room, Val tried to focus on the task at hand.

Finally accomplishing his mission, Val stepped back over to his seat and sat down, watching as Alex adjusted the chain so that the stone was centered, resting just above the neckline of her blouse.

It was funny, Val had never thought of the old stone and its beat-up chain as beautiful, but now, as worn by the beautiful woman across the table from him, Val found it to be the most exquisite piece of jewelry he had ever seen.

"Tell me," she finally prompted, "tell me the story of this necklace."

"Well," he replied, attempting to recall the scenario he had devised to try and get her to use the amulet, "you see, the necklace you are wearing is more than an ornament. It's...symbolic. Everyone who has worked at Span Global has contributed to something larger than themselves. We've made the company bigger, better, more complete through our hard work and dedication. You—your efforts—are a part of the company now, a part that will be remembered and will continue to breathe life into all we do, even though you've moved on to bigger and better things."

Val could tell from the slight curve of her lips that his words moved her. Encouraged, he continued. "Because you have enriched the life of the company, your life should be enriched by the company, in return."

Alex raised a hand to stop him. "I would say the salary I got paid every week was enriching."

"Yes, but you deserve something more. Everyone who works at Span Global deserves something more." He paused before continuing. "This necklace is associated with a tradition, and when you accepted the necklace, you accepted to carry on that tradition."

"You didn't tell me about any tradition when you gave me the necklace," she bantered, "so legally I can't be bound to something I wasn't aware of."

"Okay," he countered, trying to maintain his focus and beginning to worry that his scheme would not work, "forget that you're a lawyer for a minute, would you? I'm not asking you to do anything crazy. All you have to do is make a wish."

Alex looked at him, puzzled. "A wish?"

Panic had made Val forget the elaborate story he had concocted, and he decided to cut to the chase.

"Yes, just make a wish. It doesn't have to be right now. But soon, like maybe tonight or tomorrow. Hold the necklace, think about the thing you want most of all, and wish for that thing, okay? Please, promise me you will do that. Please. It's really important."

He knew he must have sounded like a raving lunatic to her—a pleading, desperate fool. He studied her face, looking for some sign that she would agree, silently imploring her not to think too hard about what he was asking, but to just do it. Alex didn't have to know exactly what she was doing. She just had to make the wish.

Her face gave him no clues, though, and Val asked her again, "Will you do it? Please?"

He held his breath, waiting for her response. Finally, she sighed in resignation. "Who am I to break with tradition? Sure, I'll make a wish."

He wanted to say "Thank God" but instead replied, "Good, thank you. Like I said, you don't have to do it this instant. Just think about it, okay? Make sure it's what you want the most. You only get one wish."

"And it'll come true?" she asked, smiling coyly, as if she were challenging him.

"Most certainly," he replied without hesitation. "That's why it's important that you wish for the thing you want most. So, take your time to decide, but don't forget to make the wish."

"I know what I want," Alex said, her face suddenly serious.

Of course, she knew what she wanted. Val was counting on that. He leaned back in his chair and nodded, although he could not bring himself to smile. "Good," he said finally. "Very good."

Later that afternoon, Val sat in his office with the door closed, thinking about what he would do when he got the news from Israel that FiberTech would not be going through with the deal. He knew that was the only possible outcome, now that the amulet was no longer in his hands. It would happen on Sunday, and on Monday he would have to come in to work and let everyone know. He would need to remain optimistic about the future, for the sake of his employees, but he knew it would be the beginning of the end for Span Global.

Perhaps some of his engineers would go over to work with Kurt at Pierce Industries. He was sure Kurt was already courting them. Once they found out Span Global had lost the deal, there would be nothing tying them to his company. Better for them to take their chances swimming to a lifeboat than to go down with a sinking ship.

The sound of a knock at his door pulled Val back to the present, and immediately he said, "Come in."

The door opened, and the sight of Alex peeking her head in raised his spirits somewhat.

"Is this a bad time?" she asked, still standing outside his office.

"No, no, it's fine. Please, come in."

She entered the office, leaving the door slightly ajar, and walked slowly to the two chairs in front of his desk. At the chairs, she stopped but didn't sit down. Her hands were clasped together in front of her, her head tilted down slightly.

"I just turned in my computer and was about to return my ID badge. I've said goodbye to everyone, so I guess it's time for me to go."

Val was quiet. It was ridiculous for him to feel sad. He knew the end of the day was approaching, the end of Alex's last day working at his company. It was nice of her to come and say goodbye. But perhaps it would have been easier for Val if she hadn't.

"Yes," he said finally, "there's no reason for you to stay any longer than you have to. You should go, start enjoying the weekend. It'll be Monday before you know it, and after that, well, I hear associates at law firms don't get too much time for themselves."

She smiled, "Yes. Much like the owners of

successful companies."

Val nodded. It was as though he had forgotten how to smile. How could he, now that Alex was leaving him?

"Well, there's no sense in long goodbyes," he said, knowing he was being terse, unable to be otherwise. "I'm sure we'll see each other around before too long."

"Yes, I'm sure you're right."

The smile had been wiped clean off her face, the result of Val's callous demeanor. Val hated himself for that.

"Thank you for all your hard work," he said, sounding like an emotionless robot. "You came at a very tough time for the company, and I really appreciate all you've done."

He reached his hand toward Alex in the posture of a handshake. She looked down at his hand, then put her own hand in his, shaking it. Her skin was warm, soft, and electric, and Val wanted nothing more than to leap over his desk and take Alex in his arms so she could know how he truly felt about her.

"Thank you," she replied, taking back her hand. "I've enjoyed my time here, however short it was. Thank you for Israel. It's a trip I'll never forget. Thank you for being flexible about me missing hours at work. And thank you for lunch, and the necklace. I'll be making my wish tonight, I promise."

Val nodded, not knowing what else to say.

He watched Alex turn gracefully toward the door and start to walk away from him. His mind was racing, searching for something he could do, some way to make her stay with him.

Alex reached for the handle of the door, and as she

began to pull it open wider to pass through, Val called out to her in a feeble attempt to keep her in his presence, if only for a few extra moments.

"You'll let me know how it turns out? If you get your wish or not?"

She radiated with the most beautiful smile in response. "You'll be the first to know."

With that, she was gone. And he felt cold and alone once more.

Chapter Twenty-Two

Val woke up two days later at an unreasonably early hour for a Sunday. He hadn't slept well, waking up every hour or two and forcing himself to go back to sleep. Now, seeing that it was nearly six in the morning, he gave up the fight.

Pulling himself out of bed, he shoved aside the heavy covers that he had gotten tangled up in throughout the restless night. Then he reached across the nightstand for his phone. As expected, there was a voice message from Gideon. It was one o'clock in the afternoon in Israel, the first day of their workweek. They would have concluded their board meeting just before lunch, and the board would have decided by now regarding the acquisition of Span Global.

Of course, Val already knew what that decision was going to be—had to be. Val no longer had his good luck charm. There was only one possible outcome.

To his credit, Gideon sounded genuinely apologetic as he delivered the news in his message. The board did not agree with Gideon's assessment of the suitability of Span Global for immediate acquisition. Their business was too niche for FiberTech's goals; their engineers too specialized; their research too focused. Span Global was a fine company, but it was just not the right time or the right fit for FiberTech. And so on and so forth.

Val resisted the urge to delete the voice message in

disgust. He was not surprised with the result, but the lack of surprise did not mitigate the disappointment he felt.

It was the beginning of the end, Val knew that. But he was not worried about what might become of him. He still had his company, and the company still had its customers, FiberTech being one of them. Even if FiberTech sought its fiber optic components elsewhere—and Val was quite sure they would soon be changing suppliers from Span Global to Pierce Industries—Val would be fine. Even if the company's other customers followed suit and canceled their contracts, and even if Span Global ultimately had to close its doors, he would be fine. Val would survive. He had survived on much less, and if he had learned anything from his deplorable childhood, it was that you didn't need much to get by.

No, he wasn't worried about himself. Val was worried about his employees—the engineers, the sales team, the finance group, the staff. This news would come as a huge blow to them. They would fear for their jobs, and rightfully so. Val would do the best he could to keep things going for as long as possible, even taking from his own income to pay his employees' salaries, but his fortune was not large enough to keep things going forever without a revenue stream. Sure, some of his people would find jobs elsewhere, including at Pierce Industries. But Pierce couldn't take all his engineers, all his sales folks. Many of them would have to reinvent themselves, break into a new industry, learn new skills. After all, Gideon was right—theirs was a pretty niche market, and with Pierce being their only real competition, there wouldn't be anywhere else for them to turn.

Shaking his head in disgust again, Val summoned the will to get up. He had a lot to do before Monday morning.

At ten o'clock the following morning, Val called an impromptu "town hall" meeting. Everyone tried to cram into the biggest conference room they had, which didn't have nearly enough space to hold all of them at the same time. *This won't be a problem a month from now*, Val told himself wryly, watching as some of the late arrivals stood just outside the conference room door, which was propped open, so they could hear what was going on.

Val stood at the podium that was set up for him, with a microphone pointed at him and the company's emblem draped on the wall behind him. There was an excitement in the air that even Val, in his semi-depressed state, could feel. Just as the crowds would dissipate once they heard the news, thought Val, so too would their palpable energy.

Calling the meeting to order, Val got right to the point, and he did not sugarcoat the news. FiberTech's board of directors had voted *not* to purchase Span Global, and so the sale was not going to go through. Was FiberTech still their customer? For the moment, yes, but they would likely move their business to Pierce Industries. At this point, there were a few choice terms thrown about by some of the older, bolder employees regarding Kurt Donovan, and Val couldn't help but smile ruefully.

Were they going to lose their jobs? No—Val was adamant about this point, despite his inner pessimism. They still had customers who were counting on them, and they still had the best employees and sold the best product. That was all any company needed to do well.

His employees took heart in Val's confidence and left the meeting determined to do their best to provide even better service to their customers. Treat every customer like it's your only customer—that had always been their mantra, and it was more important now than ever.

Oddly enough, in telling his employees what he thought they wanted to hear, Val inadvertently told himself what he needed to hear—that they weren't sunk yet, and that there was still hope.

Val spent the rest of the day in his office, going over customer lists and pending orders and planning trips to visit customer sites to revitalize the company's relationships with those customers. He had spent the last several weeks focused on making FiberTech happy. Now it was time to show some love to his other customers.

Chapter Twenty-Three

"Alex, you're on the invite for the Cyber Medtrics meeting at ten, right?"

Alex looked up from her computer to the middle-aged attorney who had appeared in her doorway and smiled. "Hi, Jordan. Yes, it's on my calendar. I'll be there."

He pointed a finger at her in his trademark gesture of acknowledgment. "Excellent. See you later, then."

As she turned back to the agreement she was marking up, Alex couldn't help grinning. The past two months at Farber and McCraw had been everything she'd dreamed they would be. The team she worked with was smart, friendly, and understanding, and Alex was learning so much. But best of all, her teammates treated her with respect and valued her contributions. Alex was needed and important, and, even when she made mistakes, they didn't make her feel like less of an attorney. Rather, Alex felt like her mistakes were opportunities to gain experience that would help her with the next assignment.

Glancing at her watch, Alex realized she had a meeting with Sarah in two minutes. She grabbed a notebook and a pen and hurried to her mentor's office.

Sarah had a growing practice, but ever since Alex's first day on the job, Sarah had taken Alex under her wing and helped her assimilate to being an associate.

Her mentor had shared tips about how to receive feedback, how to make her interest in new assignments known in a way that didn't rub other associates the wrong way, and generally how to navigate law firm politics while keeping her dignity intact.

Even though Sarah was in a different practice group, she had found ways to funnel assignments to Alex now and then, which gave Alex the benefit of learning substantive law from her, too.

Reaching Sarah's closed door, Alex knocked twice.

"Come in."

Alex opened the door and entered Sarah's spacious office. While associate offices were pretty nice and boasted windows with amazing views of the city from twenty-five floors up, the extra square footage in the partner offices was certainly something to look forward to.

"Hi, Sarah."

"Alex, how are you? Have a seat."

Alex stepped farther into the office and was about to sit in one of the chairs when a contract sitting at the top of a pile of papers on the corner of Sarah's desk caught her eye.

"Span Global? Is that one of your clients?"

Sarah's gaze darted to the contract, then to Alex's face. Alex had never seen her mentor flustered before, but in the five seconds of silence that ensued, it was obvious the wheels were turning in the seasoned attorney's mind as she tried to come up with an acceptable response. Finally, Sarah smiled, her features relaxing. "Span Global is one of the first clients I brought in."

"So, you know Val Nikolov?"

Sarah hesitated a moment, then nodded. "He's my main contact at Span Global. We exchange emails at least two or three times a week."

Suddenly, it all made sense. This opportunity that had come from nowhere—it wasn't the result of a résumé Alex had sent out and forgotten. It was a result of Val's intervention. Val had reached out to Sarah. He had asked Sarah to hire Alex. He had made all of this happen.

Alex wasn't sure how to feel about that. On the one hand, she was grateful. She'd never been happier with her work life than she was now, at this firm. On the other hand, though, Val had led her to believe that he only knew of the firm in passing. He had deliberately kept the fact that he worked with Farber and McCraw—with Sarah—from Alex. Would the firm even have hired her if it hadn't been for Val? Were they just trying to keep one of their clients happy by bringing Alex on board?

Before she would let herself succumb to anger or self-pity, though, Alex had to be sure.

"Is Val the reason you hired me?"

"No." Sarah's response was immediate and unequivocal, and Alex let out a silent sigh of relief.

"Alex," Sarah continued, "I will admit that I reached out to you for a phone interview because Val sent me your résumé and told me what a great job you were doing for his company. And I will admit that I wouldn't normally have reached out to someone whose only experience years out of law school is working as a contract attorney. But the only reason this firm hired you is because you impressed me. And not just me—you impressed everyone who interviewed you. Every day you continue to impress us with your work product, your enthusiasm, and your willingness to learn. In the end, that's what counts."

A different emotion threatened to overcome Alex, but she swallowed it down with a smile.

"Thank you, Sarah. It means a lot to me to hear you say that."

"Well, it's all true. You're doing great. Keep it up. Now, tell me about what you've got going on this week. What matters are you working on?"

As Alex filled her mentor in on the matters she'd been staffed on, she made a mental note to reach out to Val. Two months had passed since they had said goodbye to each other in his office. Two months had passed without a word from him—no phone calls, no text messages, no emails. She'd tried to call him in recent weeks, but the calls had always gone to voice mail, and she couldn't work up the courage to leave a message. She'd even walked by his building a few times, hoping to run into him. But she hadn't.

Alex had thought that time away from Val might help her to forget him, how she felt when she was with him. But if anything, Val was in her thoughts more and more with each day that passed. She couldn't help wondering how he was doing. She missed him.

She'd read the news stories about the deal with FiberTech falling through. It must have been so difficult for Val to tell his employees. Alex should have been there for him. She should have been there to tell him she knew his company would be okay because they still had him.

But she wasn't.

Most of all, though, Alex wanted to see Val so she

could figure out if the feelings she still had for him were just a figment of her imagination, the result of her romanticized memories of Israel and their time together, or if there was something really there between them. Something more.

As she sat in Sarah's office, listening to her mentor's good advice, Alex resolved that she would reach out to Val and ask him to lunch. If he agreed, she would soon learn the answers to all her questions.

And she would know if that amulet he had given her really did grant wishes.

****

The last couple of months had gone by in a blur for Val. He had basically been living out of a suitcase, and half the time he woke up in the morning not remembering what city he was currently in. He had spent hours in taxis and waiting around in airports, all for lunch with a customer here, an afternoon with a customer there, meeting and talking, listening and taking notes.

When he was in the office briefly between customer visits, Val spent all his time with his engineers and sales personnel. He reported back to them about what their customers liked and what they didn't like, what was working for them, and what was causing difficulties. The engineers worked overtime to design and redesign, coming up with different ways to solve new problems and better ways to address old ones. The sales team spent more time with the engineers and learned more about how to identify the customers' needs—both the needs the customers knew they had, as well as those they weren't even aware of.

There was an energy pulsating in the hallways and

the conference rooms at Span Global. Everyone was working together. Everyone felt needed, each person contributing something only they could bring to the table. When Val paused to take a breath now and then, he saw it. He felt it. His company was alive again. He didn't know how long it would last, but he was thankful for each day they got.

Although FiberTech had canceled their orders about a week after their board meeting and moved their accounts to Pierce Industries, just as Val had predicted, none of Span Global's other customers followed suit, which was encouraging. Moreover, instead of losing employees to Pierce, his company had to hire two more engineers and another junior sales rep to keep up with the volume of work. They were actually growing.

It was mid-March when Val finally took a week-long break from traveling—his longest break in two and a half months. He was exhausted, and he knew that if he didn't stop to relax and regroup, even for just a week, his body would go on strike and force him to stop.

Val got into the office a little later than usual that first Monday back, so happy to be sleeping in his own bed that he hadn't even heard the alarm clock go off. People were hustling and bustling in the halls, groups meeting in the conference rooms, and phones ringing as he passed by closed doors on the way to his office. These were all good signs, Val thought to himself. All good signs.

He waved at Judy as he passed by her desk—she was also on the phone but looked up and grinned when she saw him.

Finally, Val stepped into his office and shut the

door (Judy had an especially loud voice when she was on the phone). He put his laptop bag down on the desk, took out his computer, and docked it. Sitting in his comfortable leather chair, feeling satisfied at how things were going, he patiently waited for his computer to boot up and emails to appear on the screen.

As his inbox updated, Val quickly scanned the senders and subject lines. He had checked his phone for emails just before leaving for work that morning, but already forty-four new emails were waiting for his attention. Another good sign.

Val skimmed the list of emails from newest to oldest, and as he got to the bottom of the list, he noticed the name of a new sender—AlexW@Farber.com. It was an email from Alex, sent from the email address at her new firm.

Ignoring the other unread emails, Val double-clicked on the one from Alex.

Dear Val,

I hope you are doing well. I heard that the deal with FiberTech didn't go through—I was really sorry to hear that. I truly believe you did everything you could to make that deal happen. I don't know what else to say about it, other than I know you and your company will be fine.

I also recently discovered (somewhat accidentally) that you are a client of Farber and McCraw, THE LAW FIRM THAT HIRED ME! How could you not tell me they were your lawyers? In any case, after asking her a series of very direct questions, I got Sarah (YOUR LAWYER!) to tell me exactly how the firm came across my resume. So now I know you were behind it all. You were the reason I got the interview. You are the reason

I have this job, this job that I love.

SO, I thought maybe you would let me take you out to lunch to thank you. I'm making a big-time salary now (thanks to YOU), so you pick the place—my treat! I'm free today, and also Thursday or Friday, if you're busy today. What do you say?

Alex

What did he say? Val had tried to put Alex out of his mind over the past two and a half months. If he were really being honest with himself, Val would have admitted that part of the reason he was doing so much traveling was to keep himself mentally and physically occupied, so he wouldn't have time to think about her. So that he would fall asleep at the end of each day as soon as his head hit the pillow and wouldn't have time to picture Alex's lovely face or hear her soft laughter. Or think about that amazing kiss.

Stop it, he told himself. It was just a stupid email, and there was no reason for him to be conjuring up images of Alex huddled next to him, the two of them gazing into the sunset from the top of Mount Precipice in comfortable silence, shoulders touching. No, there was simply no reason for that.

Val had a few options here. One—he could simply ignore the email, just not respond. But that would never sit well with him. Val wasn't one to run away from problems. He faced them head-on.

Two—Val could respond and give an excuse for not being able to make it. He had been traveling practically non-stop for the past ten weeks. It would be perfectly reasonable for him to need some time to catch up on work without having to take a long lunch break to chit-chat with a former employee. But this would be another attempt to avoid seeing Alex. He couldn't just blow her off. Especially since, to him, she wasn't just a former employee.

So, Val looked at his calendar. He already had lunch meetings set up for Thursday and Friday. It would need to be today, or Alex would have to wait a couple of weeks until his schedule cleared up a bit. Which of course also meant that Val would have to wait a couple of weeks to see Alex. And now that the prospect of seeing her, talking to her, *being* with her was just within reach, he couldn't bear the thought of waiting another two hours, let alone two weeks, for it to happen.

Val hit "Reply" and typed up his response:
Sure. Let's meet at 11:30 at Miguelito's.

That was all he wrote—no names, no greeting, no closing. He had picked an Italian place he liked close to her office, even though it meant he would have to walk ten blocks to get there.

Almost immediately, another email from Alex popped up on the screen, and, eagerly, he opened it:
Great! See you soon!

There, it was done.

Despite the number of emails he had to go through, the almost continuous stream of people who stopped by to see him on his first day back, and the endless number of contracts and legal documents he had to review and sign before lunchtime, it seemed like forever before it was eleven o'clock.

Noting the time with a sigh of relief, he pushed away from his desk and stood up. It was supposed to be a warm spring day, so he left his jacket in his office and walked out to the reception area where Judy sat at her desk. She looked up as Val walked toward her.

"Heading off to lunch?" she asked, her eyes twinkling.

He nodded. "Yes."

Something kept Val from saying more, as though he was doing something wrong by seeing Alex and trying not to get caught.

The more Val thought about it, the more he wanted to hurry up and leave. He threw a "see you later" over his shoulder at Judy and walked as quickly as he could out of the office, making his way down to street level via the least populated route, hoping to avoid making conversation with anyone.

What was he doing, agreeing to have lunch with Alex?

Val asked himself that question over and over again as he walked ten blocks to the restaurant, head down and hands in his pockets. There was no reason for him to have lunch with Alex. None at all. He was getting used to the solitude again, and Israel was fading in his memory. Why did she have to email him like this, out of the blue, on his first day back in town?

And why did he have to agree to see her?

Well, the answer to that one was easy—Val had agreed because he *wanted* to see her. No matter how much Val tried not to think about it, he missed being with Alex. In whatever capacity they had been together, the point was that they had been *together*, laughing, sharing, eating, joking. He missed knowing where she was and what was going on in her life. He missed strategizing with her and hearing her ideas. He missed her smile.

Man, he was pathetic.

Amulet

All Val had to do was get through lunch, and then he could go back to the way it was, before Alex came to work for him. He would find himself a hot little number and date her for a little while, get his mind off things, focus on rebuilding his company, and forget about Alex. He never had to see her again.

And then he saw her, and the feelings came rushing back into him, almost knocking him over.

Alex was looking in the other direction, and Val took his time studying her as he approached, forgetting all about his solemn vow to forget her. A warm feeling grew in his chest and quickly spread through his body all the way to his fingers and toes, just at the sight of her.

The way Alex stood there, in a dark blue pin-striped dress with cap sleeves and a slitted neckline, her head gracefully tilted to one side as she tried to peer around some diners who were sitting at the open-air tables in front of the restaurant, presumably trying to locate Val—she was, in a word, breathtaking.

And Val was hopelessly in love with her.

****

At the sound of footsteps approaching, Alex turned and saw him. Val was even more handsome than she remembered, despite the serious expression on his face. She had never seen him look so grim, his features so severe. Although Val walked in her direction, it was as though he didn't see her, and for a moment Alex wondered if he would just keep walking past.

She shook off the feeling of disappointment and put on a smile as Val came up to her.

"Hi, Val! There you go sneaking up on me again."

He didn't even crack a smile. "Did you ever think

that maybe you're just completely oblivious to your surroundings?"

Alex chuckled, but Val didn't join her laughter, even though he had been the one to make the joke. He looked past her again to the door of the restaurant, and Alex wondered if he had only accepted her invitation to be nice. Because it didn't seem as though he wanted to be there at all.

"I think they've got a table ready for us," said Alex, turning away so he wouldn't see the tears threatening to spill onto her cheeks. "I told them to seat us inside. I hope that's okay."

"Sure," he replied flatly. "That's fine."

Alex led the way inside the restaurant, where the hostess greeted them.

Once seated, Val picked up his menu and began looking at it.

Picking up her menu, Alex said, "This was a good choice of restaurant. Sarah brought me here on my first day of work, and the food was really good. I'm assuming you've been here before?"

"Yes. A few times." His gaze did not stray from the words on the menu.

Val had never acted this way with her before. Even that last morning in Israel, after they had kissed—even then he hadn't given her the cold shoulder. He had always been kind and pleasant. He had always made Alex feel as though he cared about her.

What had changed in the last couple of months? Why did Val seem so distant?

Unable to deal with the silence between them, Alex said, "I had the rigatoni the last time I was here, but I feel like trying something new. What are you thinking of getting?"

Val sucked in a breath, still studying the menu. "I'm not sure yet."

Alex had never felt at a loss for words with him, but now, suddenly, she had no idea what to say. All she could do was look at him. His dark brown hair was tousled, as though he had been running his fingers through it all morning. Lips pressed together in a serious line, eyes dull and tired, Val wasn't himself at all. What was going on with him? Was he just exhausted? Or was it something else?

Suddenly, Val looked up from his menu and caught Alex looking at him. She quickly lowered her eyes, pretending she had been studying the lunch options all along, even as her cheeks burned with embarrassment.

Val cleared his throat. "So, how do you like having a real job with a real salary?"

Looking back up at him, Alex smiled, relieved to hear him speak. "It's great, Val. I'm so happy at Farber. Sarah is a great mentor, and everyone I've worked with is wonderful. They're all really patient and give constructive feedback. And they're so good about getting me involved. It's a lot like the environment at Span Global, where people look out for each other and are happy to be there. Your company spoiled me in terms of work environment, so I'm glad Farber can live up to the expectations you set."

Val nodded, then resumed his perusal of the menu, which he likely had memorized by now.

Their server came, and they placed their orders. Then there was more silence.

"So, what's new with you?" Alex asked, hoping he would offer more than a one-word answer.

"Aside from losing the deal with FiberTech and then losing them as a customer altogether?"

Val's expression softened as soon as he'd uttered the words, and Alex knew he regretted them. He sighed but uttered no apology, although a certain look of sadness crept into his features.

This was not the Val she knew.

Still, she had to say something.

"I still can't understand how that happened," Alex replied softly. "Our meetings in Israel went so well. Gideon practically told you outright that you had it. It just doesn't make sense. They'll be sorry. Who are they getting their components from now, Pierce?"

Val nodded.

"They'll definitely be sorry. Is that why you've been traveling a lot lately?"

Val looked up at her in shock. "How do you know I've been traveling?"

Alex felt herself blush again, and she reached for her glass, hoping the water would return her cheeks to a normal hue. Taking a sip and setting the glass back down, she answered truthfully. "I tried calling you a few times over the past month, but I kept getting your voicemail. I didn't want to leave you a message when I had nothing really important to say. So, I finally called Judy and asked her if you were out of town, and she told me. She said you'd be back today, so I thought I'd send you an email so you could ignore it if you were busy catching up on stuff. Which I'm sure you are."

"Yes. There are a lot of emails and messages I still haven't even touched."

Again, Val seemed to wince at his own words, and again Alex wished he would just tell her what was bothering him.

Looking down, Val blew out a breath, just as the server returned with their salads.

As they began nibbling on their greens, Val surprised her by speaking. "So, the job is going well. I'm glad to hear it. How's Billy doing with his injuries and rehab?"

That was the kind and considerate Val she knew, and Alex couldn't help smiling. "Billy's doing great. He started walking without a cane a few weeks ago. I think he's going to physical therapy only once a week now."

Alex saw Val clench his jaw out of the corner of her eye, but when she looked at him again, his face was relaxed. "That's great. That was a terrible thing that happened to him."

"Yeah. There are a lot of bad people out there. The funny thing is that this happened to Billy on the way to his car, which he parks in the indoor parking garage in his firm's building. You know, one of the fancy garages you berated me for not parking in, then promptly paid for on my second day working for you."

Amazingly, the stern line of his lips curved, just slightly. "That is somewhat ironic," Val replied, "but I still stand by my berating of you for parking in the sketchy lots."

Alex laughed, the tightness in her chest easing. She had really missed Val. Being with him again now only made her realize how much.

Their entrees came, and as they ate, Val began to abandon his serious demeanor, slipping back into the pleasant banter Alex knew and loved. Val asked her about what she was working on and how she liked it, and Alex asked him about all the different places he had been in the last several weeks. They talked over and around each other, and the words just flowed, effortlessly. Like they used to.

Toward the end of the meal, there was a lull in the conversation, and Alex worried for a moment that Val would resume his former distance. But before she could think of something to say, Val said, "You seem happy. I'm glad for you." He paused, but only long enough to take a breath. "How are things—I mean, between you and Billy?"

Alex glanced down at her half-eaten plate of pasta and smiled, then looked back up at Val. She was hoping he would ask that question. Part of the reason Alex had wanted to have lunch with Val was to tell him, but she'd felt awkward bringing up her love life at lunch, unsolicited.

"Things with Billy have been—resolved."

Alex had more to tell him, so much more, but before she could get the words out, Val pushed his chair back from the table and stood up. "I'm sorry, I have a meeting, and I need to get back to the office."

The server came by with the check just then, and Val handed the woman two twenty-dollar bills, telling her to keep the change.

"I was going to pay for—"

"That's okay," Val interrupted. "You can get it next time."

Confused, Alex tossed her napkin on the table and rose to follow Val to the front of the restaurant. She tried to keep up as Val pushed his way through the revolving door to the outside and waited. When Alex appeared a moment later, his hand flew up, stopping her mid-step. "It was good to see you, Alex. Keep in touch."

She shook his hand. Without a word, he turned and walked away, leaving her standing there, watching him go.

Chapter Twenty-Four

It had been a mistake. He should never have agreed to have lunch with her. It was as if Val had just torn out his stitches with his teeth, dug his fingers into the wound, then spread it open for Alex to pour salt in.

Val had been doing fine before he saw her again. It had been over two months, and he had been fine. Now, here he was, sitting in his office with the door closed and the lights turned off, staring at a blank computer screen.

In addition to the pain and sadness he felt at the renewed realization that he would never be with Alex, Val was angry with himself. He had wanted Alex to be happy, above all else, and she was just that—happy. He could tell simply by looking at her. Alex was content and at peace with herself and the world. She had the job she had always wanted, and things had worked out for her and the man she had chosen to spend her life with. Val had made all that possible, with a phone call and an amulet, and, without a doubt, he would do it all over again.

Why couldn't that be enough for him?

Val went through the rest of the day in a haze of self-pity and self-loathing. Judy encouraged him to leave when she peeked her head in his doorway at five o'clock that afternoon, on the way out herself. Val looked up at her just long enough to shake his head "no" and say goodbye before turning back to the contracts he was trying to review.

It was two hours later when he finally shut down the laptop and packed it up to go home. He would do more work later that evening. He needed to stay occupied to keep his thoughts and feelings at bay, especially tonight.

Throwing on a light jacket and slinging the laptop bag onto his shoulder, Val headed out the door. Everything was quiet as he walked down the hallway to the elevator. He was the last person in the office, as usual.

He stepped onto the elevator and pushed the button for the lobby. The doors closed, and he thought to himself how symbolic that was.

Getting off the elevator at the lobby level, Val turned toward the elevators that went down to the parking garage. After only a few steps in that direction, Val stopped short.

"Alex? What are you doing here? Are you okay?"

Alex's hair was pulled back in a sloppy ponytail, and her eyes looked red and puffy.

She took a few steps in his direction, then froze just an arm's length away.

"Are you okay?" Val asked again, more gently this time.

Alex looked at him, as though trying to understand the meaning of what he'd just said, then stretched out a fist. She was holding something.

"I-I wanted to give this back to you," she said finally. She turned her hand over and spread open her fingers, revealing the amulet. "Take it."

Val looked around. There was no one in sight

except for a security guard near the main bank of elevators. The guard was playing a game on his phone.

"Let's go back up to my office," said Val, touching her arm. "We can talk there."

Alex nodded, shoving the hand holding the amulet into the pocket of her overcoat. They walked side-by-side to the elevator bay and waited for the doors to open.

When they were in the elevator, on their way up again, Val turned to Alex. "How long were you standing there, waiting for me?"

Alex shrugged. "I don't know. An hour maybe. It doesn't matter."

Her voice was emotionless, her face expressionless. Val couldn't remember ever having seen her without a smile of some sort on her lips, even if at times it was a sad one.

The doors slid open. Without a word, she stepped out, then followed him to the end of the hall, where his office was.

The floor was quiet, and, aside from the lights in the hallway, everything on either side was dark.

Val opened the door to his office and turned on the lights. Silently, Alex walked over to the leather chair in front of Val's desk and lowered herself into it. Val followed her and sat in the other chair next to her. Perched on the edge of the seat, Alex refused to look at him, choosing instead to study the lovely hands clasped together in her lap.

Val shifted in his chair to face her. "Tell me what's going on," he implored. "Please, talk to me."

As though she had just remembered why she had come to see him, Alex looked up, her lips parted slightly in surprise. Then she pulled the amulet out of her pocket and pushed it toward him again.

"I want to give this back to you," she said, her voice cracking as she spoke.

"Why? It's yours. I gave it to you as a gift."

"I don't want it," Alex replied, raising her voice. "It doesn't work. I don't want it."

Val reached out his hand, and Alex placed the amulet in his palm, her fingers innocently brushing his skin.

"Oh, Alex. It didn't work? But I thought, I mean you said that things had worked out. Oh, I'm so sorry, Alex."

And he was. For as much as Val hated the idea of Alex being with Billy, it broke his heart to see her so sad. Alex, who brought joy and happiness to everything she touched—she didn't deserve this kind of pain.

"Maybe you didn't do it right," he offered.

Val's fingers scooped up her hand, and the warmth of her skin on his almost made him forget the reason for the contact. Flipping over her hand, Val gently pressed the amulet into it, pushing her fingers closed around it.

"I'll do it with you this time," he said, still holding her closed hand in both of his. "If you want Billy to marry you, just say it, please. It will work this time, I promise you."

Alex drew her eyebrows together into a frown and shook her head slowly from side to side. "That's not what I want. That's not what I wished for."

"What?" Val couldn't believe his ears. "But I thought you wanted him to marry you. I thought that was what you've wanted for a long time."

Alex looked down in embarrassment and tried to

pull away, but Val held her hand fast in his own. After a few moments of trying, her hand relaxed into his as she finally relented. She looked at him, eyes shining with unshed tears.

"I thought I wanted to marry Billy, I really did. I told him I loved him all the time."

"You told *me* you loved him when we were walking along the beach in Israel, and I hadn't even asked."

Ignoring the joke, Alex continued. "I think all these years I loved the idea of being married to him. I had always thought that something wasn't right between us, and I guess between Sunday school and my mom's constant lectures I had convinced myself that it was the fact that we were living together, that we weren't married. I just assumed that things would right themselves if he would just marry me. But when I finally stopped to think about it, when he finally did ask me to marry him…"

"Wait a second, he asked you to marry him?" Val was having a hard time keeping up.

She nodded shyly. "My first week of work at Farber, that Friday when I got home, I found that Billy had spent all day making dinner. I thought he had just been bored—he's not used to sitting around all day at home. Then after dinner, Billy pulled out a ring and asked me to marry him. He said that when I was in Israel and away from him, he realized that he didn't want to be without me, and if I needed the reassurance of having a ring on my finger, he was willing to do that."

Val sighed. "Far be it for me to judge, but that doesn't sound like the most romantic proposal ever."

"Well, it meant a lot to me," Alex was quick to reply, disregarding his teasing tone, "and I was going to say yes. I mean, it's what I had wanted all along, just like you said. But then, when it came right down to it, I couldn't say the words. Because I finally realized that it wasn't being unmarried that I was unhappy with. It was us, Billy and me. Our relationship."

Alex's face clouded over as her brows knitted in thought, and she shook her head. "I think poor Billy just about had a heart attack when I told him I needed some time to think about it, after all the whining and complaining I had been doing all these years to get him to marry me. But he took it in stride, even when I said 'no' the next day."

She paused to take a deep breath, then exhaled. "You can't make something right that just isn't. Sometimes, you just have to admit you've made a mistake and fix it, no matter how long you've been wrong."

A lightness crept into Val's chest, even as he was still processing the words she had spoken. "But, Alex, I don't understand. I thought you loved him."

"I thought so too, Val. But I didn't love him the way I should have, the way he loved me. If I really had loved him, I would have been able to stop thinking about you."

Val's heart stopped beating for a moment as Alex's words hit him, and his hand moved up slowly to tuck a loose strand of hair behind her ear. Her gaze moved downward at his touch, as though she could not look at him, and when she spoke again, her voice was almost a whisper.

"I blamed it on the trip, at first," she said, still

avoiding his eyes, "the long trip over, the lack of sleep, the wine, the beach, all of it. I mean, you spend twenty hours on a plane with someone and you're bound to feel like you know them. You get comfortable—too comfortable. You say things you shouldn't, you lean in too close, you look at them, you touch them, and it all feels right. That's how I always felt with you. Right. Like that was where I was supposed to be. The more time we spent together, the more we talked, the happier I became. I loved it, and I wanted more."

"I wanted more, too," replied Val, wishing she would just look at him.

"I shouldn't have felt those things, and then that night outside my room, when we kissed…" Her voice trailed off, and she closed her eyes.

"Tell me," he said, emboldened by her shyness, "if you didn't wish for Billy to marry you, what did you wish for?"

Opening her eyes but still refusing to look at him, Alex replied in a voice so quiet he almost couldn't hear it. "My wish was for you. For you to always have peace and joy in your heart, that same peace and joy that I felt when I was with you in Israel."

Val should have been furious with her for wasting the wish on him. Of all the things she could have asked for—love, health, a long and prosperous career for herself—she had wished for Val to have the thing he should have asked for, half a lifetime ago. She had wished for his happiness.

"Then today," she continued, "you were so different. You were annoyed, displeased, angry—I don't know. It just felt like you didn't want to be there, like it wasn't even you. Like the wish hadn't worked at all…"

Her voice trailed off as a tear rolled down her cheek, and Val's throat tightened with emotion.

"Oh, Alex."

Gently, Val pulled her chair closer to his, so that her knees fit between his own. Then, reaching up to cradle her face in both his hands, he wiped the tear aside with his thumb. "Don't you know I could never be happy without you?"

Her eyes came up slowly to meet his, and the effect was magnetic. Continuing to stroke her soft cheeks with his thumbs, Val drew her face to his and kissed her.

Once their lips touched, Val knew he couldn't be without her again. She was the fulfillment of everything he had ever wanted in his life. Love, companionship, acceptance, belonging. Home.

She sighed as he tilted his head, parting her lips in an invitation that he gladly accepted, and her hands came up between them to grasp at his jacket, tugging him closer.

Suddenly, Val was acutely aware of how far her body was from his, with both of them leaning forward in their chairs and meeting only at their lips. He rose from the chair slowly, never breaking the kiss, and took Alex up with him. His hands dropped from her face to her waist, and he pulled her against him. The feel of her thighs and chest pressing against him was both relief and torture. Then, when Alex reached around to stroke the back of Val's head, her fingers moving through his hair, the last threads of his self-control began to unravel.

Not wanting Alex to misunderstand the root of his feelings for her, Val reluctantly raised his head, finally breaking contact with her lips, but still keeping her body held firmly against his.

"Do you know how long I've wanted to hold you like this?" he asked, his forehead resting against hers, his mouth poised and ready to kiss her again.

Alex rewarded him with the smile he loved.

Feeling her arms slide down from his neck to wrap around his midsection, Val lowered his mouth to hers once more. Her lips were soft, her kisses sweet and tender, even as their mutual desire grew. His hands moved up from her waist to her back, his fingers making small circles, reveling in their circuitous path. He wanted to touch every inch of her, to memorize the shape of her under his hands. Every curve of her form, every bone and muscle, and every smooth plane. The warmth of her body, the movement between them—it was the most fulfilling experience he'd ever known, and Val realized that this was what felt like to be complete.

He had no idea how it had happened, how it could be that she was here with him, choosing him. Was it truly the amulet granting Alex's wish? Was this the universe's way of making up for his abhorrent childhood? Or was it just dumb luck? In the end, it didn't matter, as long as he could find a way to keep her there beside him, always.

Amid his delirious contemplations, Val felt Alex gently pull away from him. His arms still around her, chest rising and falling in time with hers, Val realized they were both out of breath. "I hope," he began, trying to slow the rapid beating of his heart, "that you're not going to tell me you just want to be friends."

Alex laughed quietly and shook her head. In a

voice that was steadier than he had expected, she replied, "No. I want much more than that."

Breathing in the scent of tangerine that he thought they had left behind in Israel, Val dropped tender kisses in her hair as she rested her head upon his chest.

"You know," he said, closing his eyes and rubbing his cheek against her soft locks, "I should have told you how I felt about you from the beginning, boyfriend or no boyfriend. I thought it would be unprofessional for me to tell you how wildly attracted I was to you—all of you. It wasn't just your gorgeous exterior, but also the core of you, your soul."

"Val." Alex breathed his name in a way that made him want to capture her mouth once more, but he sensed she had more to say. "After all that I've told you, about me and Billy, would you believe me if I said I love you?"

Val's breath caught in his chest, and he could have melted in her arms.

"Of course I would believe you," he replied, his voice unwavering.

"Why?" she asked innocently.

"Because I know you, Alex. Somehow, I know you better than I've ever known anyone. From the first time I laid eyes on you, there was something so familiar about you. You're like a piece of me that I lost a long time ago, that just now I'm finally remembering I had. More importantly, I would believe you—I do believe you—because I love you, too."

Val reached for one of her hands and intertwined their fingers, amazed at how perfectly they fit together.

"It's still a little hard for me to believe that you used your wish on me," said Val, bringing her hand to his lips. "Why ask for my happiness when you could have had anything you wanted—anything at all?"

Alex pulled Val's hand, still entangled with hers, from his lips to her cheek and closed her eyes for a moment, contentedly. "Everything was so different after Israel. When we came back to work, after New Year's, you were distant from me. You hardly smiled anymore. I hated that. And I couldn't help thinking it was my fault."

"It was," he teased.

"I love your smile. I couldn't bear to see you without one." Alex looked at him wistfully. "Your joy brings me joy. Seeing you smile, well, it makes my soul happy. How can anything else compare to that?"

Slowly, Val touched the caramel-colored hair that had fallen out of her ponytail to rest in soft, disheveled curls on either shoulder. "You make my soul happy, too."

He drew her in for another kiss, and this time he was not so careful with her. He could have kissed her all night if she'd let him.

When they came up for air, the corners of Alex's pretty mouth turned up in a coy smile. "So, it seems you were right," she said, pulling her hand out of his grasp and putting it into the pocket of her overcoat.

"Right about what? I'm right about so many things."

Alex laughed, withdrawing the amulet and holding it out to him. "You were right about the necklace. It did grant my wish, after all. You're smiling again."

Looking at the amulet in her hand, Val felt he needed to tell her the truth about the stone.

"My grandmother gave me that necklace when I

was about to graduate from high school," he began. "She said it had been passed down through her family, from one generation to the next. Her grandfather gave it to her mother on her mother's wedding day, and then her mother gave it to her when she most needed it. She told me it was one of two pieces of jewelry made by one of my ancestors, many generations back, and given to his twin children. The stones embodied the love he had for them, and for that reason, the stones grant the holder their heart's true desire—the one thing that person wants above all else. But when the holder gives the stone away, that thing the person wished for goes away, too."

Alex was quiet for a moment, and Val could see her starting to make sense of what he was saying. He didn't know why, but he needed her to see that what he was telling her was real. He needed her to know the truth of it.

"You believed her, didn't you?" she asked, finally.

"I did."

"What did you wish for?" There was a tremor in her voice.

Val took her hand in both of his, folding her fingers around the stone.

"I wished for success."

Alex was quiet again, looking down at her hand in his. Placing her other hand on top, she stroked his fingers pensively, her forehead wrinkling in thought. Then she raised her lovely hazel eyes to look at him. "That's why you lost the deal with FiberTech? Because you wanted me to have my wish?"

Val nodded, bending down to kiss her knuckles. "Yes," he replied, straightening. "And I would do it again."

A comfortable silence passed between them as each thought about what they had done for the other. Val had given up his wish for her, and Alex, in turn, had spent her wish on him. What better example could there be of selfless love?

Then it dawned on him.

Letting go of her hands, he asked, "Alex, can I see the amulet again?"

She handed over the amulet, and Val carefully examined the stone and its silver mount, turning it and running his fingers over its imperfections.

"My grandmother told me that the amulet gives the person who has it the thing their heart desires most. I may have wished for success in the words I spoke out loud, but maybe the amulet knew better. Maybe it knew that what I wanted—what I needed—was you."

Val looked from the necklace to Alex's face and ran his fingers over her perfection. "In any case, it doesn't matter anymore. You are my amulet now."

Alex smiled and placed her hand on his cheek in return. "And you are my amulet, Val. You always were. As long as I have you, I will have what my heart desires most."

He kissed her again, feeling her lips curl in contentment under his.

"What are you thinking?" he asked, moving to kiss her neck so she could reply.

"I was thinking about the amulet." She tilted her head to give him better access.

"What about it?" he whispered against the soft skin at the base of her neck.

"Well," Alex sighed, "just because we've

exhausted our wishes doesn't mean it can't still hold power for someone else."

Val lifted his head to look at her. "What do you mean? Is there someone you want to give it to?"

Her lips hinted at a smile. "Maybe."

Val grinned. "You're wonderful. What do you say about getting out of here, maybe going to get something to eat?"

"That sounds great."

He could see what Alex was thinking before she made the suggestion.

"How about Chinese food from the place downstairs?"

Val laughed, holding her hand and leading her out of his office.

"I think Chinese food would be perfect," he replied. "But we won't eat it in the conference room this time."

"Agreed." Alex squeezed his hand, and he looked over to see a mischievous gleam in her eye as she added, "I can't wait to see what's in our fortune cookies."

A word about the author…

Winner of the Georgia Romance Writers' 2020 Maggie Award for Excellence in the Unpublished Historical Romance category, Kathryn Amurra is the author of sweet and sensual romance stories with mystical and historical elements. Her newest series, Heart's True Desire, revolves around a ring and a necklace from generations past, each of which has the power to grant the bearer his or her deepest desire. Amurra is also the author of the independently published Soothsayer's Path series set in Ancient Rome. An intellectual property attorney by day, some of Amurra's best writing takes place between the hours of ten p.m. and midnight (or later) when she has "logged off" from her day job and her hubby and three girls are asleep. https://www.kathrynamurra.com

Thank you for purchasing
this publication of The Wild Rose Press, Inc.

For questions or more information
contact us at
info@thewildrosepress.com.

The Wild Rose Press, Inc.
www.thewildrosepress.com